SORCERER'S LUCK

SORCERER'S LUCK

Katharine Kerr

OSEL BOOKS
San Rafael

Cover design by Laila Parsi.
Cover photo of Ursus arctos used by permission of *Soldatnytt*.

ISBN: 978-0-9790573-9-7

Osel Books
Published by Urtext Media LLC
San Rafael, CA 94901
www.urtext.us

Printed in the United States of America

For Karen and Chaz

ACKNOWLEDGMENTS

A good many people helped me hammer this story into shape, but I owe particular thanks to Kate Elliott and Megan Beauchemin for sage advice and encouragement.

CHAPTER 1

I met him at the Alameda County Fair, an oddly wholesome place to meet a sorcerer. I was taking a summer class in portraiture at the art school where I was studying for my BFA. In mid-July, our instructor made arrangements with the fair's management to let her students set up a booth. We worked in shifts, drawing chalk pastel portrait sketches for ten bucks each, a bargain for our customers and great practice for us. Since our booth sat between the line for the merry-go-round and a ring-toss game, we also learned how to repel kids with sticky hands who wanted to draw on our paper.

On a hot Saturday afternoon, when the merry-go-round was playing its oom-pah-pah version of "Die Lorelei" for the hundredth time, a man sat himself down in the chair across from me and my drawing board and handed me a ten-dollar bill. A good-looking guy, tall, slender, with sandy-brown hair and brown eyes, he dressed with a total lack of style. He was wearing dirty jeans and a nerdy shirt: brown and white plaid with short sleeves and a big mustard stain on the pocket.

"Can you leave this out when you draw me?" He pointed to the stain and grinned. He had a cute dimple at the corner of his mouth. "I bought a corn dog. It was a mistake on a couple of counts."

"No problem! Would you like full face, profile, or three-quarters?"

He looked startled, thought about it, then shrugged. "Whatever you feel like drawing," he said. "You're the one who knows about art."

"Full face, I think, sir." We'd been told to be polite, you see, and call our customers sir or ma'am. But when I said "sir" I got a cold feeling in the pit of my stomach, as if I'd just turned myself into his servant. From the way he smiled at the word, I knew he saw it the same way.

I retreated into the drawing process. I've always been good at using my art to escape from whatever unpleasantness is going on around me. I learned how when I was a kid and my family was falling apart over my father's insistence on studying ritual magic, which my mother considered utterly fake and faintly ridiculous. As an adult, I realized that the way they fought about his obsession meant the marriage had other, deeper problems. As a kid, I just shut down.

My customer made it easy for me to concentrate on the present moment. He sat stone-still, a good model, as I glanced back and forth from his face to the pale cream paper. For this fairground exercise we'd been told to work fast, receive quick impressions, keep the lines loose, sketch in the proportions and then try to capture something of the sitter's personality. I'd done five successful sketches that afternoon, but as I worked on his, I kept going wrong.

I'd look at him and get a clear impression. Once I started to chalk in a line defining an eye, say, or the shape of his face, my hand stubbornly refused to draw what I'd seen. I felt like swearing at my fingers as they drew according to some idea of their own.

When I finished, I had a portrait sketch of someone strange, dangerous, and tormented. The shape of his skull had flattened out on top but pushed forward in front, more animal-like than human. Odd bluish shadows defined his cheekbones. Pain gleamed in his eyes, deep-set and dark, eyes that had looked on terrible things. His lips had drooped from their pleasant smile to a thin, tight, bitter line. I took his ten dollar bill out of our change box and held it up.

"Here's your money back, sir," I said. "This sketch is really bad. I must be tired or something."

He laughed and waved the bill aside. "Let me see the

picture first," he said. "Maybe it's not as bad as you think."

"Uh, no. I've got an eye for this, and I can tell crummy work when I see it."

He grinned and held out his hand. "Ah, come on! It's not like I'm going to be insulted. You're being straight with me."

I unclipped the sketch from my drawing board and handed it to him. He looked at it and nodded at the image.

"It's a perfect likeness," he said. "You've got an eye, all right."

I went cold all over. For a split-second his eyes and mouth looked like those in my drawing, although the shape of his head stayed human. He smiled, turned back into a perfectly normal nerdy guy, and said, "Aren't you gonna spray this with something?"

"Yeah. Chalk pastels smear like crazy if you don't fix them."

I took the sketch back and stood up. We had a table set up under a beach umbrella where we kept our supplies out of the sun. I found an aerosol can of fixative and treated the drawing. I also managed to convince myself that I was imagining things. He didn't really look like that drawing. He was just being polite.

"It'll take a minute or two to dry," I said, "and then I'll roll it up and put it in one of these cardboard tubes."

When I handed him the tube, he took it with a little nod of his head, smiled, and flipped the tube up to hold it vertically in front of him, like a dueling pistol in one of those historical flicks. For a moment he looked startled. His gaze caught mine and held me speechless in a web of pure desire. If he'd asked me to take off my clothes and have sex with him right there in public, I would have.

"Thanks," he said. "I'll see you later."

He turned and hurried away as if he'd scared himself, too. I was trembling so hard that I had to sit down. Maya, I told myself, you've got to get out of here. Now. My heartbeat pounded the message: out out out.

Getting out, however, presented a problem. I had to wait till the next person showed up for her shift because I had to guard the cash box and our supplies. Brittany tended to run late. I waited for an hour before she came waltzing up. She flopped her backpack down on the table and flipped her long blonde hair back from her face.

"Sorry," she said. "I had to wait for Buster's new parents to pick him up."

"Who? Oh! One of your dog rescues?"

"Yeah. A Rottie. He's got his forever home." She paused to look at me. "Are you okay? You didn't eat any of the garbage they're selling here, did you?"

"No, thank you very much, Miss Pure Organic."

"Well, sor-ree! What's wrong with you?"

"You're late, and—" I hesitated. You don't tell someone that you need to run away from a sorcerer you've just met. "I've got cramps."

"Oh." She stopped pouting and looked guilty. "Ohmigawd, I'm sorry, really sorry. What you need is some pennyroyal tea. I've got a couple of packets right here—"

"Uh, thanks, but I'd hurl. Anyway, here's the cash box and the other stuff. Your turn. I've got to find a porta-potty."

I grabbed my backpack and my hoodie and trotted off. I glanced back to see Brittany changing the name plate. We'd set up a miniature easel where we could place a piece of cardboard with the current artist's name. Mine, the "Maya L. Cantescu" card, had sat in full view while I'd drawn him. He knew my name. I wanted to run or maybe vaporize.

I had to work my way through the crowds on the fairway. Kids ran in front of me. Adults bumped into me. A couple of drunk guys blocked my way and leered. When I stepped around them, one of them laid a hand on my butt. As I twisted away from him, I snatched some of his energy in return. He deserved the loss, the creep!

I thought I was heading for the exits, but somehow I got turned around. I walked for what seemed like half a mile only to end up on the other side of the merry-go-round from the art booth. I swore under my breath, took a sighting down the line of game booths, and headed for the gate again.

This time I ended up stuck between a toddler-sized ride that featured cars shaped like ladybugs and a stand selling soda pop. I could see the merry-go-round just one row over and hear that rotten Lorelei song, too. I knew then that the sorcerer was keeping me from leaving. I couldn't waste any more energy on running around the damned fair. I'd used up too much already. I bought myself a small lemon-lime soda with extra ice, wandered over to watch the ladybugs go round, and waited.

He came strolling up a few minutes later, as nerdy as you'd want in his jeans and stained shirt. He smiled and said, "Can we go somewhere and talk?"

"No. I'm not going anywhere with you." I looked down and studied the ice in my soda.

"Please? I want to offer you a job."

This I had never expected. "A job?"

"Yeah. Spotting magical illusions."

"I get it now. You're crazy, aren't you? You should go back to your halfway house and leave me alone."

He laughed, a remarkably pleasant laugh, as soft as slow water running over stones. I looked up, and once again his eyes changed. This time I knew what was going to happen. When he tossed his sexy web over me, I threw the soda into his face. The spell shattered. I turned and ran. He yelped but stayed where he was.

I ran all the way to the exit, which appeared in its proper place, and hurried out to the parking lot. My beaten-up old green Chevy sat where I'd left it. Before I got in, I checked the back seat: no sorcerer, nor did he appear before I drove off.

As soon as I'd gotten a safe distance away, I pulled over to the side of the road. For a few minutes I just sat there and breathed, trying to summon energy from the air. As usual, I failed, but at least I got a little rest. I fished my cell phone out of my backpack and called the portrait class instructor. I told her I was having a bad period and couldn't work the booth on Sunday. She assured me that someone else would take my shift.

I was living in Oakland in a minimally furnished basement studio, a knocked-together long room with a tiny bathroom at one end, separated from an equally small kitchen area by a partition. Unsanitary, yeah, and illegal, too, but it was all that I could afford. At the other end of the room I had a twin bed, a floor lamp, and an armchair. That was it, no TV, no table, nothing else except a narrow closet for what clothes I owned and a cardboard box for stuff like underwear.

Even though I had a full scholarship, I was dead broke and in debt up to my ears thanks to miscellaneous fees, the cost of art supplies, and my unfortunate habit of needing to eat now and then. I owned a laptop only because the school required it and my scholarship paid for it. My one indulgence was a smartphone. I'd considered giving up the phone, even, because of the monthly fee, but with my health problems I needed to be able to call my friends in an emergency.

Through the only window, high up on the wall, a cold gray light seeped in to illuminate my squalor. My job was flipping burgers—minimum wage and one free meal on the days I worked. Tiring work, but I'd never found anything better or safer. Students are a dime a dozen in the East Bay. The competition for part-time work is fierce.

"Rats," I said aloud. "Maybe I should have asked him about that job."

Fail! I recognized it the second I said it, even before he knocked. I went up the steps and opened the door to the street only as far as the chain would allow, about three inches, and eyed him through the crack. He'd put a frayed gray sweatshirt on over the shirt. At least it hid the mustard stain.

"Uh, look." He sounded honestly miserable. "I've got to apologize for that transmission spell. I'm real sorry. I never should have made you feel what I was feeling. I mean, it wasn't any better than that jerk pawing you, was it?"

"No, it certainly wasn't. Hey! You saw that?"

"I was trying to reach you to deal with him, but the crowd slowed me down."

I crossed my arms over my chest and waited for him to

go on.

"Look," he said, "I'll go away and leave you alone. I'm not a stalker, honest. I got carried away this afternoon. But that's not an excuse. I'm glad you threw that ice in my face. It woke me up."

He was either a top-quality actor or sincere. I figured the latter because I'd never seen him on TV.

"I know I was wrong," he went on. "Maybe about a couple of things."

"Okay, enough," I said. "I forgive you."

"Thank you. That means a lot to me. You're really beautiful, you know."

It had been a long time since any guy had called me that.

"Well, you are." He dropped the guilt and smiled. "You must have gypsy blood, with those dark eyes and that hair. Raven hair, I'd call it, glistening like wings spread in the sunlight."

"Spare me the poetry! No romantic gypsies in the family tree." I laid a hand on my cheek. "I get this coloring from my mother. Her family came from Indonesia, but there was some Dutch blood in there somewhere, too."

"Cool." He hesitated as if he were trying to think of things to say. "Uh well, thanks for forgiving me."

I refused to answer. His eyes— I risked a look and saw the grim, tormented eyes of my drawing, but this time I felt nothing. He was keeping his word. He reached into his jeans pocket and brought out a shabby leather billfold.

"Let me give you my card," he said. "If you change your mind about the job, please, you can call me."

I took the card, then shut the door and slid the deadbolt. I glanced at the card and opened the door again. He was already about ten feet away, walking down the sidewalk, hands shoved in the sweatshirt pouch, head bent.

"Hey," I called out. "There's no phone number on this."

He swung around and gave me his 'only a nerd with a cute dimple' smile. "You won't need a phone to call me," he said. "Just my name."

He turned around again and walked off. When he reached the cross-street, he vanished.

His card said Torvald Thorlaksson, Runemaster. I considered tearing it up or even burning it, but in the end I put it into the zipper pocket of my backpack. Maybe I'd need to check that job out one day. When you live on the edge, you don't waste chances at extra income.

The portraiture class lasted for four hours every morning, Monday to Friday. After Tuesday's class, I went out to lunch with a couple of my friends: Brittany, who despite her flakiness showed real talent with fiber arts, and Cynthia, who was taking the animation curriculum and doing some painting on the side. They looked like a pair of opposites, Brittany so thin and pale, Cynthia so solid, with curly brown hair she wore pulled back in a rainbow scrunchie. They thought like opposites, too, about most things, but somehow we all got along. On class days we all dressed pretty much alike: paint-spattered jeans and old T-shirts or decrepit blouses.

Our usual café had a big front window looking out onto a tree-lined street. That afternoon we lucked out and got one of the nice wooden tables in front of the window. I sat right opposite the window while Brittany and Cynthia took the chairs to either side.

My friends ordered food. I could only spare enough money for coffee. When their plates arrived, loaded with sandwiches and salad, my stomach rumbled loudly enough to be heard. I buried my nose in my water glass and pretended not to notice. Ice water can take the edge off your appetite, or so I'd learned over the years.

Cynthia gave me a wry smile, put half her sandwich onto a paper napkin, and slid it over to me. "Eat," she said. "I can't possibly finish all this."

"No, I'm fine."

"Oh come on, Maya! We all admire how hard you work to stay in school. We know you're not a freeloader. So, eat."

"You push yourself too hard," Brittany put in. "You really do. We all see it, your friends I mean."

"Ah c'mon," Cynthia said. "I honestly won't be able to eat all of this.".

"Okay, thanks." I picked up the sandwich and tried not to drool. "I really appreciate it. But I can pay you back when I get paid. That'll be next week."

"No, don't worry about it. Good grief! It's only half a sandwich."

"Have some salad." Brittany slid her plate closer to me and handed me a plastic fork. "This kind of lettuce is a particularly good source for vitamin A."

If my mouth hadn't been full of ham sandwich, I would have cried in sheer gratitude. I swallowed the bite and said "thanks, thank you both."

They just smiled for an answer. For a few minutes we ate in silence. Standing at an easel for four hours brings on your appetite. Eventually Brittany turned to me. "How's your brother doing?"

"Same as always," I said. "Badly. He keeps hitting me up for money for drugs."

"Well, don't give him any," Cynthia put in. "It'll only make things worse."

I didn't trust my voice and just nodded to show I agreed. I looked away for distraction and noticed someone ambling down the sidewalk just outside. A man, tall, slender, sandy hair, he looked so familiar that I thought for a moment that I was seeing Torvald the runemaster. This man, however, appeared a lot older, in his fifties, I guessed. When he glanced my way, I saw that his eyes were blue, not brown, and gray streaked his hair.

Not the runemaster, then. He caught me looking at him, stopped, and stared. I could have sworn he thought he recognized me, but I'd never seen him before. When he realized that I was returning the stare, he pretended to read the menu taped to the glass. He kept glancing my way with a surreptitious flick of his gaze as if he were considering making a pass at me. I concentrated on the sandwich. Cynthia noticed.

"You know that guy?" she said.

"No, and I don't want him looking me over, either."

She turned in her chair to summon the waiter, a beefy muscle guy, not all that tall, but not short, either. When he strolled over, the man on the sidewalk walked off—fast.

"Not good," Cynthia said to me. To the waiter she said, "What's for dessert today?"

We lingered in the café for over an hour, just to give the older man a chance to get long gone. When we did leave, Cynthia and Brittany walked with me to my car.

The incident made me think about Torvald Thorlaksson. Did he know this man who looked so much like him? On the one hand, I was afraid to call him and ask. On the other, I wanted to know. And of course, there was his offer of a job.

That week I got more bad news in the mail, a letter from the landlord announcing that in September, he was raising the rent by California's legal limit. The rent control law did allow for inflation. Two per cent may not sound like much of a raise, but on my budget, it meant disaster. I shed a few tears, then pulled myself together. I could try for more hours at the burger job, or I could downgrade my phone plan to a cheaper level. The phone plan was my one indulgence, but that's what it was, an indulgence. I could live without it.

I was tired of living without stuff. Especially when I had a chance at a second job.

Still, it took me three more days to work up the nerve to say Torvald's name aloud.

I might not have done it even then if it wasn't for the stink. On Friday I got the chance to fill in for another worker at the burger joint. I loved the extra money and the second meal, but I got home just before midnight. I tossed my purse and jacket onto the chair and realized that I stank from the smoky grill, the spatterings of a hundred burgers, and worst of all, the grease from the french fries. All I wanted to do was lie down and sleep. I absolutely had to get plenty of sleep, because I couldn't risk exhausting myself. Getting sick would have been a total disaster, for all kinds of reasons. But that stink!

My shower was a big tin box, designed for outdoor use

but installed inside by the miserly landlord. The hot water ran out fast. I had just enough time for a soap down, quick shampoo, and rinse, no long luxurious showers for me. I dried off and put on clean jeans and a tee shirt, but the grease smell lingered in the air from the dirty clothes lying on the floor. Just one more school year till you graduate, I reminded myself. You can do it. You can endure.

But the thought of a job that didn't smell of grease– I nearly cried. Instead, I took the business card out of the zipper pocket in my backpack, cleared my throat, and said "Torvald Thorlaksson" three times without a pause.

He'd show up in the morning, I figured. Instead, about ten minutes later he knocked on the door. This time I took off the chain and let him in. He was wearing new dark jeans and a clean white shirt under a leather jacket, a patchwork of different browns.

"Hi," I said. What else do you say to a sorcerer?

He smiled and stood looking around my studio. Finally he sighed. "You really need this job. We're even now, by the way. You called me 'sir', but then you said my name three times and summoned me. How did you know to do that?"

"Fairy tales. My mom was big on that kind of stuff when I was little. She read aloud to us a lot."

"Smart woman, your mom. Call me Tor, by the way. Torvald sounds too foreign for the States."

"Okay. I take it you're from Sweden or somewhere like that."

"Iceland originally. And Norway. I've got ties to both places, but my family came here when I was four. I'm a citizen. I even pay taxes."

"How do you describe your job on the IRS forms?"

"Sorcerer. No one's ever asked me about it. They must think I'm a stage magician, a guy who does tricks in night clubs." He shrugged the matter away.

We were still standing by the door. My legs ached from working so late, but the apartment had only one chair. I refused to sit on the bed myself, and I didn't want him to sit on it, either. Even without the magic spell, he was a good-looking guy. I refused to give either of us ideas.

"This place of yours is dismal," he said. "Let's go to mine. It isn't far from here."

A pass, I figured, on his part. I had a reasonable response. "I'm so tired I don't even want to walk to my car. I had to park six blocks away."

"You won't have to walk far. Just down to the corner. It's a crossroad, y'know."

"You'll bring me back when we're done discussing the job?"

"I'll bring you back whenever you ask. No more forcing anything on you, Maya." He looked down and shuffled his feet like a guilty child. "I still feel bad about that."

"You promise?"

"I promise." He looked up. "On my art and upon the runes."

He spoke quietly, but I felt a cold chill, as if I'd heard his words echo inside an enormous cavern.

"Okay," I said. "Let me get my hoodie."

I lived just off Telegraph near the border with Berkeley, not a good neighborhood, especially for a girl on her own, but cheap. Tor and I walked east toward the cross street where he'd vanished before. At the corner a gaggle of dope dealers were leaning against the wall of the liquor store and passing around a bottle of wine. As we approached them, I heard the dopers swear in shock, so I assumed they saw us vanish. The next minute Tor and I were walking on a tree-lined street with the dealers and the traffic left far behind.

I glanced around and saw big houses set back from the street, surrounded by trees and gardens. I recognized the neighborhood as the fancy section of the Oakland hills. We stood high enough that when I looked downhill, I could just pick out the tree-shrouded campus of my college a couple of miles below. We'd ended up facing north, as far as I could tell, but our fast trip up had wrecked my sense of direction. In front of us I saw a white building. Behind it, the hill continued its rise.

"Here we are," Tor said.

The white two-story house, blocky and squared off despite its peaked roof and chimneys, sat behind a short green lawn. The front garden consisted of one Japanese maple stuck in the middle of the grass. A side driveway led to a ramshackle garage. With its white stucco walls and red-tiled roof, the building looked older than the other houses nearby, which tended toward split-level sprawl, redwood decks, and very arty plantings.

Tor took a smartphone out of his pocket. As we crossed the lawn on a flagstone path, I noticed a large sign in a lower window that displayed the name of a home security company. He turned his back on me, did something with the phone, then put it away. He took a key ring out of another pocket and unlocked one of the two front doors. Over the lintel hung a wooden plaque carved with strange, spiky letters—runes, I figured.

"The bottom floor's my work space," Tor said. "The top flat's where I live."

It was a lovely flat, too, with hardwood floors and walls painted in rich colors. He led me into a room with big windows: one on the east wall that looked down to the college and Oakland beyond, sparkling with lights, and a window to the west with a view of the Bay and the Bay Bridge, wisped with fog and glowing from the strings of lights along the cables. After my dark basement I felt as if I were floating in mid-air.

On the floor lay a modern Persian rug in pomegranate red and white with black accents. He'd painted one wall in the same red; the rest were white. I gawked at the leather sofa and two leather armchairs with matching hassocks, a couple of real Tiffany floor lamps, built-in bookcases, and a fireplace finished in natural stone. Here and there in glassed-in niches on the bookcase stood antique Chinese vases. I also spotted a solid jade carved mountain scene that stood about 14 inches high.

I was tired enough to be rude. "God, you must have money!"

"Yeah." He sounded sorry about it. "Investments. Family money. Here, sit down." He waved at a leather chair. "Do you want a drink?"

"No, I'd pass out."

I sat in the chair nearest the door, just in case. He took off his jacket, tossed it onto the sofa, then sat down next to it.

"First off," he said, "I went to the county fair to find you because of my rune staves. I cast them a couple of times. They told me that someone who could see through illusions was working in the middle of crowds. When I saw your name, I figured it had to be you. You do know what Maya means, don't you?"

"Illusion, yeah. My mother was raised by hippies. The name is supposed to make me remember to seek enlightenment."

"Oh." He considered this for a minute. "That's not a bad idea, I guess, assuming you want your daughter to seek enlightenment."

"She did, yeah. She's doing it herself. She's a Buddhist nun now."

"So I bet the L stands for Lila. The play of illusion."

I nodded yes and stifled a yawn.

"Anyway," he went on. "Here's the deal. I can offer you one of two jobs. Part-time means you spend three days a month here to spot the illusions and then three more for another—well, I'll get to that. Full time is full time, and I'd prefer that, but you could keep on going to school and everything. What would count is your being here in the evenings. Part-time, a hundred dollars a day. Full-time: room and board and five hundred a month."

In three days I could earn what the burger job paid me a month. I could laugh at the rent increase and keep my phone. With six days, I could start paying off my credit cards. I nearly salivated. He leaned forward and clasped his hands, all sincerity.

"I've got a spare room. Part-time, you could spend nights there. Full-time, you could live in it instead of that dump. You could get cholera from that bathroom set-up."

"I've often thought that, yeah."

"And this flat is pretty close to your school."

"There's got to be a catch. This is all too good to be true."

"There's always a catch." His smile turned thin-lipped and bitter. "Or in this case, two of them. I need you to see through illusions because weird things keep showing up around here."

"Huh? What kind of weird things?"

"Rose bushes in the middle of the floor." He held up one hand and began counting them off on his fingers. "Figures made out of mist. Big pottery jars with lids. Scrolls with strange writing on them. Small dragons."

"Dragons, huh?" I decided that he was crazy and I'd better humor him. "That could be dangerous."

"They all could be dangerous, or maybe not. They could just be a sign that things are going wrong, magically wrong, I mean, with my work. I hope not, but it could be. Look, you saw through my illusion when you went to draw me. Right?"

"Right."

"So if you were here, and the dragons started appearing, you could draw them and maybe get a fix on what they really are."

The logic floored me: air-tight and totally nuts.

"Er ah well," I said. "Yeah. Maybe."

Tor sighed and looked mournful. "You think I'm bats, and you don't want the job. I understand."

My first impulse: damn right I don't. I went with the second impulse. "Not so fast! You said you'd only need me part-time for a few days a month. Why?"

"These things only show up when the moon's dark."

"Yeah? I guess they're not made of moonbeams, then. When the moon's full, do they turn into wolves?"

"No. I—" He caught himself and gave me the foolish nerd smile. "Not exactly."

"Ah come on! Do you really think you turn into a wolf?"

"No. I turn into a bear."

"You turn into a bear on full moon nights? You mean, like a werewolf, but it's a bear?"

"Yes. It's called a bjarki." His smile vanished. "Think of it as an old Norse tradition. Well, maybe an old Norse curse. I'm a shape-changer."

He spoke so calmly, so quietly, that I was tempted to believe him. Only tempted, not convinced. The only real bears I'd ever seen lived in the zoo, fat, clumsy-looking creatures. I couldn't imagine this tall, lean maniac turning into one.

"That's the second catch," I said.

"Yeah, fraid so." He sighed. "The full moon nights? Your job would be locking me in my room when I change into the bear form. Just to make sure I don't get carried away and go out and hurt someone."

"Have you ever hurt someone?"

"No. Sometimes the temptation—" He shuddered, and his eyes turned dark. "But I've always managed to fight it off. Month after month after month. It would be great to be locked in and not have to worry about giving in. Y'know?"

"I can see that, yeah."

"Uh, do you want to go home now? You must think I'm some weird rich guy who'd be in an asylum if he didn't have money. Diagnosed with delusions."

I would have thought exactly that except for three things. When I'd drawn his face, I'd seen the torment in his eyes. When I'd called his name, he'd appeared. And we'd walked from my studio to his flat in a couple of minutes. I was actually seeing the magic that my father had so longed to have, even if the magician did think he turned into a bear now and then.

"Can I ask you something before we go?" I said. "Like, how did you become a buh-whatever?"

"Buh-yark-ee. I was bitten about a year ago. I was hiking on Mount Tam and saw this creature following me. I thought it was just a lost dog, so I didn't run. It attacked me." He sighed. "It was a wolf, a lycanthrope. I didn't know those were real."

"How did you get away?"

"A transmission spell, like the one I never should have used on you. I was terrified, so I shared my terror with him. He ran off howling."

"That's really clever."

"Thanks. Sorcery has its practical aspects."

"But if the creature was a wolf, why do you turn into a bjarki?"

"I don't know. All I know is I never made the change before I was bitten, and afterwards I did. What else could have caused it?"

He might have been crazy, or he might have brushed up against some dark and evil thing. Like in the folk tales, I thought, things like me. His eyes told me that either way, his torment was real.

"So anyway," he went on, "I had to have a series of rabies shots. Shit, those hurt!" He shook himself as if remembering. "But it turned out that rabies was the least of my problems."

"Yeah, I guess so." I went on to the next question. "You say you can't see illusions, but you're wearing one, aren't you? The one I saw through when I drew you."

"Yeah, I can cast minor ones, but I'm just learning. Casting an illusion on yourself is the first step when you're studying the subject."

"These jars and things. Are you sure they're not just something you've created by accident? Images from your dreams, maybe?"

"They can't be, because I can't dispel them. I can dispel the one on me. Like I said, that's Step One. But these must be what my books call major illusions. They last for hours, they're detailed, and I can't make a dent in them."

"What's weird is that makes sense."

He didn't bother to smile, just watched me with sad eyes, sure that I was going to do the sane thing and turn down the job. So was I.

Before I told him so, I tried to see him as he really was without drawing him first. The nerdy guy in front of me changed to the face I'd caught in my drawing: young, certainly, and good-looking, but his dark eyes narrowed with despair and old grief, and he'd clamped his lips to hold back sorrow. The pain touched me at a deep level, like a guitar when you pluck one string and the others vibrate in sympathy. I had a secret of my own, not that I was ready to tell him about it.

"When it comes time to lock you in the room," I said, "would you give me trouble about it?"

"No." He held up one hand like a Boy Scout. "I promise you that. I set up the master suite months ago. It's got a bathroom in it. I even have a little refrigerator with a pedal you step on to open it, so I can feed myself. Uh, you're not a vegan, are you?"

"I wouldn't work in a burger joint if I was."

"Right. The problem I have with the suite is staying in it. The bjarki wants to run, you see. He's desperate to get out and go back to the forest. In three days I could wake up and find myself a long way from home. Y'know?"

"You couldn't just—well—travel the way we got here tonight? Get home that way?"

"Not if I didn't know where I was starting from. It's always the beginning of the action that counts in sorcery. That's the crucial point for everything you do."

"Oh." It occured to me that believing you were a bear could be just as dangerous as actually turning into one. "So there you'd be, with no way to get back."

"And with no clothes, either. No ID. Nothing."

"Oh jeez." I refused to let myself wonder what he'd look like naked—pretty good, I suspected.

"I thought about locking the door from the inside. He doesn't have opposable thumbs, so he couldn't undo the locks. Then I thought, what if the building caught on fire, or there was an earthquake?"

"I can see why you're afraid of being trapped."

He heard the sympathy in my voice and began to look hopeful. "Uh, would you like to see the room that would be your room? I mean, if you were crazy enough to take the job. Which you aren't." He stood up. "It's just down this hall. Way on the opposite side of the flat from mine."

"Sure. Why not?"

He showed me a large airy room, painted teal with white

trim, with a big west-facing window and brocade drapes over lace sheers. When I pulled the curtains open, I saw the Bay, the Bay Bridge, and San Francisco glittering on the horizon. The single bed had an oak headboard carved with a pattern of flowers and vines. The tall dresser matched it. In one corner sat a little writing desk and a comfortable-looking upholstered green armchair. Just across the hall was a bathroom with a black marble tub as well as a shiny-clean shower stall.

Don't get me wrong. The luxury didn't change my mind. His hope did. He was watching me with wide eyes but a slack smile, a wary look that made me think of feral cats. My mom would put out food for them, and they'd watch her from a distance, wanting it, wondering if they dared take it. If he truly were a bjarki, a feral animal was exactly what he was.

"Okay, look," I said. "I've got to go home right now and get some sleep. I'm wiped out. But I'll try that part-time job."

He stared open-mouthed. "You must be desperate," he said at last.

"Yeah, I am. For all kinds of reasons."

CHAPTER 2

Let me tell you something about vampires, real vampires like me, not those slimy thugs in the old horror movies or the sparkly, sexy kind in the new movies, either. We are not undead, for starters. We aren't going to hang around crumbling for thousands of years. If anything, we have shorter lives than most people, just because it's so hard to maintain our life force habit. It's not blood we crave. It's life force, chi, élan vital, whatever name you want to give it. Blood carries more of it than other kinds of tissue, so we're always tempted to shed blood and then suck up the life force as it flows.

Some of us turn to the bad and drain anyone they can get their hands on. That's where the legends started, I guess, back in the Middle Ages in Europe, where the genetic mutation first appeared. Desperate sufferers of our weird disease probably did stalk victims at night, but not because they'd die from the touch of sunlight. When they met a defenseless person, they would have grabbed them and harvested all of the victim's life force right there and then. Do things like that in broad daylight, where you can be seen and identified, and you end up with a stake through your heart.

It's possible, however, to skim just a little bit of someone else's life, a drop here, a teaspoon there. They'll never miss it, because a healthy person can regenerate their chi, their vital energies, just so long as you don't take more than that smidgen at one time. You don't have to cut them. You just touch them. I needed crowds, like at the county fair, for just that reason. Bump into someone, smile, apologize, and move on. They never knew, and I was one day farther away from dying young.

I was still robbing them. I knew I was a thief. My father had told me that stealing a little bit here and there would hurt no one, but I didn't know if it was true, not in any absolute sense of knowing something. All I had was his word for it. I would have stopped, really I would have, but oh god, I didn't want to die, not when I was just barely twenty-two years old! But I did try to take as little as possible. The temptation, always, was to keep on taking, to swill up someone else's life like a drunk swills cheap booze, to drink and wallow and suck until the victim dropped dead at your feet. I had never done it, never licked up more than that drop or smidgen. When my father told me about our family disease, I swore that I never would.

So I knew how Tor felt on those crucial three nights a month, the longing and the temptation to break out of his flat and allow himself to run like the animal he believed himself to be. That's why I took the job.

"Can you be here Friday?" Tor said. "I never even asked when your classes are."

"It's just summer school, and I'm only taking the one class, the portrait studio. I had to work as many days as possible this term just to keep my head above water."

"You were that desperate?"

"Fraid so. The last three years have absolutely killed my savings and my credit. My cards are maxed out."

We agreed that I'd come back to his place the next Friday afternoon, the day that the moon would enter the dark part of its cycle. Tor wrote down his actual address and phone number on the back of a business card and gave me some directions, too, since we'd gotten there in an unorthodox way. He took me back to my place as promised without the slightest hint of trouble or hassle. At my door we politely shook hands.

"It's so good to see you again," he said. "I've missed you."

I put his odd way of speaking down to English being his

second language. With a little wave he turned and walked off. At the corner he vanished. I went inside and locked, bolted, and chained the door after me. After seeing Tor's gorgeous flat, my own squalor hit me hard. The smell of mildew and damp seemed suddenly stronger. I prowled around, but I found no evidence of a new leak in the ceiling, only the gray stains on the sheet rock from the old ones. The people upstairs threw a lot of water around. I don't know why. Maybe their sinks leaked, and the damned landlord was too cheap to fix them. I reminded myself that at least I could afford to pay the rent increase now, and that I wasn't going to find a better place for the same money.

Normally I worked at the burger joint from three p.m. to ten in the evening, three days a week in the middle of the week. Thursday night I was just on my way out of the door when my brother walked in, my older brother, just turned twenty-six that month. On his good days Roman was a handsome guy, tall, nicely built, with a thick mop of black hair that he wore cut just above the collar. He had deep-set dark eyes, regular features, and skin like mine, a deep olive or light tan—you could call it either way. That night, however, he was unshaven, he smelled really bad, and his eyes kept flicking this way and that, focusing anywhere but on me or the night manager.

"Let me guess," I said. "You want money."

"I could use some, yeah." His voice trembled so hard that I knew what he wanted to spend it on. "I haven't eaten—"

"Don't lie to me!"

I hooked my arm through his and walked him out of the burger joint. In silence we hurried down to my car, which I'd parked under a streetlight. The neighborhood around the burger joint called for caution. He shook his arm free of mine and leaned against the hood of the car.

"I'm not giving you money for drugs," I said.

He stared at the sidewalk.

"When do you get your next disability check?" I went on.

"Soon." He kept looking at the cracks in the cement. "It won't be much. They've stopped letting me have all of it."

"Good. They pay out of it for that hotel room, huh?"

"Yeah." He looked up. "Maya, I really am hungry."

"So am I. Go to Saint Anthony's in the morning."

"How am I going to get back to the city? Give me a ride?"

"No." I sighed, I debated, but in the end, I reached into my pocket and brought out my last five dollar bill. "Will you promise me you'll spend this on BART and not on drugs?"

"You can't buy enough for five bucks to do any good."

Which is why I handed it over. I also gave him a ride to the nearest BART station and watched while he bought a ticket from one of the machines. My brother, my lucky brother who'd never developed the family disease, the star athlete, always lucky until he'd joined the Marines and served in the Iraq War. I had no idea what he'd seen or done there. He never talked about it. He just took every drug he could get his hands on.

Friday after class, I went home to pack up a few things to take to my new job. I did wonder if I ever should have agreed to it. I was going to spend the weekend alone with a guy who might be crazy but who definitely could work sorcery. If I hadn't known my father and seen him study and work—or try to work—magic, I would never have gone back to Tor's flat. But I had, and I'll admit it, not only did I really need the money, I was curious as all hell.

When I arrived, Tor had a present for me: a calendar that displayed the lunar phases.

"You'll need this," he told me, "if you decide to keep working here. Uh, look. Let's consider this weekend a kind of job tryout. For your sake, I mean. If you really hate the stuff that happens, I'll understand. You can quit. I'll pay you for the days you work anyway."

"That's really generous of you. Okay. Let's see what happens."

I figured that nothing was going to happen, actually, except maybe he'd see things that weren't there and I could reassure him.

"You could put your stuff away," he said. "I'll cook dinner.

Do you like fish? Sea bass."

"That would be wonderful, thanks!"

I'd brought some clean clothes on a hanger and my laptop in my backpack. I also had a couple of sketchbooks and some conté sticks for drawing the illusions if they really did happen to appear. I carried the stuff down the hall to the room that would be mine on worknights. I set everything onto the bed and opened the brocade drapes.

In the golden glow of late afternoon the room looked positively medieval. Well, not real medieval. Burne-Jones medieval. I would have loved it as a child, and I liked it even as a grown-up. It had a real coffered ceiling in dark oak. Soft, thick area rugs in cheerful reds and yellows lay on the hardwood floor. In one corner stood a real Tiffany floor lamp. The oak furniture also struck me as genuinely antique, not that I'm an expert in that field. I examined the carvings on the dresser—a pattern of vines and wild roses right off a William Morris wallpaper. The pattern on the bedstead matched.

Or at least, when I'd first seen the pieces, I could have sworn that the carvings matched. In the center of the headboard, however, I found an anthropomorphic moon-face carved in profile. I took a sketchbook and stick of sepia conté from my backpack and drew the motif. The skinny moon-face looked exactly the same in my drawing as on the headboard— not an illusion, then. I decided that I simply hadn't noticed it when Tor was showing me the room.

The writing desk was another matter. Under its gazillion coats of black lacquer it might have been an antique in the Chippendale mode, but someone had first lacquered it, then used it as a background for the strangest decoupage I'd ever seen.

The artist had meticulously cut all the images out of old-fashioned wood block prints, then colored them by hand in vivid hues. In the center stood a bright green lion eating a sun. The sun was bleeding all over the lion's mouth. Around the lion motif was a circle of flying shrimp—pink shrimp like you'd find in salad, but with little wings. Fat green caterpillars crawled around the outer edge, nose to tail, to form a border.

The artist must have made photocopies of an original, I figured, to get the multiple images.

I opened the lid and found, on its underside, a zodiac with a spiky gold sun at the center, surrounded by small yellow fish laid nose to tail. Pale pink scallop shells formed the outer border. In one corner, tiny white script read "Liv Thorlaksdottir," the artist, I assumed, and I could guess that she was one of Tor's relatives from her name. She must have spent hundreds of hours on the piece, so many that I could ignore how ugly it was. Not all women's craft-art has to be beautiful, you know. Maybe the long painstaking project had kept her sane during sunless winters in Iceland. The desk was empty. I shut the lid. I'd been thinking of putting my laptop on it, but I was afraid of marring the varnished surface

I decided that I needed to make a show of earning my money, whether or not the alleged illusions showed up. I took the sketchbooks and conté with me when I left the bedroom and put them on the coffee table in the living room. I found Tor in the kitchen, a sunny room with a real slate floor, green appliances, and a big wooden butcher's block in the middle, where he was slicing tomatoes for salad. A breakfast bar separated the kitchen from the living room. I offered to help cook. When he shook his head no, I sat down on a high stool at the bar.

"I like cooking," Tor said. "Mundane stuff like this keeps me from drifting off somewhere. That's one of the hazards, y'know, of being a sorcerer. Drifting off."

"Guess it would be."

He gave me a vague nerdy smile. We chatted about this and that—was the room comfortable, when I did have to leave for class on Monday, that kind of thing. I also asked him about the writing desk.

"My sister made it for me. It's strange, isn't it? But then, so's she."

"Ah" was the only reply I could come up with. If he considered her strange—oh man! I thought. She must really be something.

"Is she older or younger than you?" I said.

"Three years younger." He paused, considering. "Almost to the day."

"Does she live around here?"

"No. She married a man from Iceland and went back there with him. I visited them last year at Christmas. I don't see how anyone stands the winters. I've been in California too long, I guess, to want to deal with the cold and the dark. Especially the dark."

"I've always wondered that myself."

"I couldn't stay long, anyway. I had to cram the visit in between full moons."

Up until that point our conversation had been so ordinary that I'd forgotten he claimed to be a shape-changer. I began to wonder if Tor did indeed suffer from delusions on that point. Yet my own strange disease reminded me that sometimes folklore exists for a reason.

My phone rang. I took it out of my shirt pocket and looked at the caller ID: Roman. I let it play—I'd downloaded a stride piano vamp for a ringtone—until the answering service took over.

"Who was that?" Tor said.

I saw no reason not to tell him. "My brother."

"You could have picked up. I wouldn't have minded or anything."

"Thanks, but you don't understand about my brother."

He tilted his head to one side and waited, his lips slightly parted, so bear-like a gesture that I was expecting him to grunt at me like the bears did in the TV documentaries. I considered, but he really did have the right to know about Roman.

"Look," I continued, "I don't want him to know the address here. He's a druggie. They steal. They can't even help it, I know, but I don't want him near your place, so I didn't want him asking me where I was."

"Okay. I appreciate knowing that."

"All this family talk reminds me of something. Do you have an older relative who lives around here? Your father, maybe?"

"No. My father's dead."

"Jeez, I'm sorry."

"So am I." He shrugged. "He had adult-onset leukemia. They can cure it in kids, but he waited too long to see a doctor."

"That's really too bad. I've heard that there isn't much they can do for adults anyway."

"That's what he tried to tell me." Tor smiled, if you could call that faint, bitter twitch of his lips a smile. "They did a bone marrow transplant. My sister was a perfect match. It helped for a while, but."

He didn't need to finish the sentence. I nodded to show I'd understood.

"He died just about two years ago," Tor went on. "It's weird, but when I was bitten by the varg, the werewolf– I told you about that, didn't it?"

"Yeah, you sure did."

"Okay. It was on the anniversary of Dad's death. I went hiking just because I wanted silence, and the woods around me. It was a comfort, because I kept remembering how he looked those last couple of weeks before he died. Skin and bones. Drugged."

His eyes filled with tears. He wiped them off on his sleeve.

"I am so sorry," I said. "That's really sad. You two must have been really close."

"Yeah. He homeschooled me until I went to college." He took a deep breath to steady his voice before he continued. "But as far as I know, anyway, the rest of my family's all back in Iceland. My mother lives with my sister and her family on the family property."

"I wondered because I saw someone who looked like you the other day, except he was like in his fifties. And he had blue eyes." I tried to call up the memory, but the image I had was oddly fuzzy and vague—odd, that is, because I was taking a class on how to form precise images of a person.

"Huh. I do have a couple of cousins who might have come to California, but they're not that old." Tor frowned, think-ing. "I'll email my sister. She might know, but it'll take her a while to answer. They live in the middle of nowhere. No cell phone, nothing. A couple of times a week she goes into town to shop and pick up her mail, and when she has the time, she drops by an Internet café that has a broadband connection."

"Good grief!" I said. "They're really isolated, then."

"Yeah. It's probably just as well."

I waited for him to explain. Instead he gave me a vague smile and asked if I minded him putting capers in the salad. I took the hint and changed the subject.

"If you're doing the cooking," I said, "why don't you let me clean up afterwards? I mean, you're paying me enough to be here. I could do something."

"Okay, if you want to do the dishes." He pointed with the knife blade. "There's the dishwasher, and there's the switch for the garbage disposal. The soap's under the sink."

That evening the moon went officially dark, and I learned why Tor had decided to hire an anti-illusionist. After dinner I was loading the dishwasher, and Tor was in the living room, when I heard him swear and call my name. I grabbed a dish towel and wiped my hands as I hurried around the breakfast bar to join him.

Tor was sitting on the leather couch, an open book beside him, and pointing to a large parchment scroll that seemed to be hanging just above the coffee table. Aside from the way it floated in mid-air, I could have sworn it was a real, solid piece of ancient parchment, yellowing and splitting along the edges. Lines of scribbles vaguely like cursive writing marched down the center. I stared open-mouthed. Oh my god, I thought, he's not crazy after all! Unless I am, too.

"Weird, isn't it?" Tor said. "You see now why I wanted to hire you?"

"I sure do."

When I tossed the dish towel onto the coffee table, the scroll stayed motionless, indifferent to the movement of the air. I grabbed the sketchbook and a stick of rust conté and sat down next to Tor to draw. I kept my eyes fixed on the scroll and let my hand do what it wanted. As soon as I finished, the scroll disappeared with a loud popping sound, as if it were a balloon stuck by a pin.

"Huh," Tor said. "They didn't do that before."

When I looked at the paper, I saw no trace of the scroll. I'd drawn a line of six runes arranged inside a narrow rectangle, three marks, then a blank space, then three more. I tore off the sheet and handed the drawing to Tor.

"Whoever this is," he said, "he's really pissed at me."

"What are they? Evil runes?"

"Not in themselves. There's no such thing as an evil rune." He paused for a smile. "They're basically letters, you know, and you can spell all sorts of things with the same set of letters. Live is evil spelled backwards—you must have heard that kind of dumb joke."

"Yeah, I have. So this spells out something not nice."

"Not a real word, but a message anyway." He pointed to the rectangle I'd drawn. "This is called a tine or a stave. Normally you'd inscribe your talisman or curse on a little piece of wood." He pointed to each rune in turn. "Hail, Ice, Need. The blank space could represent a concept called Wyrd. Some runesters use a blank that way, anyway. Then we have Water reversed, Cart reversed, Thorn reversed. It's a runescript that's meant to bring me bad luck."

Someone laughed. I looked up to see a misty figure drifting back and forth in front of the fireplace. I began to draw what appeared to be a very thin male ghost dressed like a Viking warrior. What ended up on the sheet of paper, however, was a pair of staring eyes. As soon as I showed the sketch to Tor, the apparition disappeared.

"This could get really creepy really fast," I said.

"It did last month, yeah. That's why I decided to look for some help. You, as it turned out. Huh. When you reveal what they actually are, they disappear."

"Maybe it means they won't work if you know what they are."

"That would be good. Probably too good to be true, though."

Several more sets of runes appeared that evening. First

one of the large pottery jars, shaped like a Roman amphora, appeared in the middle of the kitchen when Tor went to pour himself a glass of mineral water. My sketch revealed another tine and the same six runes that had appeared on the earlier scroll.

"I don't get this," I told him. "What does this person want to accomplish by doing this? He could just, y'know, text you if he's got a message for you."

"You can't text runes!"

"So the runes are what's important?"

"I'd guess. He wants to scare me, I suppose, or just put the harmful runescript into my house." Tor shook his head and held out his hands palm-up. "I don't understand it at all."

Which was not reassuring.

A little later, I went to use the bathroom and discovered a rose bush growing out of the bathtub. I ran into my bedroom and grabbed a small sketch pad to capture what turned out to be a different phenomenon altogether. This time I drew a withered, deformed plant, some species I didn't recognize. Instead of roses, the attached blooms were giant ears. When I finished what I'd gone in there for, I brought the drawing back to Tor.

"It's kind of like deadly nightshade," he said. "When I was a teenager I studied herbal magics, and you learn what to avoid if you find it."

"I didn't think stuff like that grew around here."

"It doesn't, not naturally, but you never know what some-one might plant in a garden. Plants escape, you know, or their seeds and shoots do, I should say. Look at all the scotch broom in California."

"I'd rather not. I'm allergic to it."

"So are most people. That's what I mean. You never know what's volunteered out in the hills. I guess this apparition was a threat, saying he wants to poison me. I don't get the ears, though. They look stuck on. Not a real part of the plant."

"Yeah, an afterthought, sort of."

We spent a jittery evening, waiting and watching, but no

more illusions appeared. Since I'd had a long day, what with my class, I felt too tired to risk staying up all night. Around two in the morning I took the pad and conté and went to my room to go to bed. When I glanced at the writing desk, I saw that the green lion motif had vanished.

In its place stood the Greek god Hermes, holding up his snake-wound staff. The pink shrimp had swum away, and white crows had flown in to form the outer circle. I grabbed the sketch pad and drew the images, which stayed exactly the same as they looked on the desk. No illusions these—under the umpteen coats of varnish the paper images had managed to change their form and coloration.

I lifted the lid but found the same sun in the middle of the same zodiac and the same yellow fish. I did notice, however, that the sign of Leo shone with a gold leaf background, brighter than all the rest. I had the awful feeling that when the sun moved into Virgo, the desk would highlight that sign instead. Tor's sister must have had as much magical power as he did. I wondered about their mother. Was she a sorcerer, as well? A family like that, no wonder they lived out in the countryside, away from other people.

When I got into bed, I spent a restless few minutes wondering if I could possibly go to sleep. At any minute some weird object might materialize in the bedroom. My long day, however, caught up with me, and I drifted off. When I woke, the drapes glowed from the perfectly natural sunlight behind them. I checked the time on my phone: 10.30. I got up and dressed.

In the kitchen Tor was making coffee cake with almonds and raisins. He poured me coffee, added a lot of milk, and handed the mug to me without my asking. He put the pan of batter into the oven, then sat down next to me at the breakfast bar.

"Did you see anything more last night?" he said.

"Yeah, the decoupage on your sister's desk changed."

"It does that. It's an alchemical barometer."

"A what?"

"The symbols tell you what's going on in the house. Psychically, that is. It displays images from old alchemical texts. The ones appropriate to the energy flow."

I stared. I was afraid to ask him how.

"But last night," Tor went on. "What did it show you?"

"Hermes with his snake staff."

"Okay. That means the illusions came from a powerful sorcerer." He snorted. "We knew that already. The barometer's real literal-minded sometimes."

This statement made as much sense as everything else that had happened: not much.

"Anyway," Tor continued, "I didn't see any more illusions, either. I'm really surprised. Last month the damn things paraded back and forth all night."

"Do you think they might have showed up downstairs?"

"I doubt it. Before I started dinner last night, I set a lot of heavy wards. I can't set them up here, unfortunately, not and expect either of us to be able to think straight."

The way he was smiling at me made me uneasy. Did he suspect that I had a secret? Maybe only people who had strange powers and stranger secrets could be affected by wards.

"Do wards have that effect on everyone?" I said.

"Oh yeah, or else why set them? A really powerful sorcerer could banish them, but most people would feel confused and uncomfortable. They wouldn't know why."

So I'd only been paranoid about it.

Tor yawned. "Speaking of confusion, I should take a nap. I stayed up till five. Once it was light, he couldn't send any more. Major illusions like that, they're too delicate to stand the sunlight and the— Well, I guess we could call them the daytime energies. I don't suppose you care about the technical details."

Thanks to that word, energies, I did care. "This is interesting," I said. "You mean like sunlight?"

"That, too. The world's full of different kinds of energy. Some of them everyone knows about: light, electricity, x-rays, forces like that. But some are hidden. Those are the ones sorcery depends on. You learn to manipulate the hidden energies and use them."

"Is it hard to learn?" Hope flared. "Does it take a long time?"

"Years. My father started teaching me when I was four."

"That early?"

"Well, only fifteen minutes a day at first. By the time I was ten, it was up to six hours a day. Studying. Practicing. It's like becoming a concert pianist. You've got to start real young, and you've got to work your ass off."

Hope faded. I'd probably die before I could learn how to save my life. "Your father was another sorcerer, huh?"

"No, not really. He didn't have much talent for it. He drank too much, aquavit, mostly, because he was so frustrated." He paused for a heavy sigh. "It probably had something to do with his getting leukemia, all that drinking."

"That's really sad."

"It was, yeah. His father, my Grandfather Halvar, was always disappointed in him. Still, my father knew how to teach. Those who can't do, teach. Dad used to say that a lot." Tor smiled faintly, then let the smile fade. "I don't understand it. Usually the oldest son inherits the family talent, but my dad didn't."

"You're the oldest?"

"Yeah, there's just me and my sister." He paused to yawn again. "I don't know where she gets her talent from. It's pretty strange stuff, what she can do."

Judging from the decoupage on the writing desk, I could agree with that. Their family magic differed widely and wildly from the system my father had studied.

"I've really got to go get some sleep," Tor said. "I set the timer on the oven. You can take that out when you hear the bell go off."

"Won't you want some of it?"

"I never eat breakfast." He smiled at me. "But I thought you'd like some."

I did. The coffee cake was wonderful. After I ate, I took

a real bath, the first one I'd had in a long time, and soaked the last of the grease smell away in the black marble tub. Once my hair was dry, I took a nap myself in my room, to get ready for the night ahead. Both Tor and I woke up late in the afternoon. After dinner we sat in the living room and waited for illusions.

About a hour after sunset the first sound appeared. Laughter poured out of the kitchen, the creepy howling kind that serial killers make in horror flicks. It gave me nothing to draw, of course, so at first I thought we had no defense against it. When it ended, we heard a high-pitched whine like a security system gone crazy or a knife scraping across a china plate. Just when I thought I'd go crazy myself, it stopped. I gasped in relief, and Tor let his breath in a long sigh.

"That must have been hell's hard work to create," he said. "Maybe he'll run out of energy."

"You keep saying he. You don't think a woman is doing this?"

"I don't, no. I don't know why, but I'm pretty sure it has to be a man."

"Not some girl you jilted, huh?"

"I've never jilted anyone. They always leave me."

I'd been trying to joke, but his quiet answer rang true.

"Well, sorry," I said. "I—"

The blast from a trumpet interrupted me, a sour, out of tune, squeaking blast that played the same four notes over and over. I clamped my hands over my ears. Tor muttered something that I couldn't hear and got up.

He stalked into his bedroom and came back with a plastic bag of little orange cones: earplugs. When I tried a pair, they brought the sound down to a tolerable level. After a few more minutes, the trumpet fell silent. I took one of the plugs out. Tor did the same.

"We could leave, I suppose," he said. "Go out somewhere for a drink."

"Do you think this guy's trying to make you do just that? Go out and leave the place unguarded?"

"If that's his game, he doesn't know about the security system. I'm hoping he'll just give up. Judging from what my books tell me, creating sound illusions is a lot harder than the visual variety. Maybe he'll run out of steam."

We put the earplugs back in when the automobiles started gunning their engines, racing around the roof. The attack then switched to gunshots pinging off the appliances in the bathroom. We clamped our hands over our ears to supplement the foam plugs. When the gunshot noises stopped, the silence seemed to ring almost as loudly as they had.

"Wait a minute," I said. "I was thinking about the things we saw yesterday. When I drew them, they went away. That gives me an idea. It's not the drawing that did it. It's the interpreting."

The laughter returned to the kitchen about five minutes later. Apparently the guy had a limited repertoire. I got up and walked over to the kitchen door. Once I picked up the rhythm of the sounds, I could match them. I laughed like a maniac in harmony for just a few seconds before words began tumbling out of my mouth. I felt them as air pressure and lip movement, but except for an English word here and there, I had no idea of what I was saying

The laughter stopped. I nearly fell, but I clutched the door jamb in time to steady myself. When I turned around I saw that Tor had left the sofa and was standing just a few feet away.

"You've got a talent for this," he said. "Do you know what that language was?"

"What language?"

"The one you were speaking. Go sit down. You're pale." He went into the kitchen.

Pale and sweaty and cold, I realized, horribly cold, as if I'd felt a blast from a winter wind. I sank into a leather chair and slid down so I could rest my head on the back of it. Tor returned and handed me a glass of cola.

"The sugar in it will help," he said.

"But it's so cold."

"Drink it anyway."

He sat down on the couch across from me. I drank about a third of the cola straight off and burped a couple of times. Sure enough, I began to feel better, physically at least. Mentally—well, something had taken over my mind and made me speak in words I couldn't understand. Terror and disbelief fought it out, and neither won.

"What was I saying, anyway? I know some of it was English. I heard the word thief. And I think I said 'bear's son' a couple of times."

"That's all I could understand, too." Tor frowned, considering. "It reminded me of Gothic or Old Norse, but it wasn't either of them. Older than they are, I bet. But I don't get it. If he wants to accuse me of something, why disguise it like this?"

"Yeah. He could've just sent you a note. A first class stamp doesn't cost that much."

Tor laughed with a breathy sort of chuckle. The sound reminded me of the bears I'd seen on TV—chuffing, the voice-overs called it. I forced out a smile, but my heart still pounded in fear. Thief. Who did the illusionist mean, me or Tor? Did he know that I was a vampire, stealing other people's lives, one bite at a time?

"I hope to all the gods," Tor said, "that the bastard's blown out his brain circuits."

"Me, too. Do you think it'll start again?"

Tor shrugged. Yeah, I thought, silly question.

As it turned out, the concert had ended for the evening. Around midnight we went downstairs to check on the lower flat. As soon as Tor opened the door, I felt the wards. I heard nothing, but the sensation fell in the same category as hearing those loud, high-pitched noises, or maybe staring into a bright light, or maybe smelling skunk—I experienced none of those physical sensations, but what I was sensing repelled me in the same way as they would have.

Tor made some gestures with his hands and said some words in a language I'd never heard before. The sensations vanished.

"Now we can go in," he said.

We did. He flipped a switch and turned on an overhead
light. We'd entered a large room which Tor had set up as a
library. He had built-in bookcases crammed with books, both
cheap paperbacks and expensive leather-bound volumes, as
well as free-standing bookcases set here and there, equally
crammed. On one side of the room stood a fireplace that, I
figured, stood under the one in the living room above. This
one was faced in antique brick instead of slabs of stone. Beside it on the hearth stood a chunk of rock about a foot across
and flat on top. Tor noticed me looking at it.

"That's for the nisse." He sounded embarrassed. "It's
something I learned from my mother. She came from Norway
originally. She's pleased I keep the old custom up, so I do it."

"What's a nisse?"

"A house spirit, like a brownie. I put food on that rock
for it now and then. On my birthday, and the anniversary of
Dad's death. Fourth of July, Christmas, days like that."

"That's kind of cool, actually. Does the food disappear?"

He shrugged and smiled in pink-cheeked embarrassment.
I let the subject thud to the floor. As well as the rock, a couple
of leather armchairs and reading lamps stood in front of the
fireplace. Heavy maroon curtains shrouded the room from
the view of the uphill neighbors.

"I inherited these books from my father," Tor told me. "I
haven't even read most of them."

Off to the left I saw a kitchen, again, under the one in the
flat above. Beyond the kitchen, a hallway led into darkness.
On the right I saw a closed door that, I supposed, opened
onto other rooms. Tor stood looking around, then shrugged.

"Nothing's wrong down here," he said. "I don't understand
this. Why would he give up so easily?"

"Because he's planning something worse?"

Tor sighed, and his face sagged into gloom.

"Yeah," he said. "With my luck that's probably it. Why
don't you go upstairs? I'll set the wards again and be right up."

I grabbed my courage with both hands and went upstairs
alone. I don't know what I expected would happen, and

nothing did. Tor came upstairs in a few minutes, and we sat down in the living room.

"Maya, look," he said. "You've got a real talent for sorcery. Did you know that?"

"No, I didn't." I tried to smile. "I don't want to, either."

"What are you afraid of?"

"Who says I'm afraid?"

Tor considered me for a couple of uncomfortable minutes. He arranged his nerdy smile and shrugged. "None of my business. Sorry. So what do you think of the job?"

I shocked myself by finding it hard to speak. I wanted to scream, I don't want this talent! I'm so getting out of here! The rational part of my mind thought about the money. I took a deep breath.

"I guess it's okay," I said. "It depends on what happens next."

"The darkest moon night's almost past. The lunar energies, they'll disrupt the sendings. And so will you if there are any."

"Well, we can hope I will. How long—"

"Prime time's over as soon as the first sliver of the new moon appears in the sky."

"So things will be cool after that?"

"I only wish. Look, he's got to be really powerful to send illusions like that. But you turned them aside. That means he's lost this first round. He'll try something different next, I bet."

"Like what?"

"I don't know, but he's not going to just give up." Tor spoke quietly, calmly. "You felt the malice, didn't you? He hates me, whoever he is."

That night I went to bed with the question, stay or quit? Rationally I knew I should turn down the job, get out of the flat, forget I'd ever met Tor Thorlaksson. The money wasn't enough to keep me there. I could find another part-time job if I really tried. No one would ever make me talk in a language I didn't know again.

But I kept thinking about the theory behind what I'd seen. I could remember my father talking about the astral tides and elemental forces that influenced magical actions. Tor's "energies" fell into the same category, I figured. If only I could figure out how to tap them! I realized that if I came to trust Tor, really trust him, then maybe he could teach me how to deal with my disease. I needed élan, life force, magical energy. He knew how to get it—maybe.

Even if it sounds far-fetched and crazy, you snatch at any hope you see when you know you could be dead before you hit thirty.

CHAPTER 3

I went straight to school from Tor's place on Monday. When I came back to my basement studio that afternoon, the smell of mildew hit me in the face. Somewhere there had to be another leak. I walked around, examined the ceiling and the walls, saw nothing—then looked behind the tin box of the shower. Gray mold clung in a filigree on the wall. I nearly screamed, but I reminded myself that I had a little extra money. I could buy cleanser to kill the mold and a bag of sponges without jeopardizing my food budget.

Monday's mail brought me my monthly check from the burger joint. I parked near my bank and walked over to the ATM in the bright hot afternoon. The sunlight hurt my eyes even though I was wearing sunglasses. Standing on the concrete sidewalk made my knees and ankles ache, a danger warning, symptoms of low élan. In a few minutes, I knew, I'd start to sweat, but I felt cold, clammy rather than too hot. In the small crowd at the machine, one rude guy stood way too close to me. As the line moved, I started forward, then abruptly stopped. He plowed into me. During the couple of seconds we were in contact, I managed to suck up some of his élan, which hovered like thick mist around him. It seemed to slide down my throat like a comforting sip of brandy.

"Jeez," he said. "Sorry."

The two middle-aged women in front of me made loud remarks about pushy young men.

"It's okay," I said to them. "I'm not hurt or anything."

Just the opposite—the pain in my legs had disappeared. The guy made sure he kept his distance after that, unfortunately. I needed more élan. In the crowded supermarket, a skinny shrew of a woman pushed past me at the vegetable display to grab the primo head of broccoli I was aiming for. As her arm swept along mine, I sucked up a long swallow of her life force. My eyes eased, and the bright light over the display dimmed to a comfortable level. She got the broccoli, but I noticed that when she turned away, she shook her head and rubbed her forehead as if it suddenly ached.

I'd taken too much from her. If I could have apologized, I would have. I hoped she'd recover, even if she was a bitch. I did no more hunting in the market. When I got outside with my purchases, the sunlight looked normal, no longer painfully bright.

The thefts gave me enough energy to scrub down the mildew when I got home, but the smell of the cleanser drove me out of the studio. I took my backpack and laptop with me so I could leave the window open to let the place air out. I owned nothing else worth stealing. I sat in my car out on the street and wondered where I could go to pass some time. Maybe I could find a crowd where I could steal more élan.

The memory of Tor's flat haunted me, the beautiful rooms, the comfortable bed, the good food he'd fixed for me. I kept remembering him saying that if I wanted, I could live there. What would it be like, I wondered, to share a flat with a sorcerer who claimed he turned into an animal now and then? Terrifying, I decided. Unthinkable. Crazy dumb idea. I refused to live with sorcery all around me, especially not if he was going to tell me I had talent. I had to have a place of my own to return to after the days I worked.

But I kept thinking about him. He'd treated me really decently, not just by hiring me, but in normal ways. No one else had cooked a meal for me in years. He'd taken the time to make me a special breakfast even though he'd been tired. No one else had given me a comfortable bed to sleep on and made sure I had clean towels and good soap for a bath. And

I liked the way he looked, lean but muscled, a strong clean jaw, thick sandy hair. I wondered what it would be like to kiss that cute dimple at the corner of his mouth.

"Torvald Thorlaksson." I whispered his name, just once, before I realized what I was doing.

My phone rang: Tor.

"Hi," he said. "Uh, you weren't thinking of summoning me, were you?"

"No. Why?"

"I was just kind of thinking about you, and then I thought I heard you." He sighed. "Sorry. I won't bother you."

"It's okay. Really."

A pause. "Do you want to go out for lunch?"

"Yeah, I'd like that. Let me tell you where I am. I'm sitting in my car."

I gave him the cross-streets and hung up. In about three minutes, if that long, someone knocked on the sidewalk-side window of the car. I yelped, turned in my seat—Tor, smiling at me. Before I could say anything, he opened the car door and slid into the passenger seat. He rolled the window all the way down before he shut the door.

"Why are you sitting in your car?" Tor said.

"I had to do some heavy-duty cleaning in my apartment, and I'm letting it air out. Mildew behind the shower."

"That apartment. It sucks."

"Yeah. I'm afraid so."

"You really could come live in my place. The full-time job. Room and board and five hundred a month." He stared out of the windshield. "It was cool, having you there."

"It was kind of cool being there. Well, until the noises started."

"You got the better of those. You'd have your own room and your own bathroom."

I reminded myself of the spell he'd tried to cast over me at the county fair. How could I trust this man? I'd only known him a couple of weeks. He watched me with sad brown eyes—the wild animal's eyes, I thought. Not quite human.

"Are you going to be able to work two jobs once school starts?" Tor said.

"I'll have to try. I won't be able to go full-time. I only need to take nine units to keep my scholarship."

"Shit, that sounds exhausting."

It would be, but I refused to admit it.

"I get this feeling about you," Tor went on, "that you're always on the edge of being exhausted."

I went cold and very still. Did he know about my disease? My heart started pounding, a dangerous waste of energy for someone like me. I tried to calm down. He couldn't know. How could he know?

"What's wrong?" he said. "Maya, hey, I didn't mean to upset you." He opened the car door. "Look, I'll go away. Think about the offer, okay? I just want to help—"

"Help with what?" I snarled at him and regretted it.

He winced. "I'm really blowing it," he said. "I'm sorry."

He got out of the car and started to shut the door.

"Wait!" I said. "I'm sorry, too. I don't mean to be rude."

He hesitated, then got back into the car, but he left the door open.

"You're right about me being tired," I said. "All my friends tell me I push too hard. I just don't know what else to do."

"If I hadn't worked that stupid spell at the fair, would you feel better about the offer?"

"Yeah, I would."

"I'll never do anything like that again. I swore it on the runes, and I'll swear it again if you want me to."

I hesitated. I kept remembering how clean his flat was, no mildew, no gray streaks on the ceiling, no dope dealers on the corner, no worry about someone breaking in. Shapechanger, I reminded myself. He told me he turned into a bear of all damn things! What if it's true?

"Think about it," he said and shut the car door. "Let's go have lunch. Not at a burger place. Like Indian food?"

"Sure do. Just tell me how to get to it."

He laughed and gave me directions to a nice little

restaurant in Berkeley. Since the lunch hour was long over, we had the place pretty much to ourselves, which meant we could actually hear ourselves talk. We ordered a dosa stuffed with curried vegetables to share, some sag paneer, and various side dishes, along with rose flavored soda for me and an Indian beer for Tor. While we ate, we chatted about nothing important, the food, mostly. At one point, the conversation drifted to pets.

"We always had cats when I was growing up," I said, "but I couldn't keep a pet where I am now. It would be animal cruelty."

"For sure. My dad liked cats. He had an old tomcat that died just before he did. I didn't tell him, though. He was so sick by then that it probably would have pushed him over the edge, so I just made up stuff about how the cat was waiting for him to come home." He fell silent for a long minute. "I don't know if he believed me or not."

"You didn't have him home? Y'know, the hospice program and all that."

"I wanted to, but the idea really freaked my mother. It would be putting death into the house, she said. Dad didn't want her any more upset than she was already, so he decided to die in the hospital."

"Was that the house you're in now?"

"No. We were living in Mill Valley then. Y'know, I'm sorry. I keep talking about gloomy stuff like Dad dying. I'm not real good at being social. Small talk. That kind of thing. I spend too much time alone."

"I'm not real good at it myself."

He smiled but said nothing more. For a little while we ate in silence.

"I like cats," Tor said abruptly, "but I was afraid to get one once I was–" He lowered his voice. "Bitten, you know." He glanced around, but no one was in hearing range. "What if the bjarki killed it? They're omnivores, bears. They eat animals when they can catch them."

"They do? Crap! I always thought they lived on berries

and honey."

"Only in the kids' movies. They even paw fish out of streams." He paused to put the last piece of the dosa onto my plate. "If you're going to be there for those days, I guess I could get a couple of kittens. You'll be locking me in. They'll be safe."

"And I can play with them when I'm there."

He smiled, and the cute dimple got a little deeper and cuter. We lingered over chai and halvah for maybe another half-hour. When we left, he shook my hand and strode away. At the corner, at a crossroads as he'd called it, he disappeared. As I walked back to my car, I had to admit that I wished he'd stayed a little longer.

Maybe I'm stuck with being a vampire, but I refused to sponge off my friends in that way or any other way. Tuesday I offered to pay Cynthia and Brittany back for the lunch they'd shared with me. They laughed and waved me off.

"What'll you bet, though," I said, "that my brother shows up soon? He always seems to know when I've got money."

"What kind of drugs is he on, anyway?" Brittany said.

"I don't know, for sure. It can't be heroin, because I've seen him in short-sleeved shirts, and he doesn't have needle marks."

"He could be snorting it. I saw this on the news. People who never would have used needles, but they breathe this stuff in through their noses." Brittany made a sour face. "Yuck! Real glamorous, huh?"

"Yeah, for sure! Maybe that's it, then. Sometimes when I see Roman he's really out there somewhere. He sees things moving that aren't moving, letters on billboards, pictures, that kind of stuff."

"That sounds more like opium," Cynthia put in.

"I'll take your word for it," I said. "The only drugs he's ever actually mentioned are painkillers, codeine and oxy-something."

"He might use those when he can't get the other stuff," Cynthia said.

"Codeine's super-addictive," Brittany put in. "It's bad all

by itself. Not as bad as heroin, but still! Yuck!"

Sure enough, Roman smelled money and tracked me down. On Wednesday the three of us had just come out of class when we saw Roman walking toward us across the lawn. In the hot bright noontide he was wearing a pair of torn-up jeans and a faded olive khaki T-shirt, but at least they looked clean. He smelled like he'd had a shower and a shave recently, too.

The T-shirt hung loose on Roman's chest. He'd cinched in the jeans with a belt. I hated seeing him look so hungry, but if I gave him cash, he wouldn't spend it on food. He smiled at me, a wan little twitch of his mouth.

"Maya?" he said. "Can I um uh talk with you? Just for a minute."

"No," I said. "I'm not giving you money. I'm not going to help you hurt yourself."

He blushed scarlet, glanced at Cynthia, then turned around and took a few steps away. I could guess that he'd just realized my friends knew about the drug problem. I'd humiliated him without meaning to. When I went after him, he kept his back turned toward me.

"I'm sorry," I said. "But I get so worried about you I have to share it with someone."

He turned around, trembling, and stared at the ground in front of my feet.

"Ro, please listen!" I used his childhood nickname on purpose. "Please! Can't you get help somewhere? You're never going to be able to quit on your own. I know that."

"Yeah, so do I." He spoke so low that I could barely hear him. "The counselor says there's a program. I could go to a group session today. But it costs twenty bucks."

I could afford to help him. I'd earned three hundred dollars over the weekend. I was just so afraid that he'd spend it on pills.

"If I gave you the money, would you go? Would you really go?"

"Why lie? Probably not." He looked up and took a step back.

Brittany had come up to join us. She considered Roman

in a way I can only call clinical.

"You need to rebuild," she announced. "Vitamins, B vitamins, just for starters. And C. Users always need C. Your aura's a mess."

"Another nut like Dad!" Roman said. "What the fuck?"

Brittany ignored the language and turned to me. "If you gave me the money, and I drove him to the session, he couldn't spend it on drugs."

I goggled, I'll admit it. Brittany, have such a practical idea? Cynthia walked up and laid a hand on my shoulder.

"I'd let her try if I were you," she murmured.

Roman took a step back from the three of us. He blushed again from sheer surprise, as if he'd turned a corner and seen the Fates spinning his thread.

"What about it, Ro?" I said. "Will you let Brittany drive you in?"

He hesitated, then glanced Brittany's way. What he saw made him stare fascinated at her. The drugs had such a hold on him that he hadn't noticed her looks before. She was slender and beautiful, with long blonde hair and big blue eyes, currently filled with sympathy.

"Look at those." Brittany pointed at his right forearm, tattooed with the Marine Corps logo and a bulldog in a helmet. "Some devil dog you are, if you can't take a challenge like this."

Roman swallowed heavily and continued staring at her.

"Well?" Brittany set her hands on her hips.

"Okay, yeah," he said. "Thanks."

I handed over the money. Brittany gave me a small, strong smile and a nod of her head, then slipped her arm through Roman's and led him off toward the parking lot. In a condition close to shock, I watched them go. Cynthia laughed under her breath.

"Brittany loves a rescue project," she said. "Usually it's stray dogs, but I think she's just branched out. Your brother's awfully good looking when he's healthy. She really does know nutrition, you know. She's not as stupid as all that occult stuff makes her sound."

"Oh yeah. I'd never deny it. And don't think I'm not really

grateful. I'm just surprised."

"At what? That she thought of it?"

"No, that he went for it. Oh god, I hope it works. The group therapy, I mean. I hope to god it helps him."

Brittany called me a couple of hours later, while Cynthia and I were having coffee in our usual café. With her pushing him, Roman had gone to the session, which, it turned out, was actually free, because a well-known local charity ran the program. He'd been scamming money out of me. No, I reminded myself. It's not him. It's the drugs, maybe heroin, maybe painkillers, everything he takes. That's what's goading him to get money out of me.

"I used the twenty to buy him some good vitamins," she told me. "And made him promise to take two a day. I hope that's okay, and you didn't need the money back."

"I didn't, no. Thanks. I really mean it, thanks so much."

"And he promised to call me every day and tell me if he's going to the session. I made him promise not to lie. He just has to tell me yes or no."

"And if he says no?"

"I won't cook him dinner on Saturday. It's like a big dog treat, really. When they sit, they get a treat. They don't, no treat."

"Wow. It sounds so simple."

"It won't be. This could take a couple of years, getting him clean. But I gotta try. I mean, he like served our country, didn't he? And there's something . . ." She paused for a long moment.

"Something what?" I said.

"You'll only laugh at me."

"I won't. Promise."

"Don't tell Cynthia, but I think he's got psychic vibes."

As promised, I didn't laugh. I did sigh.

"See?" Brittany said. "I told you wouldn't believe me. But okay. Besides that, he's totally cute."

"Cute and dangerous. Brittany, please be careful, okay?"

"I will. I've never been bitten yet, y'know, not even by

the pit bulls."

After I hung up, it occured to me that I'd spoken the truth: I really didn't need the money back, thanks to my job with Tor. Having a friend step in to help with Roman eased my mind as well. I mentioned that to Cynthia.

"Good," she said. "By the way, you don't look as tired today as you usually do."

"Thanks. I've been thinking about school. I'll only take nine units in the fall so I can work more without running myself down. I don't absolutely have to graduate in four years. I could take an extra quarter."

"That's more loan debt, though, isn't it? I mean, I think you're right to cut back. It's just that everything costs so much these days."

"Yeah, and the landlord just raised the rent on me."

"For that hole? God, he's got his nerve! You know, if you ever have to move, you can come stay with me and Jim for a couple of days while you find somewhere else."

"Thanks. I really appreciate the offer. With luck though I'll have the new place before I have to get out of that one. It really is a hole. You're right."

When I returned to my apartment, the lingering smell of chlorine and mildew brought back memories of Tor's flat and the Burne-Jones bedroom. I sat down on my one chair and tried to reason with myself. The pros: nice place, good money, not pay rent means quit burger job, start paying off credit cards. The cons: sorcery, bjarki, more sorcery, illusionist who might attack again. I wasn't sure which category Tor himself fell in, pro or con. It depended, I supposed, on whether he was in bear form or just himself. From the restrained way he'd shaken my hand at the end of our encounters, it looked like he was willing to keep our relationship on a business footing.

"Tor," I said aloud. "Torvald Thorlaksson."

I waited for half an hour, but he never called. I decided to stop kidding myself and called him.

"Good to hear from you." He sounded so pleased that I could imagine his smile, dimple and all.

"Is the offer of that full-time job still open?" I said.

"Sure. You could take it anytime."

"How about before my August rent's due? That's on Friday."

"How about today? I can help you pack."

"I don't have enough stuff to need help. I'll see you in a little while."

As soon as I got off the phone with Tor, I called my landlord to tell him he could have his slum hole back. The stuff I owned fit into one suitcase and two cardboard cartons. Most of my art supplies lived in a locker at school. I drove over to Tor's place and parked in front of the house. In the early afternoon light I could see the hillside behind it more clearly. At first glance it looked like a forest, but I could pick out a roof here and a redwood deck there. The pieces added up to two more houses with heavy plantings around them.

Tor came out and helped me carry everything upstairs. I stowed the suitcase and cartons in my new bedroom, then rejoined him in the kitchen. He gave me keys and also set up my smartphone for the security system so I could get in if he happened to be gone.

"Just make sure you arm the system again once you get upstairs," he said. "I'll show you how."

"Thanks. You've got some awfully nice things. I can see why you're worried about security. Those Chinese vases!"

"They're not tourist items, no."

"You've got all kinds of cool stuff. I'm kind of surprised you'd trust me like this. I mean, we just met."

He gave me the strangest smile. I couldn't tell if he was amused or saddened by what I'd just said. "Oh yeah," he said eventually. "But I've got ways of checking a person out. I know I can trust you."

"Ways? You mean with sorcery, I guess."

"Yeah. You're not offended, are you?"

I considered. "No," I said. "It's a lot easier than having to supply references."

I was expecting him to laugh or at least smile, but he just

nodded, as if he agreed.

"What else do you need to know?" he went on. "There's the garage. I don't have a car any more, so you might as well use it."

"You don't have a car? How do you get around—uh, sorry, never mind."

"Sorcery's a lot more ecologically sound than burning fossil fuels. It's too bad that not everyone can do it."

"Yeah, for sure. And speaking of burning things, I've got to get ready for work."

Quitting the burger job gave me my next big thrill. I went to work as usual, but as soon as I arrived, I told the manager I was leaving. I offered to stay on for a couple of days while they found someone else, but the manager had a file of students who wanted the job. No problem, he said. At the end of my shift, I was free of deep-fried grease at last. The night manager, a decent guy in his way, wished me luck with my new job.

"Thanks," I said. "Is there any way I can get my last check early?"

"They all ask that." He sighed and shrugged. "I'll hit up the boss for it. Don't hold your breath."

When I got back to the flat, Tor insisted I sit down and rest. I let myself sink into one of the leather chairs in the living room while he bustled around in the kitchen. He came out again with brandy in proper glass snifters.

"Just something to celebrate with," he said. "Celebrate you getting out of that apartment, I mean."

"Thanks. And I've quit the burger job, too. So that's something else to celebrate."

He saluted me with his glass. I had a sip of the brandy—very good, probably old, I figured, and expensive. I turned a little in my chair to look out at the view through the western window. Fog had crept in over San Francisco, though Yerba Buena Island and the East Bay were still clear. The lights of the distant city made the fog glow, shot here and there with streaks of color. In our companionable mood I came close to telling him the truth about my disease. Close, but not close enough—what if he threw me out? Rooming with vampires doesn't fit most people's definition of gracious living.

"You know something?" Tor said. "It's good to have you here."

"It's good to be here."

It was only a polite thing to say, but it gave me the oddest sensation—that I'd spoken something more true than I could know. For a brief moment I felt as if I'd been struggling to accomplish some task for a really long time, for years and years, even. I'd finally finished it. Or maybe I'd lost something, years and years ago, that I'd finally found again. None of it made sense. I put the sensation down to the brandy.

Later, when I went to my room, I looked at the decoupage on the writing desk. The green lion had returned to eat the sun, but around him the circles of shrimp and caterpillars had vanished. In their place flew butterflies.

CHAPTER 4

I slept so well in the Burne-Jones bedroom that I got to school late the next morning. During class, I had trouble concentrating on our current model, a man with an interesting but difficult asymmetric face. He had pale skin and thinning blond hair that he wore long and straggly. Trying to keep the textures of skin and hair separate drove me nuts, especially since part of my mind kept wondering how I was going to tell my friends about my new job. Cynthia noticed how distracted I was. When the model took his mid-morning break, she came over to my easel.

"Is something wrong?" she said.

"No, actually. Things are looking up. I quit the burger joint."

"That's great!" Cynthia grinned at me. "New job, huh?"

Brittany had drifted over to join us. "Sweet!" she said. "It couldn't have been good for you, breathing all that meat grease. And eating there, too." She shuddered with high drama. "Dead chemical food!"

"I'm glad to be out of there, yeah."

"Well, what's the new job?" Cynthia said.

I realized that the truth, or at least, part of it, could transform itself into the lie I needed. "Taking care of a shape-changer. Someone who turns into an animal now and then. Like in the folk tales, y'know?"

They both burst out laughing. "Oh come on, Maya!" Cynthia said. "What is it really?"

"That's it, really. This guy turns into a bear when the moon's full, and he's paying me to lock him into his room so he doesn't go out and hurt anyone." I kept my expression as serious as I could. "I get room and board, so I'm living there. Kind of an au pair for a were-bear."

"I get it now!" Cynthia was grinning at me. "You've moved in with some guy. You've been holding out on us about him."

"No, this is strictly a business arrangement."

"Oh yeah sure!" Brittany said. "Is he cute?"

"For a bear he's not bad. His name's Torvald, but I call him Tor. His family's from Iceland."

"That's probably why he's a shape-changer." Cynthia seemed to find my supposed joke worth elaborating. "The lonely glacial island and Viking settlers and all that amazing history."

"And the volcanoes." Brittany was speaking in dead seriousness. "Volcanoes are always centers of spiritual power. There's prana in them. Or something like that. They release it, anyway."

Although Cynthia rolled her eyes, I wondered if for a change Brittany was making sense. I'd seen National Geographic TV shows about volcanoes, and you could sense how powerful and strange and terrifying they were just from the footage. In person they must have inspired genuine awe. I could believe they did release some kind of sorcerous energy.

"Actually," I said, "he's a shape-changer because he got bitten by one over in Marin. There aren't any volcanoes over there."

"Just some totally weird people, huh?" Cynthia said. "Do we get to meet Tor?"

"I don't see why not. But it'll have to be when the moon isn't full."

They both laughed, and I grinned, but all I was doing was speaking the truth. You get good at weaseling when you've got a disease like mine. Their laughter made me realize something else, that the idea of a good-looking guy like Tor turning into a bear was too funny to be true. I thought of all those bears in movies for kids, the big, clumsy, furry clowns, or the sluggish critters I'd seen at the zoo. On the TV docs I'd seen some dangerous wild bears, fierce as tigers, and they could move really fast when they wanted to, but still! It can't be true, I told myself. It's just some kind of a joke on his part. A sorcerer's sense of humor was bound to be more than a little weird.

Before I left the campus I went to the Admin office and changed my address. I felt oddly solemn as I filled out the form, as if I'd made a crucial, momentous decision. I reminded myself that I could switch back to part-time at Tor's and find another place to live any time I wanted.

That afternoon, Tor and I worked out our routine around meals. He never ate breakfast, but he insisted on stocking up on breakfast things for me. He would do the shopping and cooking, and I'd clean up afterwards. I felt guilty at first. With the money he was paying me, I thought I should be doing more, but I was an awful cook, and he was a good one. He also had a housekeeping service come in twice a month to take care of the real cleaning. I began to feel like I was starting not a job but a vacation.

Tor also made a point of showing me both flats. No secrets, he told me, not like in those fairy tales. I knew the ones he meant, where the girl always opens the Forbidden Thing and suffers for it.

"There's nothing here I need to keep secret," Tor said. "You know the worst already."

He grinned at me, and I had to smile in return. That dimple at the corner of his mouth!

I'd already seen the library room downstairs, the place where you entered the flat. In daylight I noticed a washer and dryer set up in the adjoining kitchen. The rest of it pretty much followed the plan of the upper one, except of course for the chunk cut out for the upper flat's entrance and staircase. Beyond the library to the left as you came in was the smaller bedroom and bathroom, both echoing empty, though at the very end of the hall I spotted a closed door—a closet maybe—that I hadn't seen upstairs.

Off to the right of the library was the master suite. Instead of a bedroom set, though, the big room held a pair of wooden stools and a tall but narrow wooden table that reminded me of the chemistry lab in my old high school. Tor opened the cream-colored drapes over the window to let in some light. In the middle of the room lay a black carpet painted with a white circle, about nine feet across, in the center. Inside the circle an equal-armed cross cut it into four quarters. Where each line of the cross touched the circle, a red letter marked one of the cardinal directions.

"You can step on that," Tor said. "It's not active at the moment."

He led me across the room to a feature that didn't match the upstairs, a huge closet that lacked windows. I figured that someone had built it by taking space out of the master bedroom itself. One wall held a solid rank of wooden draw-ers, most of them shallow, like you'd find in the storerooms of an old-fashioned museum to hold trays of antique jewelry or prints.

"The guy who owned it before me put those in," Tor said. "I don't know why."

"You own this building?"

"Yeah. I need to, with the stuff I do."

Two luxury flats in the Oakland hills—his family must have had money, all right, heaps of it. I wasn't surprised when I noticed, on the opposite wall, a door to a combination safe.

"Want to see my secret treasures?" He was grinning at me.

"Sure."

I politely looked away while he worked the combination. One treasure turned out to be an old-fashioned oak display case, about two feet on a side. Tor laid it down on a wooden lectern in front of the storage unit. Against a background of yellowing linen, dimpled like an egg carton, it held a set of wooden disks, each about the size of a quarter. The wood looked ancient, dark and rubbed smooth by the touch of many years and even more hands. Each disk was engraved with a spiky, geometric mark, a letter of an ancient writing system.

"Those are runes," I said. "I've seen pictures of them in books on graphic design. It's the older alphabet, right?"

"The elder futhark, yes. This is a set that's come down in the family for close to six hundred years. I don't take them out, of course. They'd probably crumble if I tried."

"I hope that mount's archival material."

"It is, yeah. I had it checked just last year over in San Francisco. Even shut up like this, they have power." Tor ran one finger down the glass. His voice dropped to a near-whisper. "I can feel it even when they're in the safe. They fuel my work."

Without thinking I started to touch the side of the case. I felt an odd emanation, as if touching it would give me an electric shock. I drew my hand back fast. Tor tipped his head a little to one side and considered me.

"It's okay," he said. "There's nothing special about the case. It's something my father got at a garage sale. I think it originally held dead insects."

"I didn't want to be rude or anything. It was just my inner child coming out, I guess."

"Just so long as you don't want to put them in your mouth."

We shared a laugh. As he was putting the display case away, I noticed the only other object in the safe: a shoebox.

"What's that?" I said. "Or am I being nosey?"

"No, not at all. I wanted to show you everything."

He brought out the shoebox and opened it to reveal layers of cotton batting. He lifted those to one side and pulled out a flat golden square, inscribed with runes, big enough to cover the palm of his hand, and Tor had big hands. When he gave it me, it weighed heavy—solid gold. I whistled under my breath.

"I keep it in the safe because of the gold," he said. "I wouldn't want anyone stealing it to melt it down. They couldn't sell an item like this on the open market."

"Yeah, for sure! How old is it?"

"The experts think it dates from the last century before Christ."

I whistled again. "Where's it from originally?"

"The best guess is Gotland. That's an island off the coast of Sweden. My father had the gold analyzed, and it came from Eastern Europe, from mines on one of the ancient Gothic trade routes."

I examined the plaque more carefully. It had a hole at each corner, probably so it could be sewn onto a backing—I guessed horse harness, something leather, at any rate, because cloth would have ripped from the weight. The runic inscription ran around the edge. In the center sat a quartered circle like the one painted on the carpet—not a rune, but a very ancient and practically universal sign. On the back more runes formed a spiral.

"What does it say?"

"No one's really sure. It's most likely some kind of magical formula. Practically all the runes that have ever been found carved on objects are. The language must be some form of proto-Gothic, very old and real obscure. I made a rubbing of both sides. I've got it upstairs somewhere, and one of these days I'll work on it." He paused for a smile. "But it's got something to do with the Rime Jötnar, the frost giants. Ever heard of them?"

"No, I really don't know much about Nordic lore," I said. "When you study art history, or Western art history, I should say, but anyway, you learn a lot about the Greco-Roman myths, but not about the Norse."

"I can give you books if you're interested." Tor thought for a moment, frowning. "Yeah, I do have some in English. There are two main sources, the *Prose Edda* and the *Poetic Edda*, and I can give you translations. They're good stories."

"Cool! I love good stories." I held out the gold ornament. "I don't mean to be nosey, but where did you get this piece?"

"Where I get everything. I inherited it. I'm pretty useless on my own, or so I've been told."

Although he smiled, I heard a touch of bitterness in his voice. He took the gold ornament from me and stroked it with one finger. In a minute or maybe two, he went on, "A long time ago now my great-grandfather was digging a well on the family farm. He found a hoard of gold objects. In those days there wasn't any government archaeology board to buy up finds like that. So Great-Grandfather sold it off piecemeal, all except for this one thing, and hid the cash in a pickling crock in the farmhouse kitchen." He looked up and smiled again, but this time the bitterness was gone. "His son, my grandfather Halvar, found the cash and invested it. He's the one who made the family wealthy."

"I'm surprised he didn't sell this piece, too."

"I'm not sure why he didn't. Probably because no one knew what it was, and he was afraid of selling it too cheap." The bitterness returned to his voice. "Grandfather Halvar didn't like making bad bargains."

Tor returned the gold ornament to its batting, box, and the safe. Before we went back upstairs, he looked over the shelves in his library and found a stack of books for me to read, the two Eddas, some books on Norse history, and then a modern compilation of Norse myths.

"By the way," I said, "you don't have a TV, do you?"

"No. I hate them. They're useless noise, and they ruin people's brain waves."

I had no idea how to respond to that. He gave me a thin smile, as if he knew he'd shocked me.

"Look," he said. "Would you rub dirt into your eyes? Of course not! Well, your mind's the most important thing you have, and watching the crap they put on is just like rubbing dirt into it. Especially the commercials. Brain poison, that's what they are."

"Uh, well, if you say so."

"I won't have one in the house."

"Okay. I can live without it. I just wondered."

He was my boss, after all. I figured that if there was a show I absolutely had to watch, I could get it on my laptop or go to Cynthia's. Her husband had set up their flat screen TV on cable with a couple of DVRs, and they'd invited me over a number of times to catch up on stuff I'd missed.

That night Tor and I lingered at dinner, talking over the day. After I cleaned up the kitchen, Tor poured us each brandy, and we sat down in the living room.

"I love this view," I said.

"You've got the artist's eye. Which reminds me. Do you need more drawing stuff? In case the illusions come back. I bet whoever it is isn't going to give up after just one try."

"Probably not, no. I could use some more conté and another sketchbook. I can get them at the student store. They've got the best prices around."

"Okay, buy what you need, and I'll reimburse you."

On the way to class on Thursday, I stopped at the ATM for cash. My credit cards had hit their limit, and I refused to add an overdraft fee to my horrendous bills. When I bought the supplies after class, I made sure to get the receipt. I wanted to keep my relationship to Tor as business-like as possible.

Which was going to be difficult, I realized, when I returned to the flat that afternoon. I walked in to find Tor in the kitchen, putting away a sack of groceries. He turned from a cabinet and gave me a smile that announced how pleased he was to see me. His eyes became warm and alive. I felt myself respond, too, with my familiar treacherous thought. What would it be like to kiss that smile, that dimple at the corner of his mouth? I made myself look away and put the bag of art supplies down on the counter.

"Let me give you the bill," I said.

When I took receipt out of my purse, he walked over to take it from me. Our fingers touched, then brushed against each other's hand. I drew back fast, and he winced in disappointment.

"Tor," I said, "I hardly know you, and you don't know much about me, either."

For a moment I thought he was going to argue. He laid the money down on the counter, scowled at it, then forced out a stiff smile.

"Well, that's true enough," he said. "You're right, considering the way things are now. Sorry."

He turned sharply around and returned to putting away the groceries. I grabbed the bag of sketchpads and fled the kitchen. As I was stashing the drawing supplies in various rooms, I heard him go downstairs. When I went back into the kitchen, I found the money he owed me lying on the counter.

The next time I saw him, about an hour later, he acted as if nothing had happened. So did I—not that it worked for either of us. It's hot in the East Bay in July. I'd stood up for four hours, drawing preliminary graphite sketches of the model. When I got a good one, I transferred it to canvas, then glazed with acrylic medium. After class, I walked around the student store, where I'd picked up a surge of élan along with the drawing supplies.

"I'm going to go clean up," I said. "I know I stink."

"I wouldn't call it that. You smell good to me."

He meant it, too. His eyes had turned heavy-lidded, stripped of their usual bitterness, and his mouth had relaxed into a soft curve instead of the tight line. I wanted to walk over to him and let him kiss me. No, I wanted him to do a lot more than just kiss me. I could feel the longing where it mattered.

"Uh, I need to take a shower." A cold one, I thought. Right now.

He sighed. "Yeah, I suppose you'd better."

I hurried into my bedroom and shut the door behind me. I took a pair of shorts and a shirt into the bathroom. Once I had the door closed and locked, I took off my dirty clothes. After my shower, I put on the clean clothes behind the same closed door. When I came out again, Tor had masked himself in the illusion of the nerdy guy with the vacant eyes. He'd been reading on the couch, but he laid his book aside and stood up.

"It'll be the full moon in about a week," he said. "I thought you'd better see my lair." He tried to smile, then let it fade. "Well, it's the bjarki's lair when he's dominant. It's mine the rest of the time."

The lair turned out to be the master suite. The bedroom had soothing blue-gray walls, a green and blue area rug, and antique furniture: a big oak bed, a dresser, an oak wardrobe, and a couple of upholstered armchairs. There were yellow drapes at a window that he'd fitted with safety glass, the kind with a fine mesh embedded in it. On one wall hung the pastel portrait I'd done of him that day at the fair. He'd had it matted and framed.

"I'm surprised you kept that," I said.

"Well, it says a lot about me." He gave me a shy smile. "Besides, you drew it."

I had no idea what to say to that. I turned away and glanced around.

"What's the safety glass for?" I said.

"The bjarki tried to throw himself out of the window once. I pulled back just in time."

"Do you still know you're Tor when you're transformed?"

"Kind of. It feels like I'm dreaming." He frowned down at the floor. "That's the only reason I haven't gone out and hurt someone. It's like there's two of me. And we fight the whole damn time."

"God, that must be awful!"

"It is, yeah." He turned away and walked over to the clutter on top of his dresser. "Let me give you the keys."

On the outside of the door he'd installed a safety chain and a formidable looking lock.

"There's a deadbolt, too." He handed me a ring with two keys on it. "The bjarki gets pretty desperate, and he bangs on the door a lot. I can't stop him till he wears himself out."

I glanced at the inside of the heavy wood door and noticed long claw marks. No way could Tor have made those with his fingernails. I looked around and saw that something had chewed the edge of the flimsier closet door into splinters. I felt cold all over, and I must have turned pale, because Tor saw my reaction.

"It's really real." His voice ached with sadness. "I know it's hard to believe, but I really do turn into a bear. It's in the old sagas, too. I'll have to get you some of those to read. You'll understand more, then."

Just like my disease is real, I thought to myself. I wanted to tell him, to explain that I lived under a curse just like he did, but I'd hidden my condition for so many years, and I was so afraid of losing what he was giving me, that I kept silent.

Since I needed to buy gas, I left for school early the next morning. When I backed my heap out of the garage, I noticed the filthy windshield and got out to attend to it. I kept a roll of paper towels and a bottle of window cleaner in the back seat. I was wiping down the glass when a gray car—a sleek, expensive-looking ride—drove by the house. I would have thought nothing of it if the driver hadn't looked familiar.

I only caught a glimpse of him, but he reminded me of Tor. Even though the sunny morning was already heating up, he wore a jacket with the collar turned up, as if he were hiding his face. I watched him as he drove down to the end of the street and hung a right onto the avenue that led downhill toward Broadway. It took me a few minutes to clean all the car windows, but when I drove down and turned onto the avenue, I spotted him, parked in a driveway half-hidden by trees.

When I drove by, he pulled out and followed me. I kept glancing into the rear view mirror and caught glimpses of him, enough to confirm that he was the man I'd seen looking into the café window, the older guy who resembled Tor. At the gas station, he drove on by and merged into the lane that would eventually take him onto the freeway. Even so, I kept glancing into the rear-view mirror all the way to school. I never spotted him.

Was he the same guy who'd sent those illusions? I had no way of knowing, but who else would it have been? Maybe he was checking me out, seeing if the woman who'd thwarted him was a permanent resident at Tor's. I could come up with any number of paranoid ideas.

After class, Cynthia, Brittany, and I were walking to the parking lot together. Brittany was telling me about Roman's progress with the group therapy when I had the feeling that I was being watched. It grew so strong that I stopped and turned slowly around, looking at every building, every tree, anything that might shelter a staring creep.

"What is it?" Cynthia said.

"I keep feeling like someone's watching me, but there's no one there."

"That must be what's causing the weird vibe," Brittany said. "I've been picking up something all morning, and I bet that's it."

"What kind of something?" Cynthia said.

"I dunno exactly." Brittany considered for a moment. "Like something was disturbing my aura. A feeling of danger but not to me. I thought it meant Roman was in trouble, but maybe it applies to Maya instead."

"You know," I said. "I don't think I'll go to lunch with you guys, after all. I want to go home."

"Just be careful when you're driving," Brittany said. "Don't go on the freeway, okay?"

"Okay. I'll see you Monday."

I took Brittany's advice. Over the past few years I'd often joined Cynthia in teasing Brittany about her goopy New Age ideas, but now I regretted not paying them more attention. Maybe we'd always suspected she was right, I thought. Maybe that's why we had to tease her, so we could pretend the universe was all clean and rational, that shape-changers and sorcerers only existed in the fantasy books. Even though I called myself a vampire, I'd never put myself in the same class as those fictional creatures of the night. I was just a girl with an awful disease.

Wasn't I?

When I got back to the house, I found Tor in the kitchen, where he was cutting up vegetables for salad. He looked so normal, so solid, that I wanted to run to him and ask him to hold me. Instead I just said hello.

"What's wrong?" he said. "You look like something frightened you."

"Something did."

When I told him about the car following me and my feelings of being spied upon, Tor frowned in thought for a couple of minutes.

"Have you ever come back here when I was gone?" he said eventually. "I'm wondering if he's trying to see you re-arming the security system."

"So he can get the passcode?" I thought back over my brief time of living in the flat. "No, you've always been here, and so the system's been off."

"That's a relief. Though I don't know why he'd spy on you when you're in school, if the passcode's what he wants." He considered this for another minute, then shrugged. "I wonder if he drove by to make sure you were living here now."

"That'd be my guess, yeah."

"It's a good thing you're not living alone anymore, with this guy hanging around spying on you."

I went cold all over. "It's something you're always aware of," I said, "when you're a girl on your own, being stalked, I mean. But I don't think this guy's just the usual kind of creep."

"He can't be, yeah. Pervs don't usually know how to scry. I'll bet he's our illusionist, or at least, he's got to be connected to the attacks. Sorcerers don't grow on trees, y'know."

I managed to smile at the joke.

"Look," Tor continued, "let's not take any chances. Are you going out tonight or anything?"

"No. I was going to start reading the books you loaned me."

"Okay. That'll give me time to do a thorough job. I'm going to make you a bindrune talisman. It'll look like a piece of jewelry, a pendant on a thong. You'll need to wear it whenever you leave the house."

"Bindrune?"

"That's just the name for this kind of operation. You bind the magic into the object with the runes. It looks like a monogram. I'll use a couple of runes that offer protection and combine them into a little design, then energize them. If someone's using magic to spy on you, it'll keep the prying eyes off." He gave me a sly smile. "If it doesn't work, then maybe we should see about getting you into therapy."

I laughed and pretended to swat at him with one hand. He grinned in return, his real smile, not the nerdy illusion. I felt like my heart had turned over in my chest. He was watching me expectantly, as if he were hoping I'd give him an opening, or make the first move, or in some other way give into the raw desire I felt swirling around us. If it had been just smidgen stronger, I swear, it would have been as visible as smoke.

"I'd better clean up before lunch," I said.

His grin disappeared, but he forced out a civil expression.

"Okay," he said. "While you do that, I'm going to send my sister another email. I can't help wondering if the guy you saw drive by is a relative. I don't come from a big family, so if he looked like me, well, that's evidence. And if he is from my family, who knows what kind of magic he can work? Something strange, probably."

Tor spent the afternoon down in the lower flat, while I stayed in my room reading. The Norse myths were good stories, just as he'd told me, though kind of on the grim side. When we ate dinner, I asked him if he and his family believed in gods like Odin and Thor.

"Not literally," he said, "not like Fundi Christians believe in their Jesus. The Norse gods represent principles of the universe, true things in their way. You can contact those principles, or the forces that emanate from them, and then they feel like persons. Sometimes I do feel like I'm talking to Odin, and he hears me." His face turned slightly pink. "But that's just the human mind, turning abstract principles into something concrete." The pink got brighter. "Not that I'm divinely inspired or anything. I don't mean to preach."

"You're not preaching," I said. "This is all really cool stuff."

But when I asked a couple more questions, he gave me short, embarrassed answers, and so I let the subject drop.

After dinner Tor went downstairs to charge my talisman, or so he told me. Whatever that entailed took several hours. I was sitting in one of the leather armchairs, studying the view of the Bay and San Francisco, when he returned. I stood up to see what he'd brought me: a beautiful pendant, a thin oak roundel about an inch and a half in diameter, dangling from a leather thong. He'd incised the design, then laid rust-colored paint, or so I thought, in the grooves. He'd glazed the whole thing with acrylic medium—I recognized the faint scent—to seal it. The runes reminded me of old-fashioned peace symbols, but placed upside-down, each set at a different angle to form a kind of bouquet. Lying horizontally across their nexus were two axe-like shapes, each a line with a little triangle placed in the middle. One triangle faced down, and the other, up.

"The runes I used are Yew and Thorn," he told me. "For this kind of thing you can reverse the runes, double them, put them sidewise, whatever, without any negative effects. The idea is to make something that looks decorative, so if anyone notices, they won't think much of it."

"It looks wonderful. Thank you. What kind of coloring material did you use on the runes?" He smiled and held up his left hand to show me a band-aid on his index finger.

"Blood?" I said. "You used your own blood to stain it?"

"That what the old texts all say you should use. I like to do these things right."

When he handed me the pendant, it seemed to tremble with energy in my hand. I began to think that he was right about my having some kind of magical talent, if I could feel the energies so clearly. I refused to follow the thought down. He stepped behind me.

"You hold that where you'd like it to hang," he said, "and I'll knot the thongs together."

I considered different placements, then held the disc comfortably below the collarbone. I hate chokers, any kind of jewelry that clings to my neck. Although the sensation of energy persisted, I felt it as pleasant rather than annoying. Tor picked up the loose thongs and knotted them. When his fingers brushed the back of my neck, I felt a shiver of a different kind of energy, a perfectly natural animal feeling, run down my spine. For a moment he stayed where he was, so close, so inviting—all I had to do was lean back into his arms, and he'd take over. I stepped forward instead.

"Thank you," I said. "I want to see how this looks in a mirror. It's really beautiful."

"You're welcome."

His voice stayed steady, but when I turned around, I could see the disappointment in his eyes.

"I'm sorry," I said. "I'd just like to get to know you better before we get—well—involved. If we do."

"If." Tor looked down at the floor. "I can't blame you. You haven't seen the worst of me, Maya. I know that."

"The bjarki, you mean."

"What else?"

"I just feel like I owe you—" I was about to say, *owe you an explanation,* nothing more than that, but he interrupted with a snarl.

"You don't owe me anything but the terms of our agreement. What do you think I want? Sex with you even if it makes you feel like a cheap whore?"

I stammered out a few words. He turned fast, walked away, hurried downstairs, and I heard him slam the door behind him.

"Well, no," I said to the jade mountain sculpture. "Not a cheap whore. An expensive one."

I followed Tor downstairs. In the lower flat he'd gone into the walk-in closet that held the lectern and the wall safe. When I came in, he was standing at the lectern in a pool of light from an overhead lamp and looking at a folio of black and white prints. One of the long skinny drawers in the storage unit stood half-open.

"Yeah?" His voice sounded perfectly pleasant, and he'd sheltered his eyes behind the nerd illusion.

"I wanted to tell you," I said, "that no, I don't feel I owe you anything except doing the job you hired me for. As for the—well, the sex—if I ever decide to sleep with you, it'll be because I want to. No other reason."

The illusion vanished. Despite the torment in his eyes, he smiled. "Okay," he said. "Thank you." He paused, considered, and smiled again. "I like that. It gives me hope."

"Hope? For what?" I had the goopy idea that he meant 'hope that maybe you'll fall for me.'

"That someday I can be happy for one whole day without thinking about the bjarki."

He looked down at the open folio on the lectern. When I followed his gaze, I saw an engraving of two hunters, skinning a dead bear in blood-stained snow.

CHAPTER 5

Whatever magic Tor put into the bindrunes worked. I had no more sensations of being watched, even when I drove down to the local mall on Saturday afternoon. I'd not felt well all morning—the usual aches and pains in my joints, the clammy-cold sweat. By the time I finished buying a few sundries, toothpaste, deodorant, little things like that, my blouse was sticking to my back. I felt dizzy enough to sit down and rest on a convenient bench. The hunger kept building in my blood. I found myself staring at the people passing by, the young men arrogant in their health, the women who giggled and flirted, secure in their youth. I wanted their life. I needed it, I craved it, I had to have the élan that oozed from their bodies, a healing mist. I felt it that day more strongly than I had in years. Death was walking behind me, stalking, moving in closer.

At the same time I hated the craving. I hated my disease. I hated myself.

I got up and began to walk through the mall to places where the crowd looked thick and ripe, in front of computer stores and the kind of clothing outlets that cater to the young and healthy. In the weekend crowd I managed to accidentally on purpose bump into a number of people, just by stopping abruptly to gawk at store windows when I should have moved aside. I made sure to siphon élan only from the kind of person who could regenerate the smidgen I took in a couple of minutes—or so I hoped. They'd never done me any harm, none of the people I stole from. That thought always hurt whenever I went hunting, kind of like having a thorn in your conscience.

The sense of relief kept me going. Every time I drained élan, just a bit, just a quick slurp of life, I felt the hunger ease. For a few moments I felt healthy and strong enough to hunt again, to take a smidgen from the guy in tennis clothes, the girl gazing at a window full of sexy underwear. Slowly the level built in my body. I began to feel almost normal, almost healthy as the energy I stole seeped into my blood and bones. But the guilt rose as well. The thorn in my conscience pricked and dug.

Sometimes it hurt less than others. My big coup of the day came when I went to buy vitamins. A pair of overly muscled guys in sweats were blocking the entrance to the health food outlet. They smirked when they saw me walking toward them and stayed where they were, waiting for the pretty girl to touch them as she pushed a way between them. Fair game, I figured, and slurped up a lot of energy from each of them. As it slid down my parched throat, I felt strong enough to run and laugh or even dance out in the sunlight. When I left the shop, the pair had already gone. They probably needed naps. As for me, my death had lost my trail. It would find me again, but for a few days, I was safe.

I was heading for the exit when I realized someone was staring at me. I'd stopped for a legitimate look into the window of a clothing store, because it held a display of linen blouses that I wished I could afford. In the reflection I saw a young man with pale hair, slender, dressed in jeans and a gray hoodie across the corridor. Although he was standing in front of a computer store, he had his back to the display and was watching me. My back prickled with fear. The bindrune would protect against magic, not the ordinary physical gaze. I left the window and started walking again, but I stopped suddenly and looked behind me. There he was, and this time he'd gotten close enough to look familiar. I'd known him somewhere, some time a long time ago. He ducked into a bookstore, so fast that I knew he'd done it to hide from me.

Who was he, why was he so familiar—but then I remembered the illusionist. I paused and tried to gather my thoughts. *Who is he, who is he really?* I turned the words into a mantra and waited. When he stepped out of the bookstore, the young man in the hoodie seemed to shimmer, melt, and turn into someone else. I recognized him for real: the older man who looked like Tor except for his gray hair and little paunch.

I hurried back toward the center of the mall, where I'd seen a couple of security guards earlier. Every time I looked into a shop window, I saw the middle-aged guy still following me, weaving through the crowd, getting closer and closer. When I reached the big marble atrium, I saw the two guards talking together at a coffee stand. I stopped walking and spun around. My shadow stopped about five feet away. He had Tor's strong jaw, his height, his thick straight hair—but malice shone in his blue eyes. He wore expensive, sleek clothes, a silk shirt, tailored slacks. When he realized I was confronting him, he took a quick step back.

"Stop following me, you creep!" I raised my voice deliberately. "Leave me alone!"

He stared, absolutely stunned, as if he'd been attacked by a sheep.

"I don't even know who you are," I went on, "so stop it!"

Several older women paused, looked, and took a few steps closer to me. The guy shoved his hands into the pockets of his pale blue slacks.

"Don't give me that!" His dark voice dripped arrogance. "You know damn well who I am. You've got to remember me."

"I don't." I snapped. "Except you're a creep who follows girls around. A stalker, that's what you are! You've been following me in your car, too."

I felt rather than saw someone hurrying up behind me. I glanced over my shoulder and saw a security guard, his mouth set and grim.

"All right, fella," he said. "Leave the girl alone! In fact, why don't you just leave?"

Once again the guy stared in utter disbelief. I could

practically read his thoughts from his expression of sheer
outrage: how dare this person speak to me this way! The two
older women walked over to stand next to me. The security
guard laid a hand on the billy club hanging from his belt.
The guy turned and strode off, head up, back straight, the
picture of frustrated arrogance.

"I'll walk you to your car," the guard said. "You don't live
alone, do you?"

"No," I said. "I live with my boyfriend."

"Good. If that jerk bothers you again, call the police,
okay?"

"I will, and thank you." I turned to the older women and
smiled. "And thank you, too,"

"Just be real careful," one of them said. "Tell your boyfriend about this guy."

"I will. For sure."

Although I stayed on my guard when I was driving back,
I never saw the car I'd previously seen the stalker driving.
I did see lots of expensive gray or silver cars, which meant
nothing. It was possible, I reminded myself, that he could
rent different models if he really had something criminal in
mind—like maybe rape. Or was that too normal? If he were
another sorcerer, if he was the guy who'd sent the illusions,
who'd spied on me magically before Tor had given me the
talisman, who knew what he might have in mind?

Tor wasn't my boyfriend, of course, but I made sure to
tell him about the stalker as soon as I returned to the flat. As
he listened, his eyes narrowed, and he set his jaw in anger.

"If he comes around here," Tor said. "I'll deal with him,
all right. Look, be real careful, will you? When you're driving
back and forth to school. And especially if you go out at night."

"I will, for sure. I'll stick to busy streets. He can't pull
anything down on Broadway."

"Yeah, that's true. Okay. I'm going to go downstairs and
cast the staves. I want to see if I can pick up something more
about this bozo."

He spoke as calmly and with as much conviction as if

he'd told me he was going to look the guy up in a phone-book. Maybe it's that easy for him, I thought. I had no way of knowing, either way.

Whether it was listening to Brittany talk about vibes and auras, or to Tor explaining runes and the gods, I began to feel as if I were being sensitized to magic. My father's talk of using ritual magic to alter consciousness had always seemed plausible but distant. My mother's Buddhist beliefs had struck me as real, but I didn't want Nirvana, not yet, anyway. I wanted to live.

The things happening around me came from an older, more frightening but more immediate set of beliefs. Shaman-ism, Mom would have called it, Tor and his gods and magical markings on wood and stone. An enemy shaman could throw things into Tor's house, pictures and sounds, and he meant both of us harm. Worst of all, he could look like someone else when he wanted to. I'd have to be on guard against illusions. I took to constantly looking around me, always checking out the shadows, the corners of rooms, anything that might hide some evil thing. I flipped back and forth between laughing at the idea that Tor would turn into a bear and feeling terrified by the possibility. Once the moon became full, I told myself, I'd know if it were true or not.

Tor had become just as jumpy, he told me that afternoon. He also checked his email every half-hour or so, even though he made fun of himself for doing it. It took until Sunday night, though, for his sister to answer him. Even then, all she said was, "I'll look into it."

"I was afraid of that," Tor said. "She probably won't go into town again till next week. Oh well, I should be over the damn change by then."

We were sitting in the living room that evening with the drapes open so we could see the western view. It was a gor-geous clear summer night in the East Bay, although San Fran-cisco wore its usual halo of fog. Tor shut down his laptop and placed it on the coffee table.

"I've been meaning to ask you," he said, "how much longer

will you be in summer school?"

"Three more weeks. Then we have a month off before the regular session starts."

"Were you planning on taking any evening classes?"

"No. Pretty much all the units I need to graduate are in studios and workshops. Natural light is a must. Some of the basic drawing classes run at night, and the required English and history stuff, but I had those in my first year."

"That's a relief. Then you'll be able to be here in the evenings, the ones I'll need you for, I mean." His eyes turned grim, and his face slackened. "It'll be the full moon in a few days."

I turned in my chair to look out of the east-facing window. The moon had risen over the hills, a pale silvery gold, waxing at its first quarter.

As the week went on, Tor grew more and more silent, turned inward, frightened and yet resigned. He reminded me of a man facing a dangerous surgery, like maybe a heart by-pass or organ transplant, something of that magnitude, anyway, that could kill him. All he could do was hope that he'd come through the ordeal, because the only way to avoid it was to die.

I picked up his mood. Every day I rushed home from school, half-expecting to find that he'd hanged himself as a sacrifice to Odin. Could this bjarki business possibly be real? Something had chewed up the closet door. Tor just didn't strike me as the kind of person who'd make up an elaborate lie and provide props for it. If it was true, I wondered if I'd be able to do what he needed when he was in bear form. What if the bjarki got out of his lair? How could I put him back in? I had no idea if the Tor inside the bear would even remember who I was. The thought of those gouges in the door of his room made me shiver.

Thursday afternoon I found a stack of paperback books on the coffee table. Tor had gone shopping and bought me translations of all kinds of Norse and Icelandic literature, myths and old sagas.

"More good stories," he told me. "Kind of grim reading, but I dunno, no worse than the stuff they show in the movies."

"Thanks! This is all really interesting. Everyone hears about the Vikings, but there's this whole other side to their world. I didn't know about it before." I picked up a book and thumbed through it. "How do you pronounce this guy's name?" I said. "En-jall?"

"Nuh-yall. He gets burned alive."

Like Tor said, no worse than the stuff they show in the movies.

That night the moon rose just after we'd eaten supper. Tor got up from the breakfast bar and stared out the east window. His shoulders slumped, and he caught his breath in a near-sob.

"Gods in heaven," Tor said. "I'm so tired." He glanced over his shoulder at me. "Everything turns inward, the day before. All my energy, I mean." He turned back to look at the moon and shuddered, then walked, as bent and slow as an old man, into the living room.

I cleared off the supper dishes and put them in the dishwasher. By the time I joined him, he was sitting slouched in one of the leather chairs, so still that for a moment I thought he'd slipped into a faint or trance state.

"Tor?" I said.

Slowly, as if his neck pained him, he looked my way.

"You okay?"

"For now." He returned to staring out the east-facing window. "The moon's position starts the process, not the moonlight. That's just reflected sunlight. It's got something to do with tidal forces, I think."

"Are you in pain?"

"Not exactly. It's a weird sensation. I have to suck up energy for the change, gather it in. It's hard to describe."

"You can get this energy from the air?"

"Yeah. I always take as much as I can, just in case. It's a lot more than I need and makes me feel bloated, but I'd hate to get stuck in bear form and not be able to get back. That's my worst nightmare. I'd have to figure out some way to kill myself."

His quiet sincerity frightened me. I could no longer dismiss the bjarki as a sorcerer's weird idea of a joke. Whether or not he really turned into a bear, he believed he did, and it tormented him. I walked over behind his chair and laid my hands on his shoulders.

"Let me rub them," I said. "You look so uncomfortable."

"Thanks. I am."

I dug into his shoulders in a real massage, and he sighed, pleased. I kept it up, working on his neck, too, until I felt the tendons and muscles relax under my fingers. He was paying me to take care of him, I figured, during this part of the month. I was glad I could do something to earn the money. Now and then I felt a wisp of the élan he was gathering come my way. I never would have stolen from him, but I saw nothing wrong with capturing the stray bits and fragments that hung loose in the air behind him. He never noticed.

Tor watched the moon all evening. He staggered into his room at ten o'clock to go to bed. He slept late the next morning, staggering out again just as I got home from class. He fried up a whole pound of bacon. Although he offered me some, I turned it down, and he ate the entire pound, nothing else, just the bacon. In the afternoon, he went to the local grocery store and came back with bunches of greens and a whole salmon. He unwrapped the fish, cut it up, and stowed it in the little refrigerator in his bathroom.

"I hate having to chew the plastic wrap off," he told me. "It tastes really bad."

"I can believe it," I said. "By the way, you look exhausted."

"I am." He began to pluck at the fabric of his shirt as if it itched wherever it touched him. "You'd better lock me in now." He opened the door. "See you in three days. Whatever you do, don't let me out unless the place is on fire. Okay?"

"I promise. Look, I was thinking of going back to campus for a figure drawing session. They're informal, I don't have to go, but I hate to miss them. Would that be okay?"

"As long as you're back before dark, sure. After that, no,

don't leave me." His voice dropped. "Please?"

"Don't worry. I'll stay here till you change back."

He stepped in and shut the door. I locked it with the key, slid the deadbolt, and put on the safety chain. Despite his permission, I wondered if I should leave. After double-checking everything that could possibly start a fire, I decided that I could. He had everything he needed.

I ended up leaving the drawing session early. Since I had to stay in the flat for a couple of days, I needed to stockpile more élan. I went to the mall, which at the dinner hour was half-empty. I only managed to steal a few drips and drabs from a gaggle of teen-age girls who suddenly stopped in front of me to squeal at some teen boys they knew. I might have gone elsewhere to hunt, but I had to keep track of the time.

I returned to the house just at sunset, when there was plenty of twilight left in the sky. I drove into the garage, but before I shut the door I walked back outside and looked to the east. The full moon hung over the eastern hills like a crown of silver light. When I turned to the west, I could see a few bright stars above the sun's last glow. Beautiful, calm, peaceful—the last time I'd ever use those words to describe the full moon night.

As soon as I got upstairs, I heard the bjarki moaning, a desperate little sound, moaning and snuffling at the door of the master suite. I walked a few steps into the hallway. The bjarki heard my footsteps and moaned even louder, begging, heart-broken. He wanted to run, he longed for the forest, he ached to run free—I felt that I could hear his thoughts through those animal sounds. He threw himself against the door so hard that the safety chain rattled.

"No," I said. "You can't come out. You don't dare come out. That's why I'm here, to keep you in. Remember?"

Silence—for a minute or two. He threw himself against the door again, then growled. He chuffed, a weird breathy sound, then roared and grumbled.

"No! You have to stay in there, Tor! Eat some of the fish. You'll feel better with something to gnaw."

The silence lasted for maybe twenty minutes that time. I'd just heated myself some leftovers in the microwave when I heard him first growl, then roar, a throaty, breathy sound, different from a lion's roar though just as loud. No wonder he needed to own the entire building. Downstairs neighbors would have meant big trouble. I picked up a sketchbook and started a page for questions to ask Tor once he was himself again. First question: does it make you feel better or worse if I stand outside the door and talk to you?

The growling and roaring continued at intervals all night long. Even though my room was on the other side of the flat, I could hear him banging on the door. I could only hope that he wasn't strong enough to knock it down, locks or no locks. He'd stay quiet for maybe half an hour, long enough for me to fall asleep. He'd start in again, and I'd wake up. Around dawn I gave up. I staggered out of bed and went into the kitchen to brew some strong coffee.

As I watched it drip into the carafe, I realized the truth of my situation. The exact same ordeal would recur every month. I was going to earn every penny of my salary—if I could even keep the job. For those of us afflicted with vampirism, exhaustion is dangerous. We can't regenerate our vital forces just by catching up on a few hours' sleep. My legs ached from hip to ankle. My hands hurt every time I picked up an object. Cold sweat trickled down my back.

I nearly cried. For the first time in my life I had comfort, support, everything I needed, and I might have to throw it all away because the job could kill me. I'd promised him I'd stay for the full three nights of his change. The agony I heard in his raw animal sounds made me determined to keep that promise, too, which meant I couldn't even go out and try to steal energy from the healthy. That morning I found myself hating healthy people, the kind of deep toxic hatred that springs from envy. It would poison me, I knew, if I let it, even though it would make what I needed to do easier.

Once the moon started to wane and I could leave the flat, I'd have to turn into a dedicated hunter, go around looking for crowds and innocent victims, taking a slurp here, a smidgen there, stealing mouthfuls of other people's lives in a desperate attempt to replace what I'd lost. If I hated them, I could steal without the ache in my conscience—if I even had enough energy left to go hunting. Since I'd never been so close to meltdown before, I had no way of knowing if I would or not.

Maybe it would be better, I figured, to let the disease take its course, to let myself run down and die like a watch that never will keep the right time. Just as I had that thought, Tor began to growl and moan. I could hear him throwing himself against the door of his lair.

The day got even worse when I happened to look at the headboard of my bed and see that the carved moon had become full. I wandered over and checked the writing desk. More changes: the green lion had finished eating the sun and turned into a red lion. He looked sick, too, and all the butterflies hovered closer as if they were waiting to attack his corpse. The psychic atmosphere, as Tor had called it, in the building was as sick as I was. I raised the lid and saw that the zodiacal sun had disappeared. In its place was a bear's head in profile. Its nose pointed to the sign of Leo.

The next day was different though no better. I did get enough sleep, because the bjarki fell completely silent. When I woke, I was no longer sweating, though my legs ached so badly that I risked taking a couple of ibuprofen. I had no idea if painkillers would make my élan shortage worse or better. They did ease the ache. Once I realized, however, that Tor had been quiet for hours, I began to worry that he was dead or seriously ill. I spent a lot of time sitting outside the door of his lair and listening for the sound of him moving around, or snoring, or even just plain breathing.

I heard nothing until the moon rose again, an hour or so after sunset. The bjarki began to roar and growl, maybe in greeting, maybe in pain—I could only hope it was the former. To get away from the sound, I limped outside and looked at the rising moon. Lop-sided, for sure, no longer perfectly full. One more night, I told myself. Just one more night. When

I opened the door to go back in, pain stabbed through my fingers.

I returned to the upstairs flat and walked down the hall to listen at the door. The howling had stopped. I heard claws clicking as the bjarki paced back and forth. Now and then he whimpered or chuffed. I went back to the living room and flopped down on the leather couch. Tired, so tired—I held out my hands and saw that my knuckles were beginning to redden and swell. My vital forces had started their fall toward the danger point. My father had warned me what to expect, what to watch out for.

Did I really want to die? No. Death terrified me, that long night with no sunrise. I loved being alive, loved making art, seeing art, going for long walks, being with my friends, hearing music. But did I want to stay a predator, roaming around hungry, always on the look-out for someone I could tap for a little bit of that precious élan vital? What if I succumbed one day and took so much life force that I left someone crippled, half-alive, even dead? The thought made me tremble and sweat in terror. No, never, not that!

I could think of no solution, none. I staggered into the bedroom and lay down for a nap. The bjarki began to roar and growl. I got up and turned on the floor lamp, just because I no longer wanted to lie in the dark. I was afraid to look at the writing desk. Eventually the bjarki quieted. I took off my shoes and bra and lay down, still dressed in shorts and a T-shirt, just in case something awful happened and I had to spring into action. After a lot of tossing and turning, I fell asleep.

I woke late the next morning to a silent flat. I got up and hurried out to the living room. I could hear a strange whispery sound, a slight humming overhead. Hell! I thought. What's happening now? When I realized I was hearing water in the pipes, I started to laugh. Tor had to be taking a shower, and that meant the bjarki had changed back. I fished the keys to the lair out of my backpack.

I ran down the hall to his door and took off the safety

chain, then hesitated. Possibly the bjarki could use a paw to turn on the water in order to fool me. The sound of the plumbing stopped. I heard a different sound, a human voice singing bits and pieces of songs, opera arias maybe, some kind of classical music, in a strong tenor.

"Tor?" I called out.

"I'm back. You can open up."

His voice sounded vibrant, more forceful than I'd ever heard it. I figured he felt relieved at having the change over for another month. My red and swollen hands struggled with the key, but I finally unlocked the door, opened it, and looked in—he was wearing only a pair of jeans and holding a T-shirt in one hand. The room smelled like sweat and fish scraps.

"God, the fug!" I said. "You could open a window."

"Good idea." He grinned at me and tossed the T-shirt onto one of the chairs.

I watched him stride to the window. His muscled back glistened with damp from the shower. I realized that I was trembling, not from the sight, nice though it was, but from the feel of life force in the air. Energy poured out of him and swirled around the room. I took a few steps in before I even realized that I'd moved. Tor flung up the window and stood for a moment breathing in the fresh air. As it flowed inside, it carried a waft of his excess élan right to me. I breathed deep, soaked it up, walked in a little farther, felt it pour over me. I gasped and pulled it into my aching body and soul.

Tor turned around. I loved the way he looked at me, desire as pure as the life force swirling around us both.

"Maya," he said, "you'd better leave the room. I uh—"

I grabbed the hem of my shirt, pulled it over my head and off. My fingers no longer hurt. He stared wide-eyed at my breasts. I felt my nipples respond.

"You what?" I dropped the shirt onto the floor and began to unzip my shorts.

He strode over, caught me by the shoulders, and kissed me open-mouthed. The feel of his élan, life flowing, life restoring—I soaked it in. I'd never taken so much and so freely from anyone, but he was stripping off all the extra energy he'd gathered to make the shape-change. He was throwing away what I needed to live. I sopped it up, reveled in it, and wanted more.

"Let's go to your room." His voice shook. "There's animal hair all over the bed in this one."

"I don't care." I let the shorts drop to the floor. "I don't want to waste any—to wait, I mean."

Judging by the way he kissed me, I doubt if he even noticed my slip-up. I stepped free of my shorts, then reached down to unzip his jeans. They slid down as he walked me backward to the bed. With one hand he pulled off the blanket to expose clean sheets. We fell on the bed together, rolled over each other, clasped in each other's arms. With every kiss he gave me, every caress, he shed the excess life force.

I sobbed in his arms with excitement. Ecstasy overwhelmed me from the feast, the abundance of his cast-off élan, more than I'd ever dared to take, more than I could even absorb. Like waves the raw pleasures of feeding flowed over me.

The orgasm was just a bonus.

He never cried out, but I felt his climax. He rested for a moment, then rolled off to lie on his side next to me. With his free arm he pulled me close. I cuddled up to him and listened to his heart pounding until at last it slowed into a normal rhythm. He kissed me on the forehead and smiled at me.

"I hope you realize what this means," he said.

"Umm? What?"

"You've just become my mate. I hope you don't have another boyfriend somewhere."

"No," I said. "Even if I did, I'd call him right now and tell him goodbye."

"Good. That way I wouldn't have to kill him."

I had the distinct feeling that he meant it. I raised up on one elbow and looked at his face. His expression: perfectly calm, perfectly pleasant, perfectly sincere.

"You're kidding, aren't you?" I said. "About killing someone, I mean."

"No." He kept the straight face. "Assuming, of course, that he was another bear like me. We'd have to fight over you, then, in the autumn before we hibernate."

"Oh good grief! You had me going for a minute there."

Finally he grinned at me. I lay down again.

"Don't worry," I said. "I am so not poly. Whether it's with apes or bears."

"Good. Neither am I. I just thought we should get that clear right at the beginning."

"But look, you must have had other girlfriends. You sure know what you're doing in bed."

He laughed at that. "Yes, but that was before I was bitten. That's changed everything. Just never leave me. Okay?"

He kissed me before I could answer. He stroked my stomach, then slid his hand between my legs, and I forgot about being rational.

Later that day, after we'd gotten up, I did put some hard thought into the situation. I doubted that I'd ever want to leave him. The élan vital I'd received from him more than made up for what I'd lost in the three days of the bjarki's dominance. Besides, he'd given me his promise, taken on the runes, that he'd never again force anything upon me.

Or was that exactly what he'd said? He might only have meant that he'd take me back to my apartment when I asked him to. I couldn't quite remember his words. I knew from all those fairy tales that when a sorcerer promised you something, you needed to be sure you understood precisely what he meant.

When he started dinner in the kitchen, I sat down at the breakfast bar to watch. He uncorked a bottle of red wine and poured us each a glassful.

"Cabernet," he said. "Trite, I guess, but I like it."

I took a sip of mine. "It's good, but I can't really tell one red wine from another."

"Half the time I can't either." He saluted me with his glass. "Something I wanted to ask you. Can we sleep in the same bed from now on?"

"Sure. I'd like that."

"Okay, then I'd better change the bedding. I've got some old sheets and blankets I use for the bjarki nights."

Which jogged my memory about something I'd noticed when I was too distracted to follow it up. "You know, you said that there was hair on the blankets. I never saw any."

He put down his glass and stared at me.

"Are you sure it's there?" I went on.

"Well, I—hold on. Let me go look."

I set my wine down and followed him into the bedroom. He turned on the bright overhead light, then picked up the blankets from the floor. No hair scattered, and on the pale yellow blanket, we would have seen it. He knelt on one knee and swept the side of his hand across the carpet—no hair clung.

"I don't understand," Tor said. "This morning I saw it. Lots of it. Usually I vacuum it up right away." He gave me a sultry grin. "Something made me forget this time."

I grinned in return. "It can't be real hair," I said. "It must just melt away."

"That could be. I've got one book that takes shape-changing seriously. It talks about emanations of force-lines." He stood up, frowning in concentration. "That's a terrible translation of the German. Sorry. Maybe those lines are what I see as hair. The author thinks that shape-changing's just a matter of illusions, anyway. Which I doubt."

"I really don't understand that."

"Neither do I." He shrugged and smiled. "But when I look in the mirror on bjarki nights, I see a bear. With a pelt. A bearskin. I don't see me."

Reflexively I glanced at the battered door, striped with gouges. "You couldn't do that with your fingers," I said.

"No. Not and have any nails left. He chewed up the closet door a couple of months ago, too. That's why I got this tattoo." He pulled up his T-shirt and turned around to let me see his back.

Just below the waistband of his jeans I saw a cluster of runes, six arrows, three pointing up, three down, bundled into a shape like a snowflake. The design was small, maybe the size of a quarter, which explained why I hadn't noticed it that afternoon. He let the shirt fall and turned to face me.

"Tyr's mark," he said. "The god who bound the mouth of Fenrir, Odin's wolf, when it went on a rampage. That's his rune, Tiwaz. It helps me control the bjarki."

"That must have been dangerous, binding a wolf's mouth."

"Oh yes. He lost a hand doing it. The gods aren't invincible, you know." He paused for a sigh. "Not even the gods always win."

He turned out the overhead light. As we left the bedroom, he bumped into my shoulder. I could feel traces of the excess élan wisping around him like the scent of perfume.

"Sorry," he said. "I'm just kind of dazed, thinking about the hair and all of that."

"It's okay." I stopped walking and turned to him. "Give me a kiss?"

He put his arms around me, drew me close and kissed me open-mouthed. I felt both kinds of energy, the sexual and the vital, sweep over me. I sucked them both up and kissed him again. I'd absorbed so much of his cast-off vitality that I had energy to return to him, the raw animal kind. I'd never felt so sexually aroused. I rubbed against him and whimpered. He slid his hands down to my buttocks and pressed me against him.

"Let's lie down," he said.

"Please." I meant it, too. I was begging. "Take me to bed, Tor. Please?"

This time, because I'd fed enough, I could focus on the sex, the intensity of the pleasure he gave me, and on returning that pleasure to him. He gasped when he climaxed, gasped aloud and shuddered rather than endured a macho silence. Afterwards he turned onto his side and pulled me tight against him. He kissed my face, stroked my hair, and told me that I was beautiful.

"So incredibly beautiful," he whispered. "I've never had sex this good before."

"Me, either. You make me feel so wonderful."

He smiled and lay down on his back. I rested my head on his chest and fell asleep, suddenly and without a single thought or yawn. Eventually he woke me up and told me that dinner was ready.

Later I realized that I'd never asked him about the promise he'd made, that night when he'd offered me a job. I'd fully intended to, but it seemed so ungrateful of me, after everything he'd given me. Besides, did I really care about the answer? I didn't want to leave him. I had never felt so good in my life, so energetic, so whole, so *fed*. For a change I could laugh at Death instead of the other way around.

CHAPTER 6

That night Tor and I slept together in the master suite. We did change the bedding first, just in case some of that magical illusionary animal hair was lurking in the folds and crevices. He even sprinkled the clean sheets with lavender water. When we lay down I could smell flowers, just a hint in the air. We shared a few kisses, but we both wanted sleep more than sex by then.

Since I'd left my alarm clock in the other bedroom, I overslept. I woke at about ten to find Tor already up and gone. In my shorts on the floor, my phone was ringing. I grabbed it and clicked on, then lay back down.

"Maya?" Cynthia's voice. "Are you okay?"

"Yeah, sorry." I paused for a large yawn. "Looks like I'm missing class."

"Well, you missed yesterday, too. Are you sick or something?"

"No. My shape-changer and I just had an incredibly steamy night."

Cynthia laughed. I heard her telling Brittany what I'd said, and she laughed as well.

"By the time I got cleaned up and drove down to school," I said, "the session would be almost over. Do you feel like lying for me?"

"Sure. You had a cold, right?"

"I couldn't stop sneezing and spreading germs all over, yeah."

"I'll tell the prof that. We all know how she hates germs. Uh, you guys are using something, aren't you?"

"I take the pill, yeah, because of my menstrual problems. They're supposed to put me on a regular schedule."

"Are they working?"

"Not yet." My vampirism was the reason, of course, not that I could tell Cynthia that. "For all I know I couldn't get pregnant even if I wanted to."

"Don't take chances, okay?"

"Don't worry! I'm not ready to have his cubs."

Cynthia snickered and hung up. A good thing she did, too, because when I sat up to put the phone away I realized Tor was standing in the door. He must have been up for some time, because he'd gotten dressed. He'd dropped the nerd illusion. His eyes narrowed, and I could see the torment in them, the sign of a man who could be cruel if something drove him to rage.

"What's all this about cubs and shape-changers?" he said.

"When I first moved in with you, y'know? I told my friends that you were a shape-changer, a bear. We sort of joke around about it."

Still scowling, Tor walked into the room and stood over me. He crossed his arms over his chest.

"Well, I had to tell them something," I said. "They asked about my new job, and I couldn't think of what to say. I didn't want to lie. So I told them I was taking care of a were-bear. They thought it was hysterically funny."

"Oh." All at once he grinned. "They didn't believe you."

"Of course they didn't!"

He uncrossed his arms, hesitated, then sat down next to me on the bed.

"You're naked," he said. "You know what that does to me, don't you?"

"Show me." I smiled at him. "I'm literal minded. I want a demonstration."

"That can be arranged."

There was something about him being dressed and me

being naked that I found really arousing that morning. When he started to take off his shirt, I stopped him with kisses. When I began unzipping his jeans, he took the hint.

When we were finished, I leaned over the side of the bed and retrieved the box of tissues we'd put there earlier for the usual necessities. Tor pulled up his jeans but left them unzipped. He took a tissue from me.

"What are you grinning about?" He was smiling himself.

"I was just remembering how determined I was to wait before we fell into bed. I wanted to get to know you better."

"You know me better than you think you do."

"I sure do now, yeah."

I finished cleaning up and lay down next to him. He turned over on his side and pulled me close.

"You're so beautiful," he said. "I'm so lucky."

"So am I. I love your body. It's lean and smooth, but you're strong, too. You're not like those totally grotesque muscle guys. You know, the ones with pecs that need a good bra."

He laughed out loud and kissed me. "I'm double lucky, then," he said. "You really think that?"

"Yeah, I do. Y'know, you're a man who's got good looks and money, but you're not real sure of yourself, are you? I'd expect a guy like you to be arrogant. Why aren't you?"

"The bjarki, of course." His smile disappeared. "I used to be arrogant. I think that's a good word for it. Conceited would be another one. It shows what happens to men who get swelled heads. Something always brings their luck crashing down."

I raised myself up on one elbow and looked into his eyes. I could read his sincerity from the sadness in them.

"I'm glad I didn't find you before," he went on. "You wouldn't have had anything to do with me. You would have told me off with four-letter words and walked away."

I could say nothing to that, because he was probably right. I sat up cross-legged on my side of the mattress. He got out of bed and concentrated on tucking in his shirt and zipping up his jeans.

"You know," he said, "it hadn't occured to me before that being a bjarki might have some benefits."

"I don't think I'm worth it. What you go through, I mean."

"Now who's being humble?" He managed to smile, but I could see that it cost him. "Why don't you get dressed? It's about time for lunch, and exercise always makes me hungry."

Before I could say anything, he turned and strode out of the bedroom. I got up and retrieved my clothes from the floor. While I dressed, I remembered what Cynthia said about 'using something.' I hadn't given one single thought to using a condom to protect against STDs. It was a little late to do more than hope Tor was as healthy as he looked—aside, of course, from that little matter of his shape-change. As long as he never bit me, and he wasn't the type of guy who liked causing pain during sex, I wouldn't have to worry about that.

The bjarki would present a different kind of problem once school returned to regular sessions and the moon cycle took itself out of sync with the weekends. Over lunch I brought up the difficulties of having the full moon fall on class days.

"I'll always be here in the evenings," I told him, "but what are we going to do when the bjarki dominates and I've got class during the day?"

Tor thought for a couple of minutes.

"It's not likely there'll be a fire," he said eventually. "The security system has heat sensors, so even if there was one, the company would call the fire department. You need to keep up your work. I want you to get that degree, you know. I can tell how much it means to you."

"Thanks. Not that I know what I'm going to do with a degree in painting. I could end up doing portrait sketches down in Jack London Square."

"Don't even think it! You never know what kind of weird character you'd meet if you did that."

I had to laugh, and he joined me.

"But what you can do," he continued, "is paint, of course. You don't have to worry about money any more."

Some women might have eaten that statement right up.

The huge assumptions behind it bothered me.

"If nothing else," I said, "I've got student loans to pay off. I'll have to get some kind of job."

"No." He shook his head and smiled. "We can take care of those."

I considered arguing, but I figured it would get me nowhere. Besides, I had another year of school before I—or we—had to worry about the loans. If things continued good between me and Tor, I could even continue studying for yet another year and get a credential in art education, something a little more practical than just learning portraiture.

I still, however, valued the portrait class. The teacher had set up a model for our final project, the one that was going to carry half the class grade. This model was an Asian-American man. She'd dressed him in khaki trousers, a corduroy plaid shirt, and for the final challenge, a shiny silver vinyl vest. I made sure I showed up the rest of that week to work on the portrait. I made up studio time in the afternoons even without the model present by working on the background, a drape and a lot of artificial potted plants. On Friday I was planning on staying extra late, because the room would be closed for the weekend, but Tor called me around three o'clock.

"Uh, Maya?" he said. "Were you going to come home soon?"

"I can. Why?"

"I just got email from Liv. I uh I don't know what to say, but it's really kind of upsetting."

"I'll just clean up and come right back to the house."

When I returned, I found Tor pacing back and forth in the living room in front of the west window. The late afternoon sun shone around him, and by some trick of the light, his shadow on the floor fell in the shape of a bear. I slung my backpack onto a chair and hurried to his open arms. He held me close and kissed me. I pulled back so I could study his face.

"What's wrong?" I said. "You're practically shaking."

"Yeah, I know. I just learned something new about my family. It's changed everything."

"Whoa!"

"Yeah. Let's sit down. I translated the email and printed it out for you."

We sat down close together on the couch. He picked up two pieces of print-out from the coffee table, handed one to me, and slipped his arm around me while I read.

"Dear Tor," it began. "I asked Mother your question, and she unburdened herself to me about something that's been bothering her for years. You and I have an uncle we've never heard of. He's grandfather's bastard son. Mother and Father knew all along, but they didn't want us to know because they wanted us to respect our grandfather when we were children. I don't suppose we would have even understood, much less been upset by it, but you know how she is about such things."

I glanced at Tor and pointed to that line.

"Worried about what people would think of her," Tor said. "Not prudish, no, but wanting the neighbors to look up to us. She was a village girl from Norway, not even Icelandic. She never felt she belonged in Grandfather Halvar's world."

"Is that why your folks moved to America?"

"One reason."

I waited, but he said nothing more, and I resumed reading.

"So," Liv's email continued, "Father was not the eldest son after all. I suppose that's why his talents were so thin. Uncle Nils is not a nice man, Mother says. He hated and resented Father because he had everything, and Nils had so little. Grandfather acknowledged him and let him have his name, but when he died, he did not leave him anything in his will. Mother heard many years ago that Nils moved to New York City for a job in banking there. Grandfather did do that for him, give him education and connections. So he still probably is in the United States.

"There is a woman who might still live in California who might know more. She was Nil's mother's close friend. Her name is Bryndis Leifsdottir. She moved to the States to live with her son, Orvar Arngrimmsson. She would be over seventy now if she is still on this plane of existence. Mother doesn't know where she moved to in the state, so it could be many miles away from you of course. I'll see if I can get more information, but Mother really hates talking about this. She did give me the one photo she has, and I scanned it."

I looked up, and Tor gave me the second piece of paper. On it was a color print of the man I'd confronted in the mall, much younger but still recognizable.

"That's him," I said. "That's the guy I saw at the mall, and the guy who saw me at the café before I moved in here."

"You're sure?"

"Real sure. We're going out with my friends tomorrow, anyway, so we can take this along and show Cynthia. She got a good look at him, too."

"That won't be necessary. It's not that I don't believe you. I'm just real worried. If Nils is the oldest son, he should have had the rune set, and I bet he knows it."

"The ancient one you showed me?"

Tor nodded. "I inherited it from my dad, and I don't want to give it up."

"There's no reason you should. It's not your fault your grandfather gave it to your father instead of this uncle."

"That's a good thought. And we don't even know if Nils is the one who's behind the illusions."

"Right. If he is, though, it might explain why he's calling you a thief."

Tor considered this in silence. Finally he shrugged. "The runes probably don't blame me," he said. "They lend me their power, after all. They'd withhold it if they thought I wasn't entitled."

"Can't you ask them about it?"

"Of course." He smiled in honest relief. "I can't use them as staves, but I can bring them out and then use another set for the reading. Do you mind if we do it right now? I need to stop worrying."

Before we went downstairs, he rummaged around in the kitchen and brought out a plate of offerings for the nisse, a slice of bread, an apple, and a small glass of brandy.

"Would you carry these?" he said. "All you have to do is put them on his rock. If you feed him, he'll know you're part of my household now."

Part of his household? The words struck me as strange—antique, from some time that defined a household in a very different way.

I put the food and drink on the nisse's rock while Tor drew the drapes in his laboratory, as I thought of the big room with the crossed circle on the floor. The pair of barstools faced each other on either side of the high wooden table.

"If you'll take one of those," he said, "I'll get the staves."

I took the stool facing in the direction of the little room with the safe in it. I watched Tor through the open door as he opened various small drawers in the array. He'd bring out a leather pouch, look at it, put it back, and take out another one. I noticed that he had at least five of the little sacks, all in different colors, some leather, some velvet. Finally he settled on brown leather. He took a folded up square of white linen out of a larger drawer, then brought it and the pouch back to the table.

"Brown for protection," he told me. "That's what we need."

He spread the white linen out on the table, opened the pouch, and poured out the staves, small chips of wood about one inch by two, each with a rune carved into it.

"Will you turn those upside down for me?" he said. "I'll go get the antique set."

I occupied myself with turning the chips over while he opened the safe. He brought the wooden display case back and propped it up on the other stool as if it were a person who'd want to see what was going on. He stood next to it and across from me.

"Okay," he said. "Our first question is, does this set belong to me?"

For a long moment he stared at the rune staves. He leaned forward, shoulders hunched, back tense, eyes narrow with concentration. He held his right hand flat above the scattered chips, then pounced, picking out three staves so fast I barely saw him tuck them into his palm. He laid them down face up, one at a time.

"Cattle for wealth, Tir's mark, and ancestral property," Tor said, "all of them right side up." He glanced my way. "Which means a positive answer. Yeah, they're mine." He sighed with a little puff of breath. "That's a relief."

From his sudden smile I realized that he had perfect faith in the answer he'd received. He turned the staves back over and slid them into the spread.

"Is that all there is to it?" I said.

"For a simple question like that, yeah. I'm going to ask about this new uncle next. Would you mix those up for me? Keep them face down."

While I moved them around on the linen, Tor looked away to avoid noticing what ended up where. This time he drew nine staves, one at a time. Before choosing another, he turned each over and placed it into a complicated layout, roughly circular with four staves in a straight line down the middle.

"Othala again." Tor laid a finger on the rune in the exact center of the display. "Ancestral holdings, but I don't think it means property exactly." He pointed to the rune at the very bottom. "Because here's cattle-wealth again, Fehu. That's the property, the money and land. So Othala's more like family wyrd."

Tor fell silent and returned to staring at the layout. Finally he shook his head. "This isn't adding up," he said. "I'm going to get a notebook and a pen and write it down. I'll have to think about this."

"It must be important. It sure looks complicated."

"It is, yeah." Tor laid a forefinger on the bottom rune, which looked like a drunk F. "This bit's clear. Wealth causes trouble among kinfolk. The wolf grows up in the forest."

"What?"

"That's a quote from an old Norwegian poem about the Fehu rune. I'm not a wolf, but the first part's pretty accurate."

"Yeah, the whole world over."

He gave me a wry smile and nodded. "Grandfather Halvar

tried to prevent that kind of trouble. I'd show you my copy of his will, but it's in Icelandic. Pages and pages of detail. My dad's was almost as complicated. He wanted to make sure that Liv and I stayed close instead of fighting over who got what."

"Did he succeed?"

"Oh yeah. Liv really wanted the family land, and I'm glad she's got it. We split up the money pretty evenly. The land pays her back for taking care of our mother, I figure."

"Didn't Liv say your grandfather left Nils out of the will?"

"Yeah, I never saw his name there. I hope that Grandfather made some kind of gift-settlement on him. I think there are ancient precedents for that, buying off the illegitimate kids. But the old man could be a real cold son of a bitch. Nils must be real bitter."

"The moon'll be dark next weekend," I said. "I wonder if we'll hear from him then?"

"What'll you bet?" Tor shook his head with a sigh. "Just my luck."

CHAPTER 7

On Saturday, while I ate a late breakfast, Tor went downstairs and brought back the nisse's empty glass and the plate, also empty except for the apple core and a few bread crumbs. I gave Tor a quick kiss, just to see if I could smell brandy or apple on his breath, but he was innocent. Unless he'd sneaked down there in the middle of the night, someone—or something—else had eaten the food and drunk the alcohol. I suspected a big hung-over rat until I started to toss the core into the garbage. I noticed tiny toothmarks, flat ones, in a half-circle like a human would make, not like a rodent's two front choppers at all. Tor watched me and grinned.

"You didn't believe me, did you?" he said.

"About the nisse? I didn't know whether to believe you or not."

"Know something?" His smile reminded me of a shy schoolboy. "I don't know whether to believe it, either."

I reached up and kissed the dimple at the corner of his mouth.

"I've wanted to do that for days," I said.

He laughed, grabbed me, and kissed me in return. He was in such a good mood that I decided I could finish clearing my conscience.

"The people we're going to have dinner with?" I said. "They're the ones I told about your being a shape-changer. I thought you should know, so you can play along with the joke if someone brings it up."

"Okay, I'm glad you warned me. I'd have to answer honestly, anyway. I can't lie about myself."

"It's never a good idea, yeah."

"It goes beyond that. I just can't." He turned serious and let me go. "It's an oath I took a long time ago. I cannot lie about myself if someone asks me a direct question."

"That's why you were willing to tell me so much that first night. The one where I took the part-time job, I mean."

"I don't know about being willing. I had to answer your questions. The runes desert a liar."

"I keep forgetting how much the runes mean to you. It's like a religion, isn't it?"

"No. Religion is something you accept. The runes—you have to gain them. You fight for them. You don't just take what some priest hands you." His mouth twitched in a smile. "I'm really a barbarian, you know. Deep in my heart."

Oh yeah sure! I thought, not that I said anything aloud. I couldn't picture him in a helmet with horns.

When the time came to change for dinner, I went into my room to put on my one good skirt and my best black top, which was too low-cut for me to wear a bra. I still thought of the second bedroom as 'my room' because I'd have to sleep in it during the bjarki's domination. As I was changing, I noticed the writing desk. The green lion had disappeared. In his place a man and a woman were having sex in a big tub of water. Each of them wore a crown. Rather than being erotic, the image made me feel deeply uneasy. I finished dressing in a hurry.

We'd made plans to meet Cynthia and her husband Jim, plus Brittany and my brother, at a family-style Chinese restaurant on Clement Street in San Francisco, near where Brittany was living. I figured we'd better take my car to avoid awkward questions about travelling by sorcery. As I drove over the Bay Bridge, Tor said nothing, just watched the traffic with a slight frown.

"Am I driving okay?" I said.

"What? Of course. Sorry. I'm just thinking about the rune

cast. I can't seem to make sense of it. It's like there's a piece missing from it."

I would have asked more, but a black SUV swerved right in front of us. I pumped the brakes, turned the nose of the car, and just barely managed to avoid an accident. Horns honked, drivers swerved, my heart pounded. The SUV sped off without even flashing a signal.

"Shit!" Tor muttered. "Idiot drivers out tonight!"

"There sure are." I took a deep breath and concentrated on driving. The irony struck me hard. I worried constantly about my disease, but here we could have both been killed by another driver's careless moment.

When we reached the city and the first off-ramp from the bridge, traffic slowed way down. The cars around us began lane-hopping just as if it would do them some good. The luck of the shuffle brought us next to the black SUV in the lane on our passenger side. Tor glanced over and shook his head.

"She should know better," he said. "A middle-aged woman, no less!"

The traffic closed up and began to crawl, which gave me time for a safe look at the offending driver.

"That's not a woman," I said. "It's a guy, but I can't really see him clearly."

The driver glanced our way and hit the gas. The SUV swerved again and cut across two lanes in a blare of outraged horns. For a brief second it disappeared so completely that I thought it had gone over the edge of the elevated roadway. It reappeared from behind an RV and turned onto the off-ramp. It sped out of sight as the traffic flow swept us onward and past.

"That's a difficult minor illusion," Tor said in his usual calm way. "Looking like someone else entirely. It must be our friend, whoever he is. Uncle Nils, probably."

"Must have been. God, I hope he's not going to dog us everywhere. That's creepy!"

"Sure is." Tor laughed under his breath. "When he jumped lanes to get off the freeway, I was hoping someone would hit him, but no such luck."

"I wonder if he meant to make us hit him. This old Chevy would have taken a lot of damage, but that hulk he was driving would have barely felt it."

"That occured to me, too."

I was expecting him to say more, but he merely stared out of the window, his mouth a little slack, his eyes distant, as if he were thinking about some deep subject. It occured to me that he might be working some kind of magic, scrying for danger, maybe. I kept quiet rather than interrupt. Besides, I kept thinking about an ugly fact: I'd seen through the illusion without needing to draw it, without even half-trying. The talent Tor had pointed out was growing of its own accord in my mind, like one of those volunteer plants he'd spoken of during our night of illusions. Roses or deadly nightshade? Which would the talent turn out to be? I had no idea, and I was frightened.

We reached the restaurant without any further trouble. I even found a parking spot only two blocks away on a side street. As I locked up the car, I noticed Tor waving his hands at it. I waited till he'd finished.

"Was that a ward?" I said.

"Yes. I don't want anyone tampering with the car. If the ward's gone when we come back, I'll know that another sorcerer messed with it."

I gulped in audible terror. Tor caught my hand and gave it a reassuring squeeze. I glanced around at the houses that lined the street in the usual San Francisco style, that is, set really close together and flush with the sidewalk. Most of them had lights in their front windows. Some even had their porchlights on.

"This neighborhood should be safe enough," he said. "But keep your eyes open."

We hurried back to the bright lights and traffic of Clement. Restaurants, produce markets with bins right out on the sidewalk, the occasional odd little store selling a combination of things like movie posters and computer parts, or shoes and kitchen utensils—the street always reminded me of pictures of Shanghai or Hong Kong. Cars choked the roadway. On the crowded sidewalk people strolled along or paused to look over a vendor's supply of bitter melon and bok choy or to duck into a bakery for pork buns. Several people bumped into me, just by accident, and I took the chance to swallow a slurp of their élan. The near-accident had cost me energy.

Our restaurant was a silver building with a huge curved window jutting out from the second floor. When we went upstairs, the street noise vanished into the laughter and talk of several big parties. The hostess directed us toward the back. Cynthia and her husband Jim had already arrived and been seated at a big round family table.

"Brittany's going to be late," Cynthia said, grinning. "What do you bet?"

"I never bet on a sure thing," I said.

When I introduced Tor, Jim stood up to shake hands with him. They were both about the same height, but Jim was portly where Tor was lean. Jim's blond hairline had already decided to make a run for the back of his head, too, even though he was only in his twenties.

The two men had just sat down again when Brittany surprised us all by arriving on time. She and Roman walked in holding hands, the tip-off that she'd given him a better way to forget the war than mere drugs. She winked at me and Cynthia, then sat down while I introduced my brother to my boyfriend. They looked each other over carefully, but neither growled—a good start.

I hadn't seen Ro looking so good in years. Although he was still too thin, his skin had a healthy undertone. His dark eyes looked clear, and he smiled at everyone. I almost let myself believe that he'd solved his problem, but I'd read too much about addiction to fool myself. Brittany had a long hard job ahead of her.

Once we'd all settled ourselves at the table, the waiter came over with pots of tea and menus. With that many people to choose dishes, and the waiter offering advice as well, it took us a while to come up with a reasonable dinner. Everyone was in a good mood, laughing, making jokes. Roman said very little, but he smiled a lot. I loved seeing him smile. Now and then he glanced at Brittany to reassure himself that she was still sitting next to him.

In the midst of the general chatter, I leaned over for a semi-private word with him.

"Ro? Is this going to work?"

He knew what I meant. "I sure hope so. I've been going to the group every day. There are other vets in it. We've got a lot to talk about."

"Good for you! I mean, god, you made it through Marine bootcamp, didn't you? You can do this."

"Yeah, after that—piece of cake!"

I had to remind myself that it was too soon to hope.

Once we'd settled on the menu, Tor ordered a couple of large bottles of Chinese dark beer for the party. He told the waiter to tally the beer separately and to make sure that he got the bill. Squarish liter bottles of beer and glasses arrived with a second waiter, who poured it round. The first waiter brought appetizers, then scurried off again.

For a few minutes everyone scarfed egg rolls and bits of pork rib and drank beer with only the occasional comment. The inevitable moment, however, arrived when Brittany turned her big blue eyes on Tor and said, "Maya told us you were a were-bear. Is that true?"

"Of course," Tor said. "But only at the full moon." He tipped back his head and roared with a growl and a chuff. Though he kept the volume way down, he sounded like a bear, not a guy pretending to be one.

Everyone laughed and toasted us with their beer glasses.

"Where did you meet Maya, anyway?" Jim asked. "At the zoo?"

"No, in Copenhagen on the docks," Tor said. "She'd come down with her maid to greet her husband when he sailed into port. He was the captain of a whaling ship."

"Tor!" I snapped. "You liar! When did I ever—"

"You don't remember because it was in a past life, that's all. Not our most recent ones, though. It must have been about a hundred and sixty years ago."

More laughter and more beer toasts. Tor poured the last of the bottle into Cynthia's glass, then signaled the waiter to bring two more.

"He was gone again in the spring," Tor went on. "So we had an affair. It went on for a couple of years. I ended up having to face the husband in a duel, and he won. I wasn't much of a shot with a pistol. I died on the field."

"In her arms, I hope." Jim was grinning at us both.

"No such luck," Tor said. "She'd already run away with someone else."

"I had not!" I burst out, then covered my surge of indignation with a laugh. "It was cold and rainy, that's all, and I didn't want to stand around in the mud and watch."

"Worse yet!" Cynthia said. "You heartless creature!"

"Standing around in a corset and those awful heavy winter skirts was hard on a girl." I laid a dramatic hand on my forehead. "I would have fainted at the sight of blood."

Even the waiter was laughing by then. He uncapped one of the new bottles and began to pour around the table. I noticed Brittany, smiling, certainly, but at the same time she was considering Tor with an oddly curious intensity. Oh come on! I thought. It can't be true. But somewhere in my mind I heard a woman weeping in huge sobs—no, I was the one weeping, wrapping my arms tight around my chest, and rocking back and forth like an abandoned child. The rain-soaked man who watched me smiled, a tight-lipped narrow-eyed smile of triumph.

"Maya?" Tor said. "You okay?"

"Yeah. Sorry." I shook my head to clear it and came back to the present. "Maybe it's the beer."

No one else had noticed my fugue state—I guess you'd call it that. The two waiters were bringing the food, a perfect distraction. Everyone was helping themselves and passing the dishes around. Cynthia and Brittany began discussing school, and I joined in. We needed to finalize our schedules for fall, because we liked to have one class in common every term. Jim and Tor talked mostly about cars, while Roman just watched, smiling at the noise and laughter.

The evening became a normal night out with friends, perfectly normal except I kept trying to remember our Danish names, kept seeing a view of a city where gas lamps burned on the street corners and horse-drawn cabs clopped by. I ended up drinking more beer to drown the memories, enough so that Tor had to drive us home.

Tor's driving impressed me. He drove fast but well; he concentrated on the city traffic, took no risks but missed no opportunities, either. In my blurry state of mind I watched the lights zipping by us on the streets and thought of very little. Once we merged onto the entrance ramp for the Bay Bridge, the traffic slowed to a Saturday night crawl.

"Maya?" Tor said. "I've been thinking about that near accident. Well, if it really was accidental on his part."

"Yeah?" I realized that I should have been keeping a watch for the black SUV. "Kind of scary, huh?"

"Look, let me get you a better car. I'm not trying to buy you. I just don't want either of us to get mangled in a wreck."

I disliked the idea of letting him spend that kind of money on me, but he had made a point I couldn't ignore.

"Okay," I said. "I'm not real keen on getting mangled, either. Something solid but not too expensive."

"Anything solid will be expensive." He sounded annoyed. "Cheap means a junker. I do know something about cars."

"Okay, then, whatever you want." Totally rude, Maya! I told myself. "I mean, thank you. I really am grateful. I'm just kind of muzzy from the beer. I guess I'm a cheap date."

I glanced his way and saw him smile.

By the time we got back to the house, I'd sobered up, but the memories remained. I can't lie, Tor had told me, if someone asks me a direct question. Jim had done that. In the stuffy living room Tor opened the west window to let in the night air. He flopped down on the sofa and patted the seat next to him. Instead, I sat down on the chair opposite.

"Tor," I said. "That story you told, about Copenhagen and the duel. It can't be true, can it?"

"Of course it's true," Tor said. "Remember the day you drew my portrait? I was wandering around, and then I saw your name card at the booth. I knew you had to be the person that the rune cast indicated, the one who could see through illusions, but I didn't suspect who you actually were at first. I was wondering if you could help me with the illusions, nothing more. And then you handed me the finished drawing. Something clicked." He paused, then made an odd gesture with one hand. "Wait! So that's what—you gave me the drawing in a cardboard tube. I flipped it up like the pistol. And I recognized you. That's why I cast that stupid spell."

Just as something had clicked for me in the restaurant. My stomach twisted, and my hands started shaking. I clasped them in my lap as if I could strangle the memories, but they insisted on staying alive.

"Tor, I swear it, I never ran off with anyone."

"He told me you had. His second confirmed it. That's why I let him shoot me."

"They lied! You were the only man I ever wanted."

"Then he was even more dishonorable than I thought."

I nodded, got up, paced to the west window and looked out at the distant city. They say that San Francisco brings out the magic in people, that the city is itself a magnet if not for actual magic, then for strange happenings that border on magic. I had just felt that magic sweep me up and carry me far out on a dangerous sea.

"My mother talked about past lives all the time," I said. "I thought she was just being weird. My crazy mother. Y'know?"

"No, she wasn't." He spoke softly, calmly. "The Buddhists know all kinds of things worth knowing."

I turned around so I could see him, smiling at me, just a soft, almost melancholy smile. More memories rose in my mind, bitter ugly memories.

"In our last life," Tor went on, "I don't know where you

were. I was reborn in 1913. I grew up remembering you. I looked for you all over Europe. It was the Thirties. Jobs were hard to find, but I did anything I could to keep moving, to keep looking. Washed dishes in restaurants, did farm work, loaded coal onto trains, anything so I could eat for a while and keep trying to find you."

I stared open-mouthed. How could he remember? Why did I believe him?

"When the war with Germany came," Tor said, "I managed to get home to Norway just ahead of their army. I got my hunting rifles out of my family's attic and joined the Resistance. We ambushed Nazi supply trains. It was winter when we made the raid where I died. I don't remember the details. They don't much matter. I just remember watching my blood stain the snow while I was dying." He hesitated briefly. "And I wondered where you were. I really did. I never thought of God or eternity, nothing like that. I wondered where you were."

I sobbed, only once, with a great gulp of air. He got up, strode over to me, and gathered me in his arms. I could hear his heart pounding when I clung to him. He stroked my back the way you'd stroke a cat.

"You must have wondered," he went on, "why I clutched at you the way I did. Why I had to have you, why I wanted to move you in just as if we'd known each other for years and years."

His arms tightened around me. My mind, the rational part of my brain, the part that had studied things like English composition and spherical perspective, began to rebel.

"This can't be true. You can't— I can't know all that."

"Yes, you can. You do know. You do remember. You've got to trust them, that's all, the memories, the knowledge."

I began to shiver, suddenly cold to my bones, aching and gasping for breath, just as if the salty water were pulling me under again, closing over my head, pushing me down into the final dark.

"I drowned myself not long after the duel." I started weeping. "It was the only way I could get free of him."

"Don't," Tor whispered. "Don't dwell on it. You don't have to go back to that. We're together again now, and that's all that matters."

He kissed my face, kissed the tears away, held me, stroked my back, until at last I could stop crying. When I fished a tissue out of my skirt pocket, he let me go with a little pat on my shoulder. Everyday reality came into focus again. I blew my nose and tossed the tissue into a wastepaper basket.

"Do you believe me?" Tor said.

"Yes." I knew I'd made a dangerous confession, though I didn't know where the danger lay. "Only it's more than that. I remember things, bits and pieces, visuals, not language or events."

"If you want to recover really coherent memories, you'll have to learn to meditate."

"I don't want to!" I shocked myself by yelling at him. "I just want to be who I am."

"Okay. I'm not trying to push anything on you."

"Oh yeah sure! You bring up a past life. You make me see things. Now everything, my whole life, looks totally different and creepy. You make me remember losing you—" The tears started up again. "Oh god, I hated him! He gloated about it, killing you!"

I covered my face with both hands. When I sobbed aloud, Tor reached for me, but I tried to shove him away. He caught my hands, pulled me close, threw his arms around me before I could twist away.

"Magda! Please! Stop!"

The tears deserted me. "What did you call me?"

"Magda. I'm sorry."

"I suppose that was my name then."

He nodded.

"But," I went on, "that's not a Danish name, is it?"

"No. It's Hungarian, I think. From the gypsies, anyway. Like you were."

"That why you thought I had gypsy blood now."

"Yes. And then, in our last life, once the war started, all

I could think of was the death camps. I was fucking terrified for your sake."

"The Nazis rounded up gypsies, didn't they?"

"Oh yes. And we knew about the camps, the men in the resistance. We knew where we'd die if they captured us. I kept worrying about you, what if you'd been born a gypsy again? What if you'd ended up in a camp?"

"I don't remember anything like that."

"Good. Don't try. If it's true, you don't want to remember."

I nodded my agreement. Tor ran his hands through my hair and pushed it back from my face, then kissed the tears on my cheeks.

"I love you," he said. "You don't have to say anything back, but I still love you. After all these years."

I felt torn in half. One half wanted to scream "You're crazy!" The other half wanted to say "I still love you, too." Caught in the middle, I said nothing, just stared at him like an idiot.

"Come to bed," he said. "I'll make you feel better."

"No, I don't want to." I pulled free of his grasp and took a couple of steps away. "It's all too strange."

"Maya!" His voice turned soft. "Please?"

I stared out the window as if the view could show me secrets. Tor came up behind me and laid gentle hands on my waist. He kissed the side of my neck, then pulled me close to lean against him. I started trembling. If I turned around and kissed him, I'd be putting myself in the worse danger of my life. His lovemaking meant death for both of us. I knew it, believed it—until I realized that I was only remembering. In the memory I was looking out of a diamond-paned window through lace curtains, not this clear glass view of a bridge and a city in California. Tor slipped his hands under my top. They slid up to my breasts, stroked them, found my nipples and rubbed them, gently, slowly, until I gasped aloud. He kissed the side of my neck again. I leaned back into his grasp. His hands stroked me, one on my stomach, one on my breast.

"Come to bed?" he whispered. "Please?"

I wanted to say no, to talk things out, to ask him how

he could be so sure about that ever so distant past. My body could think of nothing but his body, pressed against me, so close and so desirable.

"All right." I could barely speak.

He laughed, just softly in victory. He stayed behind me, his arms tight around my waist, and walked me into the bedroom.

CHAPTER 8

In the morning, the click and hum of the air conditioning turning itself on woke me up. Tor still slept, nestled against my back with one arm over my hip. I listened to him snoring and watched the sun brightening the yellow curtains of the bedroom. Before I'd been thinking of it as his room, but that Sunday I started thinking of it as ours. I wondered if I was sharing his delusions as well as his bed. Not about the sorcery or the bjarki—I'd seen too much evidence that both of those were real. Why couldn't I have known him in a past life as well? Why would I remember drowning if there weren't any such thing as past lives? My mother certainly believed in them.

I wanted to talk to my mother. I wanted to call her and hear her voice and ask her if she thought I was crazy or if I'd found the love of my life. But she'd gone far away to a place where they had no telephones, no wireless access. Not even paper mail would reach her unless the abbess approved the letter. Visitors, even daughters, had to make arrangements months in advance—if they could even afford to travel to Bali to start the trek to the nunnery.

You're a big girl now, I told myself. You can figure it out for yourself. I'd have to. I'd always had to make all my big decisions by myself. My mother had believed in encouraging her children to be independent. That way she could abandon us when we turned eighteen.

Tor woke up, yawned, stretched, and kissed the back of my neck. I turned over to smile at him. He was stubbled and tousled, but I liked the sight of him anyway.

"Good morning," he said. "But my mouth's too dry to kiss you."

I laughed, just because it was such a normal thing to say.

"We should get up," he went on. "I want to start car shopping today. This is going to be fun."

We're not in Denmark anymore, I reminded myself. We might have known each other long ago in Europe, but he was a Californian now, with a California guy's definition of 'fun.'

There are a lot of foreign car dealerships in the East Bay. I swear, Tor dragged me to most of them. I looked at more models of luxury cars than I'd known existed. Salesmen followed us around from car to car and talked the whole time. When we left a sales floor, they handed us brightly colored flyers on expensive paper and all but begged us to come back. By the seventh dealership I couldn't remember what I'd seen where. And god, the prices! My idea of a solid safe car was a used Volvo. Tor had other ideas.

"I want you to have a really well-engineered car," he said. "That means top of the line."

"Some of these models, you can buy a house for that kind of money."

"Only in places you wouldn't want to live. Rural Alabama, maybe."

"Look, I don't mean to sound ungrateful. I'm just overwhelmed." I felt a sudden pang that explained my bad mood. I waffled around the subject in my mind, then decided that I might as well be blunt. "You know, I think I'm getting my period."

"Oh. We can stop for today. I've got all these fact sheets to study, anyway."

By the time we got home, I had cramps. I hurried to my bathroom for tampons. Once that was taken care of, I curled up on the sofa with my laptop and the print-out of Liv's email while Tor rummaged around in the kitchen. He came out with a glass of dark beer and set it down on the coffee table in front of me.

"This should help," he said. "But let me try something else first."

He sat down next to me and took a felt-tip pen out of his pocket.

"I see you've got those jeans already unzipped." He grinned at me. "Pull up your shirt, okay?"

I set the laptop down and did as he asked. With the pen—water-based ink, he assured me—he drew a rune right at my bikini line. The way he'd placed it, it looked like a little table with bent legs.

"Perthro," Tor said. "Some scholars call it a dice cup. I'm willing to bet it represents a woman's legs bent in childbirth. Drawn with the legs pointing down and open like this, it should help you get rid of what you need to."

He put the pen away, then laid his hand on my stomach right above the rune mark. Maybe it was just the warmth of his hand, but I felt the cramping ease.

"Wow," I said. "That's working."

"Of course." He took his hand away. "I just charged the rune. Here." He retrieved the glass of beer and held it out.

"Thanks." I took it and had a sip. "I've logged onto your wireless connection, by the way. I thought I should see if I can locate your uncle online."

"You can do that?"

"Well, maybe. His last name is Thorlaksson, right?"

"Wrong. It's Halvarsson, like my father's last name."

"Wait. Then how come you're Thorlaksson?"

He grinned. "It's the Icelandic way. You take your father's first name as your last name. So Liv's Thorlaksdottir and I'm Thorlaksson. My father, Thorlak, was Halvarsson and so is Nils, because they're half-brothers. If Grandfather had had a daughter, she would have been Halvarsdottir."

"I get it now." I glanced at the print-out. "So this friend of Nils's mother—her father's name must have been Leif."

"Right. And her son's father's name must have been Arngrimm. Do you really think you can turn them up? I was planning on searching later."

"Online, you mean?"

"No, of course not! Anyway, I'm going to make dinner first."

Although Tor believed that he could find his uncle with sorcery, I preferred the Internet. I had good starting points: Nils Halvarsson, banking, New York City. Sure enough, I found a number of limited references, including a nasty blog post from one of his ex-wives—he'd been married several times, judging from what she said. She didn't post much about the man himself, except that he was a 'pig dork who never paid his child support on time even though he was rolling in money.' Maybe that's why he'd become so good at hiding where he was. Uncle Nils was a lot more web-savvy than his nephew, because all mentions of his current address, phone number, and other such useful information had been blocked on every phone book site I tried.

I did, however, dig up some possible gold on the cached public announcement site of a major New York financial firm. Two years previously, Nils had been forced to take early retirement because of a rare blood disease. The site never gave the disease's name. According to the write-up, he was seeking treatment in a specialized clinic in California. Although the site never mentioned the exact location, I already knew that he lived in the Bay Area.

A color photo showed the man I'd seen that day at the café. He looked perfectly healthy in his expensive three piece suit. Maybe the picture was an old one, I thought. Judging from his comments, his hobby was backpacking and camping in the Catskills and on the Appalachian Trail, an activity that would have kept him in great shape until the illness hit him. Various co-workers and clients had filled up the rest of the page with farewells and regrets. As if his ex-wife's bitterness wasn't bad enough, Nils had been a popular man in his specialty field, mortgage-backed securities, which made me mistrust him more than ever.

Because like everyone else in the world I think of my own troubles first, I wondered if Nils suffered from vampirism, but

it seemed highly unlikely. When my mother had been dragging me from doctor to doctor in an attempt to find a cure for
my genetic disorder, we'd seen several specialists in the field
of hematology, because our regular physician's best guess had
been some odd form of anemia. I knew the long scary names
of a lot of candidates for the disease behind Nils's retirement.

Yet, as I thought about it, the man I'd seen had looked
as healthy as the photo. Had he been cured? Maybe he'd
never really been ill. Why would he pretend to some disease
he didn't have? I was willing to bet that he'd made enough
money to retire just on a whim if he wanted to. No one would
have thought twice about it. I bookmarked the page to show
Tor later and moved on.

Bryndis Leifsdottir was an easier proposition. I found her
son, a computer scientist, immediately. He had a Wordpress
blog and home page where he'd posted pictures of a white-
haired but vigorous-looking woman smiling at her seventieth
birthday party. He'd given the captions in both English and
a language I assumed to be Icelandic. Most of his posts were
in Icelandic, too, but I found plenty of English references on
other sites. Apparently he felt he had nothing to hide, because
I located him on various phonebooks.

"They live in Daly City," I told Tor.

"You're sure it's them?"

"How many guys named Orvar Arngrimmsson are we
going to find in California?"

"Good point. Okay."

"Maybe you should call him."

"On the phone?" He looked alarmed. "What about I send
Bryndis a note? After the way my grandfather treated her
friend, she might not want to hear from anyone in my family."

"Yeah, you're right. The note would be better."

I felt a brief but odd sensation. We were being not watched
but listened to, and the eavesdropper meant serious business.

"Tor," I said. "Someone's spying on us."

"You're sure?"

I paused, tried to be aware, picked up nothing.

"It's gone now," I said. "The sensation I felt, I mean, but I really did feel like someone was listening to us."

"That damned illusionist, I suppose." Tor got up from the couch. "I'm going downstairs to see what I can see. If you feel the sensation again, yell down the heating vent."

I never did feel it. When Tor came back upstairs, he told me that he'd picked up no hostile 'emanations,' as he called them.

Thanks to Tor's runework, I felt well enough to go to school on Monday—luckily, because our instructor gave us instructions for mounting our final project, which we needed to finish during the current week. In the last week of school, the class would critique each other's work, with of course comments by the instructor. I had the awful feeling that my attempt to render the model's shiny vinyl vest was going to doom me.

Brittany, Cynthia, and I went to our favorite café to discuss the coming ordeal by criticism. The vinyl vest was worrying both of them, too. We went over the hand-outs from class while we ate lunch. With dessert, Brittany filled me in about my brother's progress.

"He's really trying," Brittany told me. "He's going to the group. When we're alone, he keeps bringing up the war, like he'll maybe tell me what hurts so bad, but then he draws back."

"It's a start," I said. "He never got that far when I tried to talk to him."

"Good to know. He says stuff like, 'if I could only turn off the video in my mind.' But then he won't go any further with it."

"It's the war that's the real problem," Cynthia put in. "Not the drugs qua drugs."

"Yeah, I agree," I said. "That and then Dad dying while Roman was in Iraq. It happened so fast I didn't have any time to get him home on leave to say goodbye. I had an awful time just trying to call him. I finally got hold of the officer in charge of Ro's unit, and he moved heaven and earth trying to help me. But it was too late by then."

"God." Brittany laid her fork down. "I didn't know that."

Cynthia stared at me so sadly that I was afraid she'd cry. I realized that other than Roman, I'd never told anyone about Dad's death before.

"It was really horrible." My voice shook from the memories.

"I bet." Cynthia considered me for a moment. "What did he die of?"

I hated to lie, but I had no choice. Dad had died of the same disease that was going to kill me, and how could I tell my friends the truth about it?

"A heart attack," I said instead. "He'd never been really well. It was something genetic, the doctor said. A problem with the main arterial valve."

Both of my friends winced. "What about you?" Cynthia said.

"My mom had strong genes." I managed to smile. "I'll be okay."

"I wondered, because you get so tired." Brittany picked up her fork again. "You need to make sure you're getting enough B-complex."

"I'm taking those vitamins you recommended."

Brittany gave me a brilliant smile and licked chocolate frosting off her fork. Her practice at times didn't match her theories, but then, chocolate *is* one of the major food groups. You can only ask someone to sacrifice so far.

"I haven't been as tired lately," I said. "Thanks to quitting that awful job. I really should look for another one. I can't expect Tor to just support me."

"Why not?" Cynthia said. "It's obvious he worships you. And I'm betting that he's got money to burn, just from the way he acts. He doesn't walk. He strides everywhere. Head up, lord of all he surveys—that kind of swagger."

"That ratty sweater he was wearing?" Brittany put in. "Cashmere. Mistreated cashmere, but still. And that wristwatch!"

"God, I never realized you guys were so mercenary."

"Just envious," Cynthia said, grinning. "And glad you

found him. Maya, you've been pushing yourself to the limit for as long as I've known you. Let him be Lord Bountiful for a while. You need the rest."

Yeah, I thought to myself, but if they only knew what he was really like! They did know, of course. They just didn't believe it. What if I told them I was a vampire? Would they believe that? My secret was too grim, too painful, too deadly, for me to imagine making it into a joke.

When I came home, I turned into the driveway as usual. I stopped the car, killed the engine, and stared. The garage door stood open, and inside sat a beautiful blue sedan. I got out of my old heap and walked up to the car, a German make, one of the really expensive ones. I glanced inside: leather upholstery in a deep-dyed tan. When I ran my fingers along the hood, the paint job felt like fine enamel, as smooth and rich as you'd find on jewelry.

Footsteps crunched on the gravel behind me. I turned around to see Tor, grinning as he held out a set of keys.

"The title's going to be in your name," he said. "I've already called about the insurance."

Lord Bountiful. Cynthia had nailed it.

"Tor." I could barely speak. "I can't take this from you."

"Of course you can, because I want to give it to you." He hesitated, and the grin disappeared. "Don't you like it?"

"I love it, but, god, it must be so expensive."

"It's also the best engineered sedan on the market. It'll keep you safe. Me, too, if I happen to be in it if—" He paused for emphasis. "If we have another incident like we did Saturday night. Steel frame. Top of the line air bags, front and side. All that good stuff."

When he held out the keys again, I took them. A gadget hung from the ring that would open or lock the doors, make the car beep if I lost it in a parking lot, turn on its lights from a distance, do just about everything but phone home. Tor opened the car door and began pointing out all the other gadgets and sensors on the inlaid wood dashboard. Now and then he paused to run his hand over the upholstery or to stroke the glossy paint job.

I realized that although the car would legally be mine, he'd gotten it for himself, too, an expensive toy that he couldn't have justified otherwise. Because he loved it so much, I could accept it.

"We should donate that old car of yours to charity," Tor said. "They'll probably get fifty bucks at the junkyard."

"No," I said. "Can't we keep it? It's a two-car garage."

He tilted his head to one side and gave me his puzzled-bear look.

"I'll need to drive it to school."

"Why?"

"The paint on my clothes. I'd hate to mess up that gorgeous leather."

Tor laughed. "Ever hear of seat covers? We can get some cheap ones. Terry cloth. You can throw them out when they get filthy."

"Okay, yeah, that would work."

The Chevy seemed to be staring at me reproachfully, as if it wanted to live, not end up squashed in a junkyard.

"I still want to keep the old one," I said. "I bought it with my own money. My first car. I hate the thought of junking it. It's like a pet."

Tor rolled his eyes. "Oh okay," he said. "Whatever."

I got back into my old car and drove it into the garage, next to the shiny new one. I wanted to keep the Chevy just in case, I realized—just in case he found out about my disease. I'd need to leave in a hurry, and I wouldn't want to take his generosity with me. As I was getting out of the car, Tor trotted into the garage.

"How are you feeling today?" he said. "Do you need to take a nap or something?"

"No, I feel better. Whatever you did with that rune really worked."

"Well, then." He paused to grin. "Let's go for a drive."

"Okay, but there's a couple of things I have to do first."

"What?"

"Here's one." I reached up and kissed him. "Thank you," I said. "It's a super-sweet ride. Thank you so much! I really really love it."

He slipped his arms around me and gave me a hug. He was grinning, so pleased and proud, so normal and happy that I hated my thoughts like this most recent one: keep the old car, just in case. Leaving him would be painful.

"And now I've got to change my clothes," I continued. "My jeans have globs of paint on them. It's acrylic, but it might not be totally dry."

"Okay, while you do that, I'm going to get some olive oil and paint runes on her bumpers. For the protection." He tilted his head to one side and considered me with a small smile. "What about a name?"

"How about Gretel? Like in the fairy tales."

"Sure. That'll do. She is German, after all."

When we took Gretel out, I drove her first. Since the engine wasn't broken in yet, we stuck to the streets and back roads rather than the freeways. Eventually we hit the curving roads that led through the Oakland hills. I'd never driven anything that handled so well, so smoothly, as if the car were doing half the thinking for me. Tor watched all the digital readouts on the dashboard as avidly as a co-pilot on an airplane.

When we reached a view turn-out on a wide road, I took pity on him. I pulled over and turned in my seat to grin at him.

"Want to drive?" I said.

"Well, if you don't mind." Tor looked as eager as a small boy who's just been offered ice cream. "I mean, it's your car."

"I want you to see how wonderful it is."

He smiled, leaned over, and kissed me—just once. He wanted to get his hands on that wheel.

Tor decided to head back down to the city to see how Gretel handled in stop-and-go traffic. As we came down from the hills, I noticed in the side mirror another car following us, a black dot on the blacktopped road. At first the car stayed too far away for me to identify. It could have been anyone, I reminded myself. For some miles, however, it kept to the same distance.

"Tor?" I said. "Slow down, okay?"

Gretel responded so smoothly that I might not have known he'd done so—except that the other car abruptly got a lot closer. I stared into the mirror and caught sight of the black SUV before he too slowed down.

"He's back," I said. "We have our friend on our tail."

"Shit!" Tor muttered. "Ruining a perfectly good day."

He drove a little faster. The tail sped up but kept a good distance between us—about a city block's worth. By then we'd reached the streets of a quiet residential district, bungalows and brown-shingled houses behind small lawns. When Tor stopped at a stop sign, the SUV turned into a driveway rather than come up directly behind us. When Tor started up again, the SUV pulled out and followed, still at that long distance.

"We could try going downtown," I said. "The traffic will fill in behind us and cut him off."

"I've got a better idea."

When we reached the next cross-street, Tor pulled over and parked. The SUV did the same thing down at the other end of the block. Tor began unbuckling his seat belt.

"What are you doing?" I said. "You can't get out of the car! What if he tries to hit you?"

"Too many witnesses around here. He wouldn't dare."

I grabbed him by the arm. "If he's crazy, that won't stop him."

"No, but the power of the runes will."

Before I could protest further, Tor shook my hand off his arm, opened the door, and got out. He shut the door again, then turned to look down the block toward the SUV.

"Nils!" He was yelling at the top of his lungs. "Come on, come talk to me!" He switched into Icelandic and yelled something else, then went back to English. "Tell me what's so wrong! Let's have it out!"

I sat paralyzed. I remembered Tor calling himself a barbarian at heart. I was seeing it in the way he stood, warrior-straight, his head tipped a little back, his hands on his hips, daring his enemy to come forward and either bargain or fight. In the bay window of a nearby house, curtains twitched, and the shadowy form of a woman looked out. I was praying she'd call the police—just in case. I had my phone in my backpack, but I knew Tor would be furious if I called.

Out in the street, Tor fell silent, panting a little for breath. I returned to keeping watch on the SUV in the rearview mirror. The black hulk pulled away from the curb but hesitated out in the middle of the street.

"Come on, Nils!" Tor yelled. "Are you afraid to talk to me?"

The SUV sped forward with a grind of gears. I screamed and covered my mouth with both hands. The huge car lumbered down the street fast, too fast. It swerved toward us. Tor never moved. At the last second the SUV swerved back to the middle of the street. It sped past Tor and lurched around the corner. I could hear the engine roaring through the quiet neighborhood, then slowly fading, dying away into the distance.

Tor flung open the car door. "Fucking coward!" he said. "That had to be Nils, all right. He looks a lot like my dad."

I caught my breath with a gulp.

"What's wrong?" Tor said. "You look scared."

"Of course I was scared, you idiot! What if he'd side-swiped you?"

"Oh." Tor slid back in behind the wheel. "Yeah, that would have messed up your new car."

"It's not the car I was worried about."

"I know." He smiled. "A joke. Do you have a sketchbook in your backpack?"

"Yeah. Why?"

"I got a good look at the license plate. I want to write it down in case I forget. Maybe we can trace it. He'll try to confront me again. This was just the first step."

"First step of what?"

"Breaking him down." Tor gave me a totally out of place grin. "He could have killed me. But he backed off. I figured he would, and because I was right, he lost—well, I don't know what to call it. He lost status, I guess. Or lost face. Something like that."

I kept a constant look-out while he drove us home, but the SUV never appeared. None of the other cars that at times might have been following us turned into it, either, when I tried to puncture possible illusions. Tor said little until we reached the house. He let me out at the sidewalk, then parked Gretel and shut up the garage for the night. As he walked back to join me he was jingling the keys in his hand.

"I've made up my mind," he said. "I'm going to figure out a way to challenge him. It's stupid, sitting around waiting for his next move."

I wanted to scream. Instead I said, and pretty calmly considering the circumstances, "You mean to a duel or a fight?"

"No, no, just to see if he'll come forward and talk. I—" He stopped and looked away.

"What's wrong?"

"You just gave me an idea. Let me think about this."

He strode off, and I followed him into the house.

CHAPTER 9

Since we'd turned off the air conditioning before we left, the summer heat had toasted the inside of the flat. We turned it on again, but it would take an hour or so to cool the place down. Tor put together a cold dinner in a picnic basket, I grabbed one of the old blankets, and we went outside to eat in the cool of the evening.

The landscaping out in back of the house was as uninspired as the front, a big rectangle of grass, dotted here and there with dandelions and other weeds. Off to one side stood a Japanese maple that badly need pruning. Since the house stood on a terraced hillside, a stone retaining wall, about six feet high, edged the rear of the lawn to keep back the hill. Beyond the wall, the property sloped up in a profusion of scrawny trees and shrubs to the neighbor's house a good long ways above.

"One of these days," Tor said, "I should hire a landscaper, I guess. Unless you like to garden."

"I don't know anything about it," I said. "I grew up in apartments."

I spread out the blanket, and we sat down in the beautifully cool air. Tor opened the basket and brought out a bottle of white wine and two glasses. I poured while he set out the food. The sky had turned the velvet blue of approaching twilight. I saw off to the east two bright stars. The fluttering gold lights of an airplane climbed slowly between them as if they were beacons marking a safe road. Above us on the slope the trees rustled in a rising breeze.

"This is actually kind of fun," I said.

"Yeah, we should do it more often, these hot days. We could even get a picnic table."

For a while we ate in a pleasant shared silence. A few flies tried to crash the party, of course, but when Tor snapped a napkin at them, they kept their distance instead of coming right back as flies usually did. Magic, I wondered? I would have felt foolish asking him outright. Tor poured us each a second glass of wine and brought out fresh pears for dessert.

"I've been thinking about Nils," he said. "The idea you gave me when you talked about a duel. I wonder if he was Björn, back then."

"Back when?"

"When you were married to him. Björn, I mean, not Nils per se. In Copenhagen."

"Oh. That." I had a swallow of wine. "Do we have to talk about it?"

"Yes." Tor looked at me with puzzled eyes. "It could be important. Look, that day he followed you around at the mall. He told you that you had to recognize him, right?"

"Right. Oh god, I never even thought much about it!"

"That's because you didn't know about us then. Huh." He thought for a couple of minutes. "You might be one of the things he wants to take from me. Not that you're a thing, not to me, anyway. He might see you as some kind of object he wants back."

"I understand, yeah. Ohmigawd, the thought makes me feel sick."

"It makes me furious. Do you remember why you married him?"

I started to snap at him, but I did remember, or at least, a story came to me as fast as a memory would have. I had a long swallow of wine before I said, "My father sold me to him when my mother died. I was fourteen. Björn didn't have to marry me, really. I guess it was decent of him."

Tor started to speak, merely stared.

"Well, gypsies didn't have any legal rights or anything, did they?" I said. "Way back then."

"No. Shit, I didn't remember that part. About you being sold, I mean."

I finished the wine in my glass and reached for the bottle.

"Do you remember Björn's last name?" Tor said. "Details like that?"

"No." I concentrated on refilling my glass. "I don't want to."

"I don't remember a lot of them myself. Your name, his name. Then there was your maid. We had to bribe her. I don't remember her name, but she was a skinny little rat of a girl. The cook was on your side, though. Elsa, her name was."

He paused for a sip of wine. I realized that he believed his story about the past life and his death, just as I believed I remembered the look on Björn's face when he returned from the duel. And the drowning. I knew I remembered that. I no longer felt like eating anything. I put the wine bottle back into the basket. Tor put his glass down, picked up a pear, and bit into it. He swallowed, then glared at the traumatized pear in his hand.

"These could be riper," he said. "A thought. Those protection runes? You could get them tattooed somewhere on you. You wouldn't have to worry about wearing amulets then. I could put together new bindrunes, too, if you wanted a different pattern."

Bindrune. The word bothered me. Would he bind me to him with magic, just as Björn had bound me with guilt and terror? I realized that I remembered more than I wanted to about my marriage after the duel.

"Needles freak me out," I said. "No tattoos. Yuck! I'd be sick the whole time the guy was doing it."

"It was just a thought. When you go out, what about I draw them on you, like I did for the cramps?"

"But the ink—isn't it going to be toxic?"

"I can get some of that stuff clowns use to paint children's faces. It should be perfectly safe. You might need a more powerful bindrune if Björn is—"

"I don't want to talk about him any more."

"We'll have to sooner or later."

"Not now!"

"Okay, okay." He looked mildly surprised. "What did you want to do tonight? We could go to a movie or something."

The calm normal way he offered a night out, coming right after his talk of past lives, made me want to scream at him. Instead I just said, "No thanks. I'm really tired. I'm still bleeding."

"Maybe later in the week, then. I need to go down to my workshop and cast the staves, anyway."

"Workshop? Oh, the lower flat."

"Yeah. It'll take me a couple of hours, probably, to do all the things I have in mind. I've got to email a college buddy of mine. He's a total hacker, and I bet he can trace that license number I wrote down."

While Tor worked downstairs, I took my laptop into my room. I found my earbud, then logged on and watched clips from really dumb TV shows on YouTube. I felt like a rebellious child, but I enjoyed the clips anyway. When I heard Tor coming back upstairs, I logged off. I was just returning the laptop to my backpack when Tor appeared in the doorway.

"I heard from Aaron," he said. "My hacker friend, y'know? He tried to find data about Nils for me. He couldn't. He can break into the blocked phonebooks without much effort, but there was nothing on the name Nils Halversson. He must have set up a false name and identity a long time ago. Probably to get money out of the country into a Swiss bank or one of those tax-shelter islands in the Caribbean."

"Oh god! We're back to square one."

"Yeah, we sure are. Now, as for the SUV, Aaron found that license plate number on the DMV site. The plates were stolen from a car in the airport parking garage a week ago. So they're not going to tell us anything about Nils, either."

"That's a real cold shot."

"Yeah, isn't it?" Tor paused, thinking, then shrugged. "I don't know what to do."

"Can't we tell the police about the plates?"

"Not without telling them how we know. I don't want Aaron arrested."

"I can understand that. He's an old friend, huh?"

"The oldest one I have. We were college buddies. We still get together, go to Raiders games with a couple of other guys. Sometimes we all goof around playing basketball, too." He tilted his head to one side to consider me. "Do you like football, by the way?"

"I like to watch it on TV. But you can go to games without me. I mean, you should get to spend time with your guy friends."

"You won't mind?" He raised one eyebrow.

"Of course not!"

"Okay. I always end up missing a game or two, anyway, thanks to the damn bjarki, but we get season tickets for the Black Hole. You probably wouldn't like sitting there. It's kind of a rowdy crowd."

"I've seen them on TV. If you went in bjarki form I bet no one would notice."

He laughed at that. "We were some of the weird guys, back at Cal. Freaks and geeks. You never would have gone out with any of us, if you'd known us then."

"Maybe with you. Maybe. You clean up pretty good."

He grinned and agreed.

We spent the evening reading in the living room, Tor with one of his books on magic, me with the pile of Icelandic sagas he'd given me, stories of kings and treachery and evil sorcerers from the Hebrides—good stories, all right. One thread ran through them that I didn't really get. At one point I looked up to see Tor laying his book aside.

"Want something to drink?" he said. "I think I'll get myself a beer. I've read all I can tonight of this heavy stuff."

"None for me, thanks. Can I ask you something? In these sagas, the men are always talking about their honor and killing people over it. Why? I don't get it."

"It's a shame culture, that's why. Once a man is shamed, he's less of a man. And that's the worst thing, to give up your manhood."

"But the way they define manhood creeps me out."

"It's a real archaic way of thinking, yeah." Tor got up from the couch and stretched. "But it hasn't disappeared."

"That's sure true. That's what Nils lost today, isn't it? Honor points."

"It's not exactly a point system. But yeah, you're right enough."

I frowned at the copy of Njall's saga in my lap. "All of these guys pride themselves on facing death and being super brave, but they're terrified of being shamed."

"You bet. You can't kill shame with a sword. That's what makes it so frightening."

I supposed so, and Tor went into the kitchen to fetch his beer.

Around two in the morning I had a nightmare. I was standing on the high wooden bridge in the Japanese Tea Garden in Golden Gate Park. As I looked down into the little stream that runs underneath it, a creature rose up, formed of mud and slime. Huge, and shaped like a man—it reached for me with fingers dripping green rot. I stood transfixed as it grabbed my ankles and yanked me off the bridge. The water beneath spread and swelled to a deep dark pool that reached for me with green fingers. I screamed and screamed again. The water churned with waves and tossed me this way and that.

"Maya! Maya, wake up!"

I opened my eyes and stopped screaming. A light went on in the bedroom. I was curled up so tightly that my arms ached. A naked man with sandy brown hair and a dimple at one corner of his mouth knelt beside me on the bed.

Tor. It took me a few seconds to recognize him.

"You were thrashing around," he said. "What was the dream?"

"I was drowning. Again."

I stretched out on my back and felt my pounding heart slowly return to normal. He lay back down and turned on his side to look at me.

"A memory dream?" he said.

"No. There was a monster involved." I forced out a smile. "And a black hole. Symbolic stuff everywhere. Was I screaming?"

"Oh yeah." He leaned over and laid his hand alongside my face. "Sort of a weird muffled scream, but I could hear it, all right."

His touch, his concern, comforted me. He kissed my mouth, the side of my face, my forehead.

"Can you go back to sleep?" he said. "Are you okay now?"

"Yeah, because you're here."

He smiled with a glowing, pure pleasure as if I'd given him the best present in the world. "Yeah, I'm right here," he said. "And I always will be."

At that moment his words soothed me further, but as I lay awake, they began to bother me. He was assuming that we'd stay together forever, or if not forever, at least for some long time. Why wouldn't I want to stay? He was kind, sexy, generous to a fault, supportive when it came to my art. Yet he frightened me at moments. With his sorcery Tor seemed like a man from another world, an alien world. He brought strange experiences with him, memories of past lives, sorcerous enemies, hints of dark things hiding in my own mind.

Like the talent to speak in an ancient language, one I didn't know, didn't even recognize. That alien world could be mine, too, if I had the guts to travel there. The thought made me shiver and squirm. I realized that night, as I lay next to him, that I was afraid of myself, not of Tor.

I did feel guilty about lying to him. I'd never told him about my disease, and that night I questioned my motives. I found myself remembering that seriously old-fashioned term for girls who took guys for expensive gifts: gold-digger. Did it come down to that, after my working so hard to take care of myself and earn my own way? The beautiful flat, a fancy car—I was willing to bet that if I asked him to buy me expensive clothes and jewelry, he would. Fortunately for his cash flow, I'd never do such a thing.

I decided that I was going to have to tell him the truth. I promised myself that I'd do it first thing in the morning, but I never quite got the chance in my hurry to leave for class. When I came home, Tor was sitting in the living room reading. I changed my paint-spattered clothes, then came out to join him. For a moment I stood in the doorway and studied his face and his body as if I were going to do a portrait of him. I wanted to fix his image in my mind, just in case my ugly secret lost him for me. I wanted to remember the strong line of his jaw, the way his thick, straight hair fell over his forehead when he looked down, and his broad hands that knew my body so well. He glanced up and smiled at me.

"Need something?" he said.

"I've been thinking about getting into your jeans all morning."

He laughed and followed my lead into the bedroom. The sex—it overwhelmed me that afternoon, just how good it was with him. He teased me, worked me up, and coaxed me into lying on top of him. I'd never had a climax like that before, sensations so strong that they edged close to pain without ever crossing into it. We rested, didn't need to talk, just lay in each other's arms. When things started up again, I crouched on my hands and knees so he could take me from behind. Like bears, I thought—but he fondled my breasts like a man.

When we finished, he lay down, smiled at me, and fell asleep. I wanted lunch badly enough to get up without waking him. I took my shorts from the floor and crept out of the room to put them on.

After I'd scarfed some leftovers I found in the fridge, I went back to the bedroom. I'd left the door open, and through it I could see Tor, still naked and sound asleep, perfectly relaxed and sprawled. He was lying on his side but tipped a little back to reveal everything he owned. He'd crooked one arm over his face to shelter his eyes from the light. On an impulse I got one of the big sketchbooks and some rust and sepia conté sticks. I sat down on the floor, half-naked myself, and drew him just as he looked. I considered adding a twist of sheet for modesty but decided against it. I liked all of him, and I wanted a record of it, right down to the scar on his left thigh from the werewolf bite. I turned the page and did another figure study, more polished this time.

Making those drawings made me wonder why I kept downgrading my feelings for him. *Just physical attraction.* You hear that, and it's a sneer. Only physical. Only great sex. Well, it's not that easy to find. When you do, it's just as wonderful as any other kind of love. The truth hit me hard. At last I knew what I felt about him, even though it meant that I was going to have to lose him. I loved him, and I couldn't keep lying to him. After I finished the drawing, I took the sketchbook and sticks into my room. I didn't want him to see the drawings, even though I couldn't say why.

That evening at dinner I decided to try approaching the subject of my disease sideways, as it were, to work up some courage. Tor gave me an opening.

"I've been thinking about Nils," he said. "Well, I did some magical work today that I guess you could call thinking. He's not Björn, or not his latest incarnation, I guess I should say. I'm sure of that now."

"Good," I said. "That's one less thing to worry about."

"Yeah, it would have been a real nasty knot if that had been the case. But you know, sooner or later he's bound to show up. Björn, I mean."

My stomach clenched. I laid down my fork.

"God, I hope not!" I said.

"Unless he's worked through the wyrd he set in motion. He never struck me as the type who would. It means admitting you're wrong. But it'll haunt him until he lets you go." Tor considered for a moment. "And until he apologizes to me. The bastard, lying to someone during an honor duel! Whoever he is now, he'll have to pay for that."

"Wyrd is like karma?"

"Pretty much, yeah. Sooner or later, you reap what you sow." He paused for a smile. "Just to quote from another tradition."

And what had I done to deserve my vampirism? I had wondered about that for years. Thinking in terms of past lives, and my mother totally believed in them, had made me feel that I deserved it. She'd never said so. In fact, she'd told me the opposite. *Not everything is karma, sweetheart. Never ever think you deserve this.* Had I believed her? No. Kids blame themselves for things they don't understand. Blame hurts, but it gives you the illusion that you have some control over your life.

Tor returned to eating his dinner. I realized that I could open the subject with a casual remark about a hypothetical situation. What if he did throw me out when he heard the truth? I'd lose him, but I'd never have to learn why I could speak in a language I didn't know. The monster of my dream would have to sink back into his black hole.

"Suppose someone has a fatal disease," I said. "Did they do something to deserve it? Or could it just be bad luck, genetics, or some kind of accident?"

"Sure." Tor looked up from his plate. "Any of those. That's why no one should blame anyone for being sick or poor or whatever. It really pisses me off when I hear people do that, say someone's responsible for getting sick or being out on the street because of what they did in a past life."

He'd given me the perfect segue. My heart started to pound in such terror that I could not speak.

"Are you okay?" Tor said.

"No." I made myself force the words out. "There's something you don't know about me."

"You've got some kind of disease, don't you? Is it leukemia?"

I felt my entire body turn hot, then cold. "How did you—"

"Maya, look!" Tor laid down his fork and swiveled on the chair to face me. "You've got olive skin, right? A little darker, maybe. Which hides things like turning pale pretty well unless someone's really looking at you. I like to look at you. So I can tell that when you're tired, the blood leaves your face. You get tired real easily, too. At first I thought, well, you've been working too hard. But that's not true any more."

"I thought I was better at hiding."

"No." He held out a hand. "C'mon, tell me. I'll take care of you. You should know that by now. I've been thinking lately that I should put you on the health insurance."

"That won't do any good. What I've got, they won't cover. It's not leukemia, no. That's too normal."

"Well, I've got investments I can call in to pay for—"

I shook my head no and struggled for words. I finally realized that there was only one thing to say, the brutal truth. Tor let his hand rest back in his lap and waited.

"I'm a vampire," I said. "A real one. I'm not dead or undead or anything like that. It's not like the movies. I just can't regenerate my life force like a normal person. I have to steal it from other people."

Tor stared with his mouth half-open.

"It's a disease, a really rare one, and it killed my father. It's going to kill me, too, sooner or later. Probably sooner." The words broke through my fear. To tell someone the truth, to admit it, to explain at last—the relief turned into a bitter pleasure. "It's a gene mutation from Central Europe. My father explained it to me, and it's the root of all the old vampire legends. It's real, Tor. You should understand if anyone can. It's like the life force you give off after the bjarki change. I call it élan, but it's probably got another name. I can harvest it when you throw it away."

"Chi. It's called chi or sometimes etheric substance or magnetism." He crossed his arms over his chest and went on looking at me, merely looking, his eyes unreadable, his face set into a mask.

"You can throw me out," I said. "I always knew it would happen, once you knew the truth."

"What?" The mask split and let me see Tor again. "I'm not going to throw you out. Why do you think I would?"

"Because I'm a thief. I take life from other people without them knowing. Just a little bit at a time, not enough to hurt them. My dad told me it wouldn't really hurt them, if I only took a little bit from people who were young and healthy. I hope to god he was right."

"He probably was, yeah. Okay. So. What are we going to do about this?"

The room lurched to one side. Tor got up and caught me by the shoulders.

"Let's go into the living room," he said. "I feel like a jerk, perching over my dinner like a raven while we talk about this. Come on."

It was my turn for the idiot stare.

"What's wrong?" Tor said.

"You're not going to throw me out?"

"No. Don't be stupid!"

"Then you don't believe me."

"Of course I believe you. Why wouldn't I?"

"Don't you think I'm crazy? Delusional?"

"No! I wondered why you could take the bjarki in stride. I guess I know now. We both have a problem, don't we? Why do you think I'd judge you?"

I had never seen it that way before. Why hadn't I? Because you've been so damn wound up in your own illness, I told myself. Paranoia is a kind of vanity, I realized. I'd thought that I was the only pariah in the world. I got up and let him lead me into the living room. When I sat down on the couch, he sat next to me, but he turned so he could look right at me. I leaned back against the cushions and trembled. The sense of relief had deserted me. I felt like I'd had too much to drink and done something horribly embarrassing, maybe even criminal, that I was now going to pay for.

"Just one thing." He spoke quietly, but I heard menace in his voice. "Have you been stealing from me? I don't mean taking what I need to get rid of. I mean stealing. Like, when I don't know it."

Even though he never moved, I was abruptly aware of just how much taller than me he was, how much stronger.

"No!" I stammered. "I never would, Tor! Not from you, not from my friends, either." I twisted my hands together in my lap to stop them shaking. "It was only after the bjarki change."

"That's okay!" He relaxed and smiled. "I was casting it

off, and if you wanted to use it, why would I care?"

I'm not sure why I found it so hard to believe him, maybe because I felt like two people fighting inside one skin. One of them felt a hard knot of disappointment that he wasn't making it easy for me to leave him. The other knew I wanted to stay.

Tor started to speak, then looked away with a little twist of concentration to his mouth. His eyes became distant, unfocused. I wondered what was wrong until I felt the élan began to gather. He pulled it from the air and from the sunset light coming in the living room window, summoned it with his sorcery. He turned, raised both hands, and like a flood of pure water let it pour over me. I gasped, sobbed, breathed it in, and fed—ah god, it felt so good to feed, to feast on life without stealing it from some person who'd never done me any harm. And so much! I glutted myself, soaked up far more than I could process. Letting some of it slide away again felt as luxurious as stroking silk velvet.

"You'll never have to steal from me," Tor said. "All you have to do is ask. Maybe not even that. I'll probably be able to tell when you need it. I'll give it to you, Maya. A gift." He smiled with an ironic twist to his mouth. "Some gift! It's free. All I've got to do is harvest it."

I sprawled back on the cushions in the ecstasy of having fed. He slid over close to me and let the remnants of élan drip from his hands. I sighed and stretched in the luxury of it.

"Tor?" I said. "I love you."

He smiled at me like the sun breaking through fog. When he held out his arms, I turned into his embrace and kissed him. Only much later did I realize that he'd bound me to him with chains stronger than any rune.

On Wednesday, when I came home from school Tor was working, as he called it, in the lower flat. I got myself some lunch, then brought out my laptop and put it on the coffee table while I sat on the couch to do some banking. I'd attached both of my credit cards to the online billpay, nice and convenient, though the total of what I owed was anything but. It would take me a long time to pay them off, but at least I could make a start. I needed to leave a certain amount in my checking account to keep it open, of course. Beyond that, I wanted to divide up the balance between the cards. If I sent it all, it would leave me without any cash on hand. I could keep out enough for gas and maybe a lunch with my friends, but how much? I was going back and forth about this when Tor came back upstairs. I wondered if I could still consider myself his employee.

"Something wrong?" he said.

"Well, um, I've—god, this is embarrassing—but I've spent my last check from my old job. And I need gas for the car."

"Right." Tor pretended to slap himself in the forehead. "And you need the salary I promised you. I'm the one who should be embarrassed, not you. You've been here a month, haven't you?" He grinned at me. "The best month of my life. Even with the damned bjarki."

"Really?"

He sat down next to me on the couch and kissed me for an answer. "Let me just stick a note about it on the refrigerator door."

"Thanks, I really appreciate it. I feel like I shouldn't take it from you, now that you're my boyfriend."

"Boyfriend." He grinned at me. "What a word for it! Anyway, I don't want you to go without spending money." He let go of my hand. "Is the five hundred a month enough?"

"I'd take less if it weren't for my credit card bills. I mean, I can't spend that kind of money just on stuff."

He sat forward on the couch and frowned at the laptop screen. "You weren't kidding when you said you were in debt."

"Yeah, fraid not."

"We should just pay those cards off. Why give the bastards all that interest?" With a shrug he stood up. "You've changed your address, right? At the post office, I mean."

"Yeah, I did."

"Do you get ebills or paper?"

"Paper. They should come any day now, probably with new penalties, too. I kind of missed a payment."

"Kind of." He rolled his eyes. "Then I'll take care of the bills when they get here. Don't worry about it any more." He went into the kitchen to make the note.

Lord Bountiful. I tried to make myself object, but the thought of being out from under that debt stole my voice. I salved my conscience by deciding that I'd make the five hundred last as long as possible before I asked him for money again. I was good at making money last. While he wrote the note to himself, I logged off of the bank site and shut down my laptop.

Tor came back and sat down next to me. "Anything else?" he said.

"Just this." I put my hands behind his head and pulled him down for a kiss.

He sighed, drew me closer, and kissed me again.

"I think," I said, "we need to get more comfortable. Like in the other room."

I got up and held out my hand, but he stayed on the couch and looked up at me with a troubled expression.

"You're not paying me back, are you?" he said. "With sex, I mean. For the money."

"No! This is why I hated to ask you for it. I don't want you to think that, not ever."

"Okay. I wanted to make sure."

"Look, why don't I just get a job, just part time, until my student loans come through? All I need cash for is gas for the car and lunch with my friends now and then. Since I'm not paying rent now, the loans will take care of my art supplies and studio fees and stuff like that."

He shook his head. "I don't want you to get a job. You don't need the loans any more, either. You're part of my household, and I'll provide for you."

I sat back down. "This thing about your household—I don't get it."

"Do you know what the word husband really means? It's got nothing to do with Christian marriage."

"No. What—"

"A house-bound man, a man bound by law and custom to support his house and the people who live in it, the householder. That's what I am." He crossed his arms over his chest. "I own this house, I protect it, and I take care of you."

"That sounds like something out of the Dark Ages."

"Pretty much it is, yeah. So?"

That's where the runes come from, don't they? I told myself. Why are you surprised? Tor uncrossed his arms, but he went on waiting for me to answer him.

"Okay," I said. "I get it now."

"Good." He smiled at me. "Now look, if ever I start coming on to you, and you're not in the mood or something, just say no. I don't want you to feel like you've got to earn anything. I'm giving you stuff because that's the way I am. Some of it's my duty to give you, and some of it I just enjoy doing."

"Your duty?"

"Maya! You ended up drowning yourself because of me. Damn right I need to take care of you now."

His typical logic again: air-tight and totally nuts, or it would have seemed crazy if I hadn't remembered the water, the cold and the dark, and the weight of my heavy Victorian winter clothes pulling me down. Tor leaned forward and put his hands on either side of my face.

"What's wrong?" he said. "Something is."

"Just remembering ugly things."

"I bet I know what." He kissed me, just softly. "Don't."

"Make me forget them."

When he kissed me open-mouthed, I felt my entire body respond. I caught his hand and laid it on one breast so he could feel my nipple harden.

"You do want this," he said. "Well, hell, who am I to argue?"

Around sunset we got out of bed. I took a shower while he cooked dinner. When I returned to the kitchen, he was standing by the refrigerator in a pair of faded, torn jeans and a black Oakland Raiders T-shirt. His hair was tousled, he could have used a shave, and he smelled of sex and sweat.

He still struck me as the most attractive man I'd ever known.

The next morning, before I left for school, Tor handed me a check for five hundred dollars. I deposited it on the way.

I finished my final project for class early that session. Brittany and Cynthia agreed that there was nothing more I could do to the portrait without overworking it. I gave it a coat of clear acrylic medium, put it on its easel to one side of the room, and left school. When I got home, Tor had just brought in the mail. He held up a small square envelope.

"From Bryndis Leifsdottir," he said. "She must have gotten my note."

We sat down together on the couch. Since Bryndis had answered in Icelandic, I had to wait for Tor to read the note through and translate it for me. She'd been very surprised to hear from him, she said, but she was quite willing to see him and his fiancée, as he'd apparently termed me. She suggested that we drive down to Daly City one afternoon for coffee.

"I would be happy to talk to you about Nils," the note finished up. "But I've not seen him for many years now. I have often wondered what happened to him. His mother, you know perhaps, committed suicide some years ago."

I winced. Tor shuddered. "Shit," he said. "That's pretty sad."

"Very, yeah." I paused for a moment to honor her death before I continued. "Uh, Tor? What's this about calling me your fiancée?"

"Does it bother you?"

"Kind of. I mean, I've only known you for a little over a month."

"No." He shook his head. "You've known me for a hundred and sixty years."

"That was another life. I'm talking about this one."

He sighed and rolled his eyes at my scruples. "What else was I going to call you?" he said. "The girl who's living in sin with me?"

"That'd be better than kept woman, anyway."

"The proper word for that is concubine." He grinned at

me. "But that's not what you are. You're the mistress of this household."

"There's a difference, huh?"

"A big one, yeah. You're the highest status woman. You'll have to approve any concubine I want to take, and you can smack her to keep her in line, too, if she gives you any trouble."

For a few seconds I felt like slapping him, but his grin—the dimple told me he was teasing even before he laughed and pretended to duck.

"When I'm gone a-viking," he continued, "you have to manage the household and my land."

"Do I get first choice of the loot you bring back? Well, of the jewelry, anyway."

"You bet. That's a promise. The guys in my warband get the weapons."

We both laughed. He reached over and took my hand in both of his.

"Bryndis is over seventy," Tor continued. "In that online picture you showed me, she's wearing a silver cross pendant. I know the stereotypes about Nordic people, but not all of us are open-minded free spirits." He looked sour. "A lot of the old people still stick to Christianity, and it's a real grim version, too. Calvinistic Lutheran. I don't know why they believe it, but they do."

"Okay, so saying we're engaged makes sense. About the visit, it'd be better for me if we didn't go next week. That's when the critiques are happening. I'm probably going to be totally stressed."

"I'll tell her that. And we've got the next couple of nights to get through, too."

It took me a moment to realize what he meant, that the moon was entering her dark phase.

"What do you bet Nils is planning something?" Tor went on.

"I guess. It's strange, isn't it? He'll try to hurt us, but then he backs off."

"He's testing me, I bet. Seeing how strong my sorcery

is. I've got an idea about that. I'm sick and tired of sitting around waiting for him to cause trouble, so I'm going to take the fight to him."

I caught my breath in a gasp before I could stop myself. "What are you going to—" I began.

"I'd tell you but you wouldn't understand."

The flat assurance in his voice annoyed me, even though he was probably right.

"Well, sorry I'm so stupid," I said.

"What? That's not what I meant! You just haven't studied the runes, that's all. Do you want to come watch?"

"Will it bother you if I do?"

"No, as long as you don't say anything or get up and leave in the middle." He paused and tilted his head to one side to consider me. "There won't be a lot to see, and the chanting's going to sound weird, but at least you'll know what I'm doing down there."

"I'd like that, if you're sure it's okay."

"I wouldn't have offered if it wasn't." He got up and turned to look out the east-facing window. "There's no use in working till it's dark, when the energies change."

"Is that like astral tides?"

He spun back to look at me. "Exactly," he said. "How do you know that?"

"My father talked about it. He studied ritual magic."

"So that's why you knew I'm a vitki. When we met, I mean."

"A what?"

"A sorcerer. The name means someone who knows stuff."

"Stuff, huh? Let's just say I knew magic was a possibility." I decided to forestall any questions about my father. "You're not going to be in danger, are you?"

"No." He shook his head. "I'm just going to explore the field tonight. Try to find him. If I can't find him, I can't challenge him."

"Do you think you can find him?"

"Probably. We're blood kin, after all. Not his address or

anything exact like that, but it'll be good enough for what I have in mind."

"What's that?"

He smiled and said nothing.

"Sorry," I said. "Is there something I can do to help?"

"No." He paused and looked at me for a long minute. "Unless—well, we'll see how things go."

CHAPTER 10

Even though I'd finished my project, I went to class Friday, just to check in and show the prof that I took her course seriously. She told me I could go home if I wanted, so I did. Tor had already made arrangements with his guy friends to play basketball in a nearby schoolyard, but he suggested that I come pick him up around noon.

"We're only good for a couple of hours," he said, "and I'd like you meet my friends."

"Sure. After all, you've met some of mine."

"But look, let me warn you about Aaron. He can be real hard to take at times. Asperger's Syndrome. Know what that is?"

"Oh yeah. He's the hacker guy, right? I guess it's really common in people with that kind of computer skill."

"Well, that's what I've read. I guess it's true." He shrugged. "The other guys are okay. We all kind of look out for Aaron, though." All at once he grinned. "Well, we like to think we're okay. Some people would think studying sorcery is weird."

I said nothing—really loudly, apparently, because he laughed.

"It doesn't take sorcery to know what you're thinking," Tor said. "Okay. I'm strange. I know it. In fact, when I was in kindergarten I got labeled a high-functioning autistic. That's why my father took me out of public school."

"You're certainly not! Why—"

"We'd just come to this country about eight months before.

My English wasn't real good. People acted differently than they did in Iceland. I'd been raised to be quiet and not get in the grown-ups' way. The other kids all ran around shouting. I didn't know what in hell I was supposed to do, so I sat in a corner and just watched. When my father tried to explain all this to the school, they brushed him off. I wasn't real sure what was happening, but I do remember him coming home in a towering rage. He told my mother, that's it! Homeschooling!"

"I can see why. Were you part of an organized program? Play dates, science classes with other kids, that kind of thing?"

"Oh yeah. My mother saw to that. And I learned early not to tell people that my father was teaching me sorcery. So did Liv. He homeschooled her, too."

Before Tor left, he warned me that the cleaning women would be coming. Although he vacuumed out his workshop himself, Tor had hired one of those franchise housecleaning services to take care of the heavy work in the upstairs flat. Every month he consulted the lunar calendar before he made the appointments, just to make sure they wouldn't arrive on a full moon day.

Around ten in the morning, a pair of business-like young women in matching black pants and striped shirts appeared at the door. The shy one set right to work in the kitchen, where Tor had left a plastic basket of cleaning supplies. The other woman, Meg, whom I judged to be a few years older, stopped to talk with me.

"How long does it take you to do the flat?" I asked. "I'm just curious. It won't be a problem."

"Only a couple of hours, with two of us. Say, is Mr. Thorlaksson ever going to get those doors in the bedroom replaced?"

"Eventually, I guess."

"I hope so. Come look."

We walked down the hall to the master bedroom. Meg opened the door and pointed to the damage. "Look at those grooves. The splinters catch the dust. Sometimes they stick in the carpet, too. They could maybe ruin his vacuum cleaner."

"I'll talk to him about it."

"Thanks." She smiled at me. "I'll bet you're glad he got rid of that crazy dog."

"Very, yeah." I smiled in return. "I'll just get my stuff and get out of your way."

She trotted off to start on the bathroom on the other side of the flat. I took a minute to look at the scratched door more closely. The damage had left an odd pattern. You'd expect a bjarki's claws to leave three parallel grooves from the three strongest claws in the middle of his paw. These looked like they'd been made one at a time because they weren't quite parallel. I walked over the closet and examined at the damaged door there. Instead of a pattern of teeth marks, the damage looked more like it had been done with an ice pick.

Maybe the bjarki had weird teeth, I thought. I knew little about real bears and less about bjarkis. I shrugged and left the room. When I went into my bedroom to fetch my backpack, I glanced at the writing desk. The design had changed to an innocent bouquet of roses. Somehow it knew that normal people were in the flat.

I slathered on sunscreen and made sure to wear my sunglasses. Here and there in the sky a few wisps of yellowish smog hung in the heat of the day. I drove down to the schoolyard in Gretel, because I figured that Tor would want to show the guys his new car. I did think of it as his, even though he'd registered it in my name.

I parked just outside the chain link fence that surrounded the play yard. The four men were playing two on two at a basketball court marked by white lines on the pale, cracking asphalt. I found a wooden bench nearby and sat down to watch. Someone had left a black plastic cooler with the Raiders' logo on it under the bench. I touched it, found it was cool, and figured it belonged to the guys.

It didn't take me long to see that Tor wasn't much of a basketball player. The other guy on his team, who had glasses and an amazing head of light brown curly hair, did most of the shooting while Tor did most of the guarding. On the other team the chubby redhead and the fourth guy, an African-American man with a shaved head, seemed pretty evenly matched. All four were laughing as much as shooting, though, pretending to elbow each other out of the way as they scrapped for the ball. Tor darted at the Black guy and stole the ball from a dribble, then did a layup that finally went into the basket.

"One for the wizard!" the redhead called out.

"Ah, he cheats!" the guy with the shaved head said.

The curly-headed guy caught the ball and stopped the entire game by cradling it and standing still. "Tor doesn't cheat." He sounded puzzled.

"Aaron, yeah, I know." Shaved Head grinned at him. "It was a joke."

Aaron tossed him the ball, then took off his glasses and wiped them on the edge of his T-shirt while he thought about it. "It's not real funny." He put the glasses back on.

"True enough," the redhead said. "Chalk it up to the heat of the moment."

Aaron shrugged, and the game resumed. Although Tor was no polished athlete, I loved watching him move. He had a certain grace for all his lack of aim. His thin T-shirt, soaked with sweat, clung to the muscles of his back. He was wearing a pair of cut-off jeans, a little too loose in the waist, so that they slid down an inviting few inches. I began to hope the game would get itself over soon. Finally, after a few more skirmishes, the redhead maneuvered toward the basket, made a perfect shot, and shouted out, "Sixty! We win!"

"Again!" Tor said. "Ah shit!"

They all laughed and strolled toward the bench, the cooler, and me.

"Hey, look!" the redhead said. "The beer's attracted prey."

"That's not prey," Tor said. "That's my girlfriend."

Everyone laughed but Tor. Shaved Head raised a hand like a warning and made a face at the redhead, who ignored him.

"Dude! You've got the luck, wizard," the redhead said. "Gonna introduce us?"

Tor stopped walking, turned toward him, and gave the

redheaded guy a narrow-eyed look so cold that the redhead stepped back fast. Before either could say anything, Shaved Head moved in between them.

"Tor," he said, "no one's going to try to mess around with your lady. Okay?"

"Sure." Tor arranged a normal-looking smile that I read as false as a pair of drugstore eyelashes. "Sorry."

"My bad." The redhead turned to me. "I apologize. I disrespected you, and I'm sorry."

"I forgive you," I said. "I'll put it down to the thrill of victory."

More laughter, a little bit strained, this time, but at least it was laughter, not shouting. Tor made introductions like a gentleman. The redhead was Billy, another computer person like Aaron, though without the Asperger's. It turned out that he worked for the same company as Cynthia's husband Jim, just on a different shift, a coincidence that got everyone grinning. The last of the tension eased up. The African-American guy was JJ, who was doing a PhD in linguistics. His thesis, he told me when I asked, explored semantic issues in the construction of theoretical computer languages for artificial intelligences. I couldn't even begin to understand it.

"They keep telling me," JJ said with a wave at Billy and Aaron, "that if I keep working on AIs I'll get rich."

"Practically guaranteed!" Billy put in.

"It's sure not my thing," I said. "I'm getting my BFA with a painting emphasis. I'm doomed to be broke all my life."

Billy and JJ both groaned. Tor sat down next to me and put an arm around my shoulders. "That's why you've got me," Tor said. "Your doom's been cancelled."

"Whoa!" Billy said. "This is serious, huh? Between you guys, I mean? I apologize again for my big mouth."

"I don't get it." Aaron was a couple of beats behind the tune. "Some painters make a lot of money."

"Yeah," I said, "but they're all men."

"Oh." Aaron considered this statement. "Y'know, I've read about that."

JJ hunkered down and pulled the cooler out from under

the bench. "Who wants a beer?" he said.

"None for me," I said. "I'm driving."

"Since I'm not," Tor said, "I do."

"Always you do." JJ grinned at me. "It's the Nordic genes. These White guys, they drink like fish."

We stayed at the schoolyard for maybe a half an hour more while the guys finished the beer, only a tall can apiece, nothing extravagant. When Tor decided we should leave, the others came with us to admire the new car. Everyone made the appropriate noises of envy and approval. As we drove off, Tor asked me if I wanted to go out to lunch.

"Though I bet I need a shower first," he said.

"Yeah, you do if we're going out. But you smell totally sexy to me."

"Oh yeah?" He grinned at me.

"Yeah. We could eat lunch later."

"Later? After, you mean."

"Do you mind me asking for sex?"

"Hell, no! Do you think I'm crazy or something?"

"Only a little bit. Not about the things that really matter."

We both laughed. I pulled up at a red light.

"JJ," I said, "he's the guy who prevents trouble, huh?"

"Yeah. He's the oldest of five kids. His dad worked as a security guard, and he got shot and killed during a robbery. His mom worked two jobs after that, and JJ kind of ran things at home. Shit! Sometimes I realize how lucky I am."

" I see what you mean. Did he get scholarships to go to college?"

"You bet. His high school teachers saw to that." He hesitated briefly. "Never tell him this, okay? But I set up a grant to pay for that doctorate. I hope he never suspects who it comes from."

"I'm impressed."

"Don't be. I did it out of guilt, y'know, because I've got so much."

I could think of nothing to say to that. The light changed, and we drove on home.

The cleaners had long since finished and left. We went

upstairs, and Tor paused to arm the security system. I went straight for our bedroom and began taking off my clothes. There were times with Tor when I turned into a female animal in heat. He followed me, but he stood by the door and watched me strip before he strode over, caught me by the shoulders, and kissed me with all his usual intensity. We made love once, as good as ever. I was expecting we'd do more, but he only kissed me a couple of times, then lay still.

"Don't you want to do something else?" I said.

"I've got to save it for tonight." He let go of me and moved a little away. "The energy, I mean. For the ritual. I'll need it if I'm going to find Nils."

I stopped being the animal in heat and began to think again. I finally understood one strand of the arguments between my parents. Since we'd lived in apartments, I'd overheard way too much as a kid, not that I'd understood what I was hearing. They made sure to keep any sexual noises hidden from me and my brother, but the fighting was too loud to hide.

"I'm sorry." Tor raised himself up on one elbow so he could look me in the face. "Are you mad?"

"No, not at all. God, Tor, I'm not insatiable or anything. You just make me feel like I am."

He laughed and lay back down.

"My mother used to fight with my father about this," I said. "I heard them talking about rituals and channeling sex energy. She thought it was really unhealthy."

"It is if you do it wrong. Hey, how much do you know about ritual magic, anyway?"

"More than I thought I did. I didn't understand much when I was a kid. I just soaked up what I overheard. Y'know?"

"Kids do that, sure." Tor considered me for a moment. "Then you know what chanting sounds like?"

"Yeah. We got kicked out of an apartment once because my dad was practicing it, and the people downstairs complained about the noise. The vibratory formula, he called it."

"That's it. Okay, then it won't freak you out when you hear me tonight."

"Not the sound of it, no."

The memories it might bring up were another matter entirely.

Tor got out of bed, picked up his T-shirt from the floor, and made a sour face. "I've got to go shower," he said.

When he went into the bathroom, I stretched out luxuriously and stayed in bed. It felt so good to rest, to just lie still and rest without worrying about money and school and whether the car would die and all the other things that had tormented me for years. By the time he returned, all damp and clean, I'd nearly fallen asleep.

"Do you want to just have lunch here?" Tor said.

"Yeah." I paused to yawn. "If that's okay with you."

"No, it's fine. I need to do some preparation, anyway."

I found out that evening what he meant by preparation. Once the last of the sunset faded away, we went downstairs. Tor had vacuumed out the room with the magic circle and scattered a mixture of herbs around in the corners. The place smelled like fruit as well as flowers, because he'd also put out a peeled and segmented orange for the nisse, then tossed the peels into the herb mix. We went into the room with the cabinets, where we both stripped off our clothes. He handed me a clean white T-shirt to wear, one of his, which fit me like a draped tunic. He put on a pair of loose white boxer shorts.

We returned to the magic circle. He sat me down outside of it against the western wall and told me to stay there, then lit four thick candles on earthenware plates. He walked clockwise around the circle and placed the candles, scented with cinnamon, at each cardinal point. By then I felt half-drunk from the smell in the room and wondered exactly what those scattered herbs were. Not marijuana—I would have recognized that—but something powerful was scenting the air. Tor, however, looked intensely focused and fully in command of himself.

He walked into the circle and took up his stance at the point where the arms of the cross met. For a moment he stood in a relaxed pose with his arms hanging loosely at his side while he looked off to the east. He drew a deep breath and seemed to grow taller. He began to chant a long but simple string of vowels. It was a good thing I knew what he was doing, or the sound might have driven me out of the room and ruined his working. His normal voice deepened, slid lower in his chest somehow, growled and hissed and vibrated the vowel sounds until they sounded like nothing a human being would normally make. They came from deep within him, from the root of his soul and his body both. I turned icy cold, felt the hair rise on my neck and arms, felt my own breathing come in gasps to match his.

As he chanted, he turned to face the different cardinal points, one-quarter turn at a time, always moving clockwise. He returned to facing east, then made a half-turn to look in my direction. When he fell silent, I felt as if he'd been holding me by the throat but had suddenly let go. He never moved, simply stared off to the west while the candles guttered and threw more shadows than light around the big room. The scent of herbs strengthened in the warm night air. Thinking, even remembering, became impossible. I'd always existed in this room, in this ritual, in Tor's powerful grasp upon my soul.

He tossed his head and chanted again, on and on until I began to sway from side to side with the rhythm of his chanting. He stopped, stood silently, then sat down on the floor with a motion graceful enough for the dancer. He looked at me out of the pools of shadow that had become his eyes.

"Maya," he said. "Undress and come here."

I knew what he wanted from me. I knew this ritual, not that I could have told him how I knew. My father never would have talked about such things in front of me.

I got up, took off the T-shirt, and walked into the circle. He lay down, then arched his back and pulled down the shorts. I knelt next to him and slid them off the rest of the way. He was already erect. I straddled him and felt him enter me, but he lay without moving his hips. I leaned forward to put the pressure on the part of my body that counted. He raised his hands and cupped my breasts. I gasped at the touch, but he never noticed. For a long time we stayed that way, silent, still, while I felt the pleasure mounting inside me. I must have climaxed several times, but he never moved. His eyes stayed wide open, staring at the ceiling. The herb scent wrapped us around like the heat from a fire.

Someone watched us. I knew it, looked up toward the east, and saw a shadowy form, just a patchwork of light and shadow at first. It became slightly more distinct, like a figure seen in mist or clouds. I saw blue eyes gleaming through the smoke-mask of its face.

"What do you see?" Tor whispered.

"A mask. Some kind of image of a face."

The smoke began to coalesce into a likeness: the man I'd faced down in the mall.

"Nils," I whispered.

The face turned solid, a real face attached to a ghostly pale body. The eyes glittered with sheer hatred.

"You broke him," the face said. "You ruined my captain and my friend."

"Who?"

The face sneered. It began to speak in a language I didn't know, then stopped with a choking, gasping sound.

Tor spoke one word.

The face started to speak, then choked and spat. Tor never moved or spoke again, but he smiled, the icy, deadly smile of a warrior who raises a sword against an enemy. I heard a scream of sheer terror. The figure disappeared.

"He's gone," I whispered.

"Good."

He raised his hands to my shoulders and pulled me down. I bent at the waist and lay against his chest. He began to move and released his sexual tension. I wouldn't call it pleasure, just a release, because his fixed warrior's smile never changed. Élan swept over me as he dispersed the life force he'd summoned to work the ritual. I gobbled it shamelessly, fed on the élan he was tossing away like garbage. My mind cleared, and I could think again thanks to the flood of raw energy. I felt the ecstasy of feeding, so different from sexual ecstasy and so glorious. We lay still, just briefly, until he smiled normally and patted my back. I rolled off him.

"Sorry," Tor said. "I should have brought some kleenex down. Hand me those shorts, will you?"

The ritual mood broke—deliberately shattered on his part, I figured. I handed him the shorts. He sat up, wiped himself, handed me the sticky cloth so I could so I could clean up, too. He got up and turned on the floor lamp in the corner, then walked around the circle counter-clockwise and pinched the candles out.

"Was that really Nils?" I said.

"Who else? You know what? He's crazy, completely over the edge. Do you remember when I did that reading with the nine runestaves? And I told you I was missing something?"

"Yeah, I do."

"That's one of the things I was missing. That he's nuts."

"That makes him more dangerous, doesn't it?"

"I don't know yet." Tor frowned and looked away. "It might just make him sloppy. In the way he works, I mean."

He sounded as if he doubted it. I wondered if Nils had seen me the way I could see him. I shuddered when I remembered the eyes shining through the face made of smoke.

"Who do you think he meant, when he told me I ruined someone?"

"Björn, probably. I think I know who Nils was, the second at the duel. The guy who lied to me. The first mate on the whaling ship."

I felt as if the normal world around us had just cracked open. Through the crack I could catch a glimpse of the past, see a man with mutton-chop whiskers saluting another man with a glass of liquor. The crack healed itself. The sight disappeared.

"How can he blame me?" I said. "And for what? The affair, I guess. Björn won the duel."

"If anyone was broken, it was you," Tor said. "I told you. Nils is one damaged guy. Crazy. Let's get dressed. I've got to vacuum up the herbs. I don't want the nisse eating them. He could get sick."

"Uh, what are they?"

"Marjoram, dried lavender, laurel leaves, and dittany of Crete."

"Isn't that dittany stuff dangerous?"

"Poisonous, yeah. That's why I don't want the nisse eating it."

But it was, or so I hoped anyway, okay for us to breathe its scent. I went upstairs to shower away the smell of the herbs that lingered in my hair and on my skin. I'd just finished when a fully dressed Tor came back up and joined me in my bedroom. I could smell cinnamon wafting around him with the last traces of the jettisoned élan. When I breathed in both, the room seemed to grow larger.

"Everything cleaned up?" I said.

He nodded and wandered over to look at the decoupage on the writing desk. I put on my jeans and joined him there. The green lion and the shrimp had disappeared. In their place stood a hermaphrodite: half-man, half-woman, joined down the middle, but with two heads, each wearing a crown. They stared out at us blankly with thin little lines for mouths. Tiny red lions made up the decorative circle around it or them, whatever you'd call that figure. Tor frowned and laid a forefinger on one of the lions.

"Is something wrong?" I said. "You looked worried."

"These lions should be something else." He took his hand back and looked at me. "We might have revved things up a little high. Released too much power, I mean. I've never done this before, used sex like we did. You've got real talent for sorcery, Maya, but still, I'm kind of surprised it worked."

I had to steady my voice out of fear of those words, *talent for sorcery*. "Well, it did work. That's good, right?"

Tor shrugged as if he wasn't sure. "I've been thinking. You know, maybe I never should have asked you to—well, uh, join in. I'm sorry. I ran up against his defenses and couldn't break through, and when I'm working, hell, I can't think of anything else. I'll do whatever I need to. So I invoked you, and maybe I shouldn't have."

He'd grab any weapon he could find, even me, was my take on the matter. "I could have told you no," I said. "But I don't know if I ever want to do it again."

"I hope I won't need to ask you. I scared the hell out of him, and he didn't have a partner to help him out. I bet he leaves us alone for a while. I only wish I could scare him off once and for all."

We spent all day Saturday at home while Tor worked his minor sorceries downstairs. He came up late in the afternoon and told me that he'd been casting the runestaves.

"Look, we know that Nils hates me," Tor said. "Probably because he was left out of the will. We know he's gone off the deep end. But that's not reason enough to do what he's doing."

"Hatred makes people act like real dorks."

"Yeah, but he's studied the runes. He's a vitki. He should know better." Tor smiled briefly. "Dorks yell at people and turn into trolls online. They don't use magical energy to attack their enemies. They don't blame them for things that happened in past lives. They usually don't try to run them off the road. Nils has played car games twice now."

"You've got a point."

"He wants something from me. It's not you, and I'll thank Tyr for that. I don't think it's the rune set I was so worried about. It can't be cash, because he must have money of his own. So what is it? I keep getting Fehu and Othala showing up in the staves when I cast them. Family something, family wealth."

"Well, you don't have any cattle." I'd been reading about the basic rune meanings. "And the only land you own is this house. What does that leave? Gold?"

Tor's eyes got very wide. "The ornament! That's the only gold I've got, and it's got runes all over it. I've always thought they must spell out an incantation. Huh. You might have answered the question. You've got talent, all right."

I arranged a fake smile. After a moment he shrugged and

went back downstairs.

When evening fell, we went on guard. I was dreading more illusions, not because I feared them, but because I hated the thought that I had the talent to dispel them. But although we stayed up half the night on watch against the waning moon, Nils never sent a single illusion our way.

Sunday was the day when everything changed.

Working the Friday ritual and then our broken sleep on Saturday had left Tor so spent that I did the grocery shopping that Sunday. Although he was reluctant to let me leave the house, I pointed out that in broad daylight in a crowded parking lot and supermarket, I'd be perfectly safe. "Besides," I told him, "if you're this tired, I bet Uncle Nils is worse off."

He grinned at that and agreed.

Shoppers crowded the supermarket. Every time someone got too close to me, I reminded myself that I no longer needed to steal their élan. The relief was so profound that at moments I teared up, just because I was no longer afraid. I wasn't going to run down and die. I wouldn't feel my heart knocking desperately in my chest. Best of all, I was no longer a thief. That tempting slob of a teenage boy, the rude woman and her obnoxious kids—they were safe from me, and I was safe from myself.

When I returned home, I drove the car into the garage, took out the two bags of groceries, then locked up. As I was carrying the bags to the side door, however, someone came walking down the driveway to meet me. He must have been seven feet tall or nearly so, a gangly thin kid wearing a Minnesota Timberwolves jersey and a pair of jeans that showed a lot of ankle, an attempt to disguise him as a basketball player, I assumed. His irises were a gray so light that the eyeball seemed almost uniformly white. His hair was dead-white, as were his eyebrows and the hair on his pale arms, but close up I saw the smooth, unlined face and soft jaw of a young teenager.

I immediately thought he might be an illusion, Nils's masterpiece, maybe, even though the sun was shining.

"Hello, this is the sorcerer's house, is it not? You are the sorcerer's woman, yes?" His English sounded like a parody of a Wisconsin Swedish accent. "I have the note. You will take it in to him, yes? The runes above the door, they keep me out."

With a flourish he held out a square envelope of expensive cream laid paper. On the back I saw a lump of gold-colored sealing wax with a rune stamped into it.

"You've asked me three questions," I said. "I get to ask you three in return."

He took a sharp step back. "You are too clever."

"If you won't give me three answers, I won't take in the note."

He debated, looking down, scuffing the toe of his enormous running shoe on the ground like a normal teen might do. Eventually he looked up again.

"Very well," he said. "Ask."

"Why are you bringing a note?'

"You asked to send the note. We heard you when the other sorcerer made the silly noises."

I did vaguely remember making a joke about a note. "Okay. How old are you?"

"Thirteen of your years."

"Third question. Are you a Rime Jotunn?"

Again the scuff, and this time he gave me an agonized look. Sweat beaded on his face from the hot sun. I could barely hear his answer. "Yes."

"I thought so! Now I'll answer. This is his house, and I'm his woman, and I'll give him your note."

I took the envelope from his huge hand and saw a line of runes on the front. As I tucked it into one of the grocery bags, I noticed the two family-sized bottles of cola I'd bought. I took one out.

"You must be thirsty," I said. "Here, try this."

He risked a trembling smile. I unscrewed the cap and handed the bottle over. He took a sip, grinned, and drank off a third of the bottle in one long gulp.

"Careful!" I said. "It's got air in it. It makes you—"

He burped so loudly that the nearby window rattled. No,

he was definitely not an illusion.

"So good," he said. "I keep, yes?"

"Yes."

He grinned again, took one step away, and disappeared. The bottle disappeared with him. He'd gone back to Jotunheim with a bottle of off-brand cola in his hand.

When I got upstairs I found Tor sprawled on the couch asleep, a book open in his lap. He woke up, mumbled something under his breath, and sat up straight with a stretch and a yawn.

"I have a message for you," I said. "From the Rime Jötnar."

I set the bag down, found the envelope, and sailed it into his lap. He took it and stared at it without speaking for so long that I picked up the bag again and carried the groceries into the kitchen. I'd just set them down on the counter when Tor came hurrying in with the envelope in one hand and a piece of cream-colored notepaper in the other.

"Maya," he said. "You weren't kidding." He turned the envelope over and pointed to the broken seal. "See that rune? It's Thuraz, thorn. It's the sign of the Jötnar."

"Oh." My voice shook. "Well, that's what the kid told me he was."

"The kid?"

"The guy who brought the note. He was a giant kid. Thirteen, he told me."

Tor stared at me.

"He told me he was a Rime Jotunn," I continued. "Well, I pried it out of him, but he had to be telling the truth. He was all white, hair and all, but he was still a kid."

"He wouldn't lie about that, no."

"How did he get here?"

"I don't know." Tor hesitated, his mouth slack. "Unless uh. Oh shit!"

"What?" I snapped at him.

"We released a lot of power Friday night. That's what the red lions mean. I might have opened something up. A bridge or something. To some place."

One of the beings I'd read about in the mythology books had crossed over that bridge and walked down our driveway. It finally dawned on me that I was frightened. I forced myself to concentrate on unpacking the grocery bags while Tor stared at the note. Now and then he sounded out a word or two. I put the last carton away in the refrigerator and turned to lean against the counter and look at him.

"What does it say?" I said.

"I don't know." He looked up wide-eyed. "It looks like the language on the gold ornament. Y'know, the one I keep in the safe, and it could be the same language you started speaking last month. During Nils's attack. Proto-Gothic again. The only words I recognize are thief and bjarki. I don't even know what case they are."

"What what?"

"It's a grammar term. Case endings, like the difference between he and him. They show you what the word's doing in the sentence."

"Oh. That."

"Yeah, that. It could be real important. I wonder—one of my old profs at Cal might be able to help me read this, but shit, it's summer, and he won't be there."

"Do you think you can puzzle it out?"

"Maybe. I'll try, and if I can't—" He shrugged. "I'll wait, I guess, until the guy who can gets back." He hesitated. "I'd better cast the runes. I'll be in the other flat, okay?"

"Sure," I said. "Good luck."

He gave me a sickly smile and left the kitchen. I'd believed from the beginning that Tor was a runemaster. I'd recognized him as a sorcerer, a vitki as he called it. He'd shown himself to be so powerful that I hadn't realized he could make a mistake. Apparently he could and had. I had the horrible feeling that when a sorcerer made a mistake, it would be as powerful as he was, neither more nor less.

I poured myself a glass of cola and went into my bedroom to fetch my laptop. On the writing desk the hermaphrodite stared out at me. Both of its faces were smiling.

CHAPTER 11

Even though the moon still hid in darkness, Monday morning brought me back to ordinary life, school, and the start of critique week. My nerves got me to class early. As I walked down the hall, I saw a small mob milling around the door to the painting studio. Students like me, I thought, also nervous. But as I walked up, I realized that our instructor stood at the front of the crowd. She always called herself by her last name, Harper, a tall woman, skinny, with rich brown skin and black hair that she kept in long dreds. That morning she wore her usual denim overalls and an old gingham shirt, as paint-spattered as any of her students' clothes. She was talking with one of the campus security guards.

I found Cynthia at the edge of the mob. "What's happened?" I said.

"I'm not sure." Cynthia shrugged and held her hands palm up. "It can't be anything good."

"Yeah, I guess not." I glanced around and saw a man in a dark blue uniform striding down the hall. "Because here comes a real cop."

The Oakland police officer joined the security guard and our instructor at the door. They conferred for a few more minutes, while the crowd of students grew and began to spill down the hallway in a murmur of questions. Finally Harper turned to face us and held up her hands for silence.

"We've got a big problem," she said. "The room's been vandalized. A lot of your work has suffered. Brace yourselves.

We're going to let you in a few at a time."

You probably could have heard the groans all the way across the bay in San Francisco. Those projects represented hundreds of hours of work and important grade points, too.

Harper rose on tip-toe and looked over the crowd. "Cantescu," she said. "You'd better come in first."

I felt too sick to say a word as I made my way through. The security guard opened the studio door just enough to let me and Harper slip in. As soon as I got a good look at the big, open room, I felt even sicker. Slashed canvases littered the floor. Thrown paint spattered what was left of them. Paint tubes, squeezed empty, lay everywhere among broken brushes. It took me some minutes to find the remains of my project. Rather than merely slash it, someone had shredded it. Tiny bits of paint-encrusted canvas lay on the floor like dead autumn leaves. The vandal had even broken up the stretcher bars, not an easy thing to do with that thick wood.

"I got here early," Harper said. "And found this. Yours is the worst mess of all, which makes the security people think someone particularly had it in for you. Though I dunno, the motherfuckers might just have grabbed yours first and then run out of steam later. They shredded a couple of others, too, just not so thoroughly."

"There had to be more than one person, you think?" I found my voice at last.

"I'm just guessing. There's bound to be fingerprints with all the lousy paint they threw around." She sighed. "Unless they had the sense to wear rubber gloves."

"How did they even get in?"

"Through the window." She turned and pointed at one of the old-fashioned wood-framed panes. "They used a glass cutter to make a hole so they could reach that little gizmo that keeps it shut. Once they turned that, they could just push up the whole window and climb on through."

I squatted down and leafed through the shards of my dead painting. They could have ruined it with a lot less effort if they'd only wanted to cause trouble. Did they think it was dangerous, somehow, and so they had to destroy it? I picked up one of the bigger pieces, maybe three inches of the silver area that had once formed part of the model's vinyl vest.

"Can I take this?" I said. "Or will the cops mind?"

"I doubt if they'll care. Why do you want it?"

"I dunno." I stood up and pocketed the fragment. "Nostalgia, maybe?"

She gave me a twisted smile. "You don't have an ex-boyfriend who'd want to hurt you, do you?"

"No. I'm living with a guy now, but the guy before him, he was the one who dumped me. I was single for over a year."

"Okay. Let's go out. I need to make a general announcement. The good news is that I've already made notes on everyone's work. Did it last Friday, just so I could compare my first impressions with the student critiques. So there will be grades."

"That's a relief!"

"I knew it would be particularly hard on scholarship kids like you if there weren't. Don't worry, you did a good job. I made sure the police know that no one's failing this class. If someone was, I suppose they might have done this to get out of the critique, but no one needed to, especially not you."

"Thanks." My eyes filled with tears. I snuffled them back. "God, this is so awful!"

"Yeah, I know. Maybe it was just a class project, but you put a lot of work into that. And then the bastards tore your baby to bits."

I nodded. I didn't trust my voice because I didn't want to cry in front of her. A class project, sure, but art is art, and that painting contained a little bit of my soul.

We returned to the crowded hallway. Pretty much the entire class had arrived, as near as I could tell, except of course for Brittany. While Harper told everyone what had happened, I made my way back to Cynthia.

"There's not much use in holding the last week of class," Harper finished up. "I'll post the course grades online as soon as I have time. Tonight, probably."

Harper went back into the classroom. The security guard and the police officer began letting people in to join her four at a time.

"I'm in no hurry to see," Cynthia said. "Shit! All that work!"

"Yeah. They turned mine into confetti. Brittany's was a real mess, too. I saw yours, though, and it could be patched. Just a couple of slashes."

She shrugged and made a small groaning sound. Was it Nils? I wondered. I wished that Tor were there. Somehow he'd know if his uncle were responsible, I thought, not that he could give the police information he'd gained through sorcery.

"Where *is* Brit?" Cynthia said. "I suppose she'll come dragging in later." She began rummaging through her backpack. "I'll call her, if I can find the damn phone in here."

I glanced around to look for Brittany. Instead I saw Tor, striding down the long hallway. For a minute I thought I was hallucinating, but he waved to me and hurried over.

"What's wrong?" he said.

Cynthia stared at him in complete open-mouthed surprise.

"I'll explain later." I was too shocked to think up a good lie. "Uh, Tor, let's move over here, okay? Cynthia needs to call Brittany."

I laid a hand on his arm just to ensure that he was really there. I felt solid flesh. He caught my hand in his, and we walked some ten feet down the hall, away from the crowd. He dropped his voice to make sure no one could overhear us.

"I picked up your message," Tor said. "That you wished I was here, I mean, and I could tell you were upset. So I came over. Leapt the distance. You know."

"Thank you so much! Something awful's happened. The studio got vandalized." I dug into my pocket and took out the scrap of canvas. "Everyone's work is ruined. Someone cut my project up into little pieces like this."

Tor took the scrap and held it between his palms. His eyes went unfocused, his entire face slackened. After a few seconds he scowled and shook his head.

"Nils," he said. "What do you bet? I'm picking up some kind of trace from him. I never should have brought you into the working. I'm so sorry. It was stupid of me, dragging you in."

"He must have seen me, then, when I saw him."

"Why else would he do this? He wanted to get back at you." Tor scowled at the fragment of portrait. "His vibes, yeah. I'm sure of it. Fucking coward! Going after you instead of me. I bet he's trying to drive you away."

"Why would he want to?"

"He's almost as strong as I am. You tipped the balance in that working. Without you around, he'd have a better chance at me."

Since I'd spent most of my life afraid of dying, I thought I was used to fear. The icy-cold terror I felt at that moment caught me by surprise. I gasped aloud. Tor threw an arm around my shoulders and pulled me close.

"I really wish," Tor said, "that I could just go to the cops about this. They wouldn't believe me. Magical attacks. Sorcerers fighting it out. They'd probably try to get me committed. And they might even be right about that."

I managed to smile. He kissed my forehead.

"This is all my fault," Tor went on. "My damned conceit again! Arrogance—yeah, you nailed it. I thought I was strong enough to punch a wasp's nest and not get stung. I'm sorry, Maya. I really blew it."

"You don't need to keep apologizing. He's the one who attacked you first. I feel awful because he had to go and wreck everybody's work. I feel like I brought all this down on my friends, y'know?"

"Well, that's not your fault. That's his fault. You didn't make him do anything. What a crappy thing! Do you remember when you felt like someone was spying on you at school?"

"Yeah, I sure do. It must have been him, all right. He must have seen this studio room."

I was about to say more when Cynthia hurried over to join us.

"I reached Brit," she said, "and she's on her way. She was just leaving the house, she told me, when I called, so she won't be here for another half-hour."

"Late as always," I said, just because it was such a normal thing to say.

Cynthia glanced at Tor and raised an eyebrow. "On the other hand, you're here early."

He nodded but kept quiet.

"He needed to use the car." Luckily I'd never sworn any vows to the runes against lying. "So he was just going to drop me off." I glanced his way. "You must have seen the police car drive up."

"I wanted to know what was going on," Tor said, and of course that was true. "Make sure you were all right."

"Well, thank heavens, we're all okay," Cynthia said. "But oh my lord, all our work! At least we're going to get grades." She tried to smile. "I suppose we should be grateful for getting an extra week off."

"Your instructor's cancelling the last classes?" Tor said.

"Yeah," I said. "She announced that just before you got here. The police probably don't want us in the room. They'll have to go over it for evidence."

Tor brightened. "Maybe they'll find fingerprints."

"Maybe," I said. "You know, we could go visit Bryndis this week after all, if you want. And if it's convenient for her." I glanced at Cynthia to include her. "An old friend of Tor's family from Iceland."

Tor pulled his smartphone out of his jeans pocket. "I'll just call her."

Visiting during the week proved to be very convenient for Bryndis. Over the phone they arranged that we'd go to her house on Tuesday afternoon. After Tor clicked off, we hung around in the corridor with the class in order to keep Cynthia company. When she came out of the studio, I was glad that we'd stuck around. She'd gone pale, and her voice snapped with anger.

"I'm too upset even to swear," Cynthia said. "Did you

realize that whoever did this peed in the corner? It's so disgusting!"

"No, I didn't see that when I was in." I felt more guilty than ever, even though Tor was right. Nils was the one who'd chosen to throw this nasty little temper tantrum, not me. "God, how sick!"

"Crazy," Tor muttered. "Way out there somewhere."

"Oh yeah," Cynthia said. "Devon found it when she picked up her share of the pieces. He did it right on a pile of paint rags. Well, sorry. We don't know it was a guy."

"It's not the kind of thing women do," Tor said. "It's not as convenient for them."

Cynthia managed a small, twisted smile at that. "Yeah," she said. "You're right. I—" She paused and looked down the hall. "Here's Brit, and your brother's with her, Maya."

I turned and looked where she'd pointed. Brittany and Roman came striding down the hall arm in arm. With a khaki T-shirt he was wearing a faded pair of camo cargo pants left over from his days on active service. The flap pockets had his name printed on them, Cantescu. The military gear reminded me that there were worse things in life than having one of your paintings destroyed. When they joined us, Brittany let go of him to give first Cynthia, then me, a hug. Roman and Tor shook hands.

"Well, Sis," Roman said, "this is a pile of shit, huh?"

"Fraid so," I said. "It's a real mess in there. Brit, Harper's signaling to you."

"I'm probably the last one in," Brittany said. "I always am."

"There are reasons for that," Roman said darkly.

They shared a grin, and she hurried off to join Harper in the studio.

"Time means nothing to Brittany," Roman remarked.

We all nodded our agreement. Roman looked good enough that I was willing to bet he'd stayed drug-free since the last time I'd seen him. He seemed nervous, though, shifting his weight from foot to foot, slipping his hands into his pants pockets, taking them out again, glancing up and down the hall, always looking around as if he expected someone to jump out at us. Tor, on the other hand, leaned against the wall of the corridor and hid his face behind the illusion of the nerdy guy with the meaningless smile.

"What did you think of yours?" I said to Cynthia. "It looks to me like it could be patched from the back, and then you could paint over the slashes."

"It's not worth it," Cynthia said. "It's just class work, and let's face it, it's not real good."

"Oh come on! You really caught his facial expression."

"Yeah, but the rest of him. . ." She let her voice trail away.

I sighed. Neither of us could think of anything more to say. When Brittany and Harper came back out, Harper returned to consulting with the police, and Brittany hurried over to us.

"I could feel the guy's psychic vibes," she announced. "He's really a nutcase."

Behind her back Roman rolled his eyes. Cynthia set her lips together to prevent sarcasm escaping, or so I figured. Tor, however, peeled himself off the wall and ambled over to join her.

"What kind of vibes?" he said. "Can you describe them?"

"Yeah, he's an old guy," Brittany said. "Like, maybe fifty. He's really scared about something. He shredded my project like he shredded Maya's. I bet he picked up that I'm psychic. I got the impression he thought our paintings were magic somehow, and so maybe that's what he's scared of."

"That could be it," Tor said. "Thanks."

For an awkward moment no one spoke. Tor glanced at each of us in turn with his nerdy smile. "Say, do you guys want to go to brunch? My treat! Roman, I bet you'd like to see the car I got for your sister."

"Sure would," Roman said. "That old Chevy of hers wasn't real safe."

The two men strolled off together, leaving the three of us hurrying to catch up.

"Men and cars!" Cynthia muttered.

"Well, it's a totally cool one," I said. "I forgot that you

guys haven't seen it yet."

As we walked along, Brittany said nothing. I realized that she was thinking hard as she stared at Tor's back.

"Brit?" I said. "Is something wrong?"

"Tor's some kind of magician, isn't he?" Brittany said. "A mage, I mean, not some guy who does card tricks."

"Oh for crying out loud!" Cynthia broke in. "Brit, you should write fiction, with your mind."

"No, she's right," I said. "He studies rune magic. He's pretty good at it, too."

Cynthia opened her mouth and shut it again without speaking. None of us spoke again until we reached the parking lot, where we caught up with the guys. Spotlessly blue and gleaming in the sun, Gretel sat at the end of a row. When I pointed her out as Tor's car, he laughed and corrected me. "No, it's your car," he said, "I registered it in your name, remember?"

"He bought you that?" Roman said. "Just bought it for you?"

"Yeah."

"Do you know what a car like that costs?"

"No." I smiled and shrugged. "A lot, I guess."

"Jesus fucking God!" Roman muttered, then winced in Brittany's direction. "Sorry, honey. I'm trying to clean up my language, but it'll take time."

It was Brittany's turn for the rolled eyes and the little skeptical shake of her head. I was more worried about the way my druggie brother looked at Tor, narrow-eyed and speculative. Tor, who was talking with Cynthia about where to go for brunch, never noticed Roman's expression. Brittany did, though, with a frown that edged toward a scowl. Eventually we all agreed on our usual café, the one near Lake Merritt with a view of trees.

Although half the morning had passed, we were still early enough to get our favorite table by the window. The waiter helped Tor and Roman move a second table up against it to give everyone room. We all settled in with menus. Tor and

Roman ordered beer and began talking about baseball, Giants versus the A's, mostly, while Brittany and Cynthia discussed what had happened in the studio room. I kept touching the bindrune pendant Tor had made me, only half-consciously at first, until I realized I felt watched.

I turned a little in my chair and glanced out the window. No one was looking in. Stupid, I thought, if it's Nils he doesn't have to be right here! But he was right there, I was sure of it, and turned a little more. Someone was standing across the street and looking our way. Tor must have noticed my motion.

"Shit!" Tor stood up so fast that he knocked his chair over. "There he is!"

He turned and raced out of the door of the café. I got up and ran after him, but I stayed in the doorway. For a moment Nils stood stunned on his side of the street. Tor strode to the curb on our side and yelled in Icelandic. Nils yelled right back. At the corner the light changed, and cars began to stream past between them. Nils turned and started walking away. Tor kept yelling and moved along the edge of the sidewalk to keep pace with him.

When Tor stepped out between two parked cars, Nils broke into a jog.

"Tor," I called out. "The traffic! Be careful!"

I have no idea if Tor heard me, but Nils suddenly stopped and turned to look back. He flung up both arms in Tor's direction. Tor swung up his left hand, palm outward. Nils screamed, twisted around, and took out running for all he was worth. Tor set his hands on his hips and watched him go.

For a moment I thought my eyes were giving out. A cloud of fog settled between me and Tor. A man coalesced out of the fog, standing behind Tor, still shadowy, a figure of mist, but tall, huge, towering over Tor. He raised his hands—raised his left hand and a stump, because he'd lost his right. Beside him stood a huge dog—no, a wolf, made of the same mist.

"Fenrir," I whispered.

The wolf turned its head and looked my way. The man laughed and waved to me with his whole hand. They both disappeared into a long wisp of fog that vanished in the hot sun. Tor, perfectly calm, came walking back to me.

"Sorry," he said. "I got carried away."

"What did you do, when you held up your hand, and he screamed like that?"

"Just sent his ill-will back to him. He sent me a curse, so I turned it around." Tor grinned at me. "That'll teach him."

I could say nothing. We returned to our friends in the café. As we sat down, the waiter came hurrying over. Tor ordered a ham sandwich with fries as if nothing had happened. I managed to point to a salad on the menu, though I had no idea what it was until it actually arrived. I gulped ice water. Tor had a couple of sips of beer.

"Can I ask what was all that about?" Cynthia said.

Tor looked at me. I knew he wanted me to do whatever lying was necessary.

"Family troubles," I said. "Over the inheritance, y'know, money and stuff like that. His uncle feels cheated. That was his uncle, by the way."

"I saw the resemblance, yeah," Cynthia said. "Oh my god, fighting over the will! It's always so nasty. Doesn't matter if they leave you a lot or a little. My sister still resents the way I got our grandmother's engagement ring, and it's only an amethyst."

"I'm sorry," Tor said. "I never should have gone out there. He just infuriates me. He won't let things go. I guess I said a few things I shouldn't have." He managed a weak grin. "I'm glad you ladies don't understand Icelandic."

"So am I." Cynthia raised an eyebrow, grande dame fashion, then grinned. "It's okay. We're tough. We're artists, not ladies."

We all managed to laugh at that, except Brittany, who merely smiled, a small knowing kind of Mona Lisa smile. I wondered what she might have seen out there on the sidewalk, but I was afraid to ask.

By the time we finished eating, the café was filling up. We abandoned the tables to the busboy, straggled out onto the sidewalk, and stood around talking for a few minutes. Roman and I walked a little way away from the others.

"The group therapy's going well," he told me. "I'm sure glad you and Brit got me to go. Most of the other guys in there are vets, too."

"I'm glad you've kept going. Ro, that's supercool."

He shrugged the praise away. "Are you okay?" he said. "Your anemia hasn't come back, has it? Y'know, that crap you had in high school."

"Just a little bit, yeah. I'm not working at the burger joint any more, so I feel better."

"Good. I wondered. You look worried about something."

It was the first time in a couple of years that he'd paid attention to someone else's troubles. I began to allow myself to hope that he really was recovering.

"It's this business with Tor's Uncle Nils," I said. "He's seriously crazy. He doesn't have any kind of legal claim on the estate, so he's made threats. Tor doesn't like to talk about it."

"Yeah, I can see why." Roman smiled with a wry twist to his mouth. "Well, that's one thing we don't have to worry about, huh? Our huge inheritance."

Our dad had left us fifty bucks each and a couple of bad debts.

When Tor and I returned home, I decided to do some drawings. No, not a decision, a need—I needed to draw, to immerse myself in drawing like I had as a child when I needed to make the troublesome world go away. Tor went downstairs to study the note from the Rime Jötnar. I got my biggest archival-quality sketch pad and my selection of conté sticks and sat cross-legged on the sofa with the pad in my lap. I made a rough drawing, very gestural, of the scene outside the café, with Nils and Tor, the trees and the cars just laid in almost as scribbles. I turned the page and held the sketchbook vertically.

All at once I felt as if I'd had a couple of drinks. An image forced itself into my mind, the mist-figure with the missing hand and the bound wolf. I began to draw, another rough gestural sketch, then went to a fresh page and drew again from memory. Or more than memory, because the man and wolf began to fill in and build up so easily that I felt as if I'd left my body and joined them in the picture. It was more like seeing than drawing. I used four different colors of conté and found an old tissue in my shirt pocket to twist and use as a rough stump. When I finished, I fell out of the picture again and realized that I felt exhausted. I set the pad and my supplies down on the coffee table and went into the kitchen to get some water.

I drank two glasses straight down and was pouring myself a third when I heard Tor come upstairs. I returned to the living room to find him staring at the drawing.

"What's this?" he said.

"I saw that guy standing behind you," I said, "when you were yelling at Nils. Do you know who it is?"

He nodded. I realized that his face had gone slightly pale. "You saw him?" he said.

"Yeah. What's wrong?"

"Nothing. That's Tyr and Fenrir."

"I figured it was Fenrir, yeah." I paused for a sip of water. "Wait a minute! Isn't Tyr one of the gods?"

Tor nodded again. "The god I feel the most affinity with," he said. "I showed you the tattoo, didn't I? I wear his mark. You saw him?"

"Yeah, backing you up, I guess."

Tor smiled, an amazing open smile of delight, of joy, really. That's when I realized that he truly believed in his ancient gods of the northlands. I'd been ready to talk about hallucinations, or to call the vision a psychic phenomenon, or even say that maybe I'd just imagined it, but I held my tongue. How could I spoil his moment of pure joy?

"Thanks," he said. "I mean it. Thank you for drawing that." He paused and looked at the drawing again. "It's really good. Your art, I mean."

That particular picture did work for me. I could look at it objectively as one of the best conventional figure drawings I'd ever done, strong and clean lines, definitive shading. Even the wolf—and I'd never even drawn dogs before—had the look of life about it. I wondered if I'd really drawn it, or if the god had been guiding my hand. I'd certainly felt entranced.

"I'm glad you did it on decent paper," Tor continued. "I'll take it to a frame shop and get it matted and framed."

"Thank you," I said, "but I probably shouldn't take credit for it. Maybe Tyr wanted it drawn so you could see him."

"That could be. I'll hope so." Tor hesitated, his eyes solemn. "I'm really sorry about what happened to your class project. I mean, about the whole thing. Everyone's work, messed up like that. I want you to know that."

"Well, I figured, yeah, but thanks. You know, maybe you shouldn't keep pushing on Nils. He's really out there somewhere, isn't he?"

Tor nodded and looked away. He caught his lower lip between his teeth and thought for a couple of minutes.

"Maybe so," he said eventually. "Maybe I should just fend him off if he tries any more shit around here and let it go at that. It'd gripe me to do it, but it might be smart."

"Maybe he'll just give up. You keep winning the challenges."

"No, we won the big one. Together, I mean. And the trouble is, he knows it. But yeah, if he leaves us alone, I'll do the same for him. We'll have to see."

"See what? What he does next?"

"If he does anything, yeah. And I want to hear what Bryndis has to say. She knew him and his mother when he was a kid. That always seems to matter, what someone was like when they were kids."

Tor sounded so reasonable that I felt relieved. Maybe Nils would just leave us alone now that he'd had his cheap little revenge. But when I thought of the slashed paintings in the studio, I felt fear down my back like a slide of ice. It took a lot of rage to cut through paint and heavy canvas, rage and a real good knife.

"You look pale," Tor said. "Do you need chi?"

"Yeah. I don't know why, but doing this drawing really

took it out of me."

He led me over to the window where I could stand in the sunlight. With a little frown of concentration, he summoned the élan. I could feel it oozing from him and began to tremble in anticipation. Tor raised a hand and let the élan fall over me like a perfumed shower, warm and delectable. I fed with half-closed eyes, and when I'd had enough, I rubbed against him like a grateful cat.

"Feel better?" Tor said.

"Yeah, I sure do. Thank you. I could purr."

He laughed and kissed my forehead. "Something I meant to ask you," he said. "Does Roman know about your disease?"

"No. I mean, he knew I was a sick a lot as a kid and a teenager. My mother told everyone that I had a rare form of anemia." I called back the few pleasant memories of those years, like cheering my brother on at games. "Roman was really wrapped up in sports, his teams, his workout schedule, that kind of thing. And he had girlfriends, too. He wasn't home a lot when we were both teenagers, especially once my folks divorced."

"Ah. I wondered if they had. Do you know why?"

"The real question is why they ever got married." I tried to smile and failed. "I guess no one could really blame Dad for finding a girlfriend. He and Mom fought all the time."

"Not a good atmosphere to grow up in. Jeez, I'm sorry. The girlfriend—do you have a stepmother?"

"I guess. Not that she'd ever think of herself that way. She wouldn't have done a thing for me and Roman even if we were starving at her door." I smiled, but it wasn't a nice smile. "Not that we'd ever have asked her to."

"Too bad. She's a bitch, huh?"

I merely shrugged and scowled for an answer. Tor allowed me my silence.

In my memory I could see my father so clearly, his narrow face with the high cheekbones, his dark eyes, his hair that had gone gray so early in his life, his droopy moustache. I remembered my stepmother, too, and her hatred, *the way she'd hissed at me from the other side of his death bed. "You've killed him," she said. All I could do was stare at her. Her blue eyes glittered, her painted red mouth twisted in hatred. Even at my father's death bed she wore make-up.*

Hatred like Nils's hatred, I thought as I looked back on it. It hurt her more than it hurt Roman and me.

But I knew why she hated me. For years my father had robbed his own élan to feed me. He'd hunt, take a little of the life energy for himself, then funnel the rest to me. He'd kept his young daughter alive until she could hunt on her own. While he fed me, his heart grew weaker. His own life ran dry like a well pumped one time too many.

That night I had a dream that wasn't precisely a nightmare, even though I found it deeply troubling. I was standing in the living room of the flat. I ran down the hall to my bedroom and found two rooms instead of one, mine with its familiar furniture and beyond it, an empty room. *That's impossible.* It was one of those dream voices that come from everywhere and nowhere. I ran back the other way, crossed the living room, and found the bedroom I shared with Tor, but although the west window looked out on the usual view, wooden shutters covered the other window. I tried to open them, but they were locked.

I woke in a cold sweat. *That's the way the flat really is.* I knew it with the muddled certainty of someone who wakes from a particularly vivid dream. This insight, however, stayed with me instead of fading like dream-truths usually do.

Beside me Tor lay on his side, his back to me, breathing heavily but comfortably. I slipped out of bed without waking him and made my way through the dark living room to the hall that led to my own room. I could see the open door to the bedroom and across from it, the door to my bathroom. The hall seemed to end just beyond those two doors. I walked down to the door into my bedroom, reached inside, and flipped the switch that turned on the floor lamp. The room itself extended well beyond the wall that marked the end of the hallway. Since from the outside the building had no odd bay or extension to hold that extra space, something had to lie behind the end of the hallway. I wondered if I was about to have a Bluebeard moment, but by then I had to know.

I'd taken two steps toward the end wall when I heard someone walk up behind me. I spun around and screamed before I could stop myself. Tor stood blinking at me in the spill of light from my bedroom door. He'd put on a pair of jeans.

"What the hell?" he said. "What's wrong?"

"I just—uh—well." I was gasping for breath.

"Were you sleep-walking?"

"No." I took a couple of deep breaths and steadied myself down. "I had a dream about the floor plan of this flat." Saying it aloud sounded stupid, but I forced myself to continue. I pointed down the hall. "Like, is there something behind that wall?"

"Yeah. A closed-off room. Do you want to see it? It's probably dusty as hell."

"Not if you don't want me to."

"Huh? That's got nothing to do with it."

He flipped on the overhead light and walked down the hall with a wave to me to follow. He stroked one hand down the seemingly solid end wall, frowned, moved over a few inches and repeated the gesture. He grinned and pressed on something. As the door creaked open, I saw what had concealed it. Its vertical edges ran along the stripes of the wallpaper, and at the top it lined up with the bottom of the dado strip. The dim light at the hallway's end had made the cracks invisible to a casual glance. Behind the door lay an empty room littered with dust bunnies. One wall held a set of cheap shelves with nothing on them. A light fixture with no bulb hung from the ceiling.

"The guy who owned this place before me had weird ideas about storage," Tor said. "You've seen the bank of drawers in that big closet downstairs. I found this room after I moved in, but I didn't have anything to put into it. He must have kept something valuable here, though. Why else hide the door this way?"

The explanation was perfectly rational and normal-sounding.. "But what about the shutters?" I said.

"Huh? What shutters?"

By then I had no idea what I meant. I turned away and hurried back down the hall. I heard Tor close the door to the hidden room. The overhead light went out as he followed me. As dreams do, mine was fading and breaking up into pieces of imagery.

"But the room was real," I said.

"You've seen the downstairs. You must have noticed the door there, the one under the hidden one up here."

"Of course! And I must have made the connection without really thinking of it." I turned around to look at him. I fought my memory, finally recovered the image. "What about the shutters in the bedroom?"

"There aren't any shutters." Tor looked so puzzled that I figured he was telling the truth. I needed to be sure.

"You didn't install any magical shutters or find any ordinary ones when you moved in?"

"No, none. But they might be the point of the dream. There's something you're not looking at. You've shut something away from yourself."

As soon as I heard the words, I knew he was right. "Now I'm afraid to go back to sleep," I said.

"You need to start drawing these things. The things you see in your dreams, I mean."

I stayed silent. Tor cocked his head to one side. "Why don't you want to?" he said. "They're just dream images. Nothing's going to jump off the paper and bite you."

"That's not what I'm afraid of."

"Okay. What are you afraid of?"

"I don't know. I've got to figure that out first."

"Fair enough." He yawned again. "Let's go back to bed. I need more sleep."

We returned to the bedroom. The first thing I did was check the windows, but of course, there weren't any shutters. When we lay down again, Tor fell asleep almost immediately.

I lay awake and listened to the hum of the air conditioning. I heard voices in it, talking to me, but in a language I didn't know. When I finally fell asleep I had no further dreams that I could remember in the morning.

CHAPTER 12

B ryndis Leifsdottir and her son Orvar Arngrimsson lived
in a tidy little house in the middle of the Westlake neighborhood, a lot of other tidy little houses just off the freeway in
Daly City. As we drove through the development, I noticed
four basic architectural plans, turned on their lots to add variety to the look of the place. Each house had a bay window, and
each sat behind a short green lawn. Over the years, though,
the houses had acquired some character thanks to different
paint jobs and plantings. Bryndis's freshly-painted white house
sported a flower bed, blooming with purple flowers, under the
bay window. Over the front door I spotted a wooden plaque
with runes carved into it. Tor smiled at the sight.

"It's basically a kind of prayer to keep the house safe,"
he told me.

When we rang the bell, Bryndis herself, a white-haired
woman with piercing blue eyes, answered and ushered us
into the warm yellow living room, set with a sofa and two re-
cliners upholstered in a vaguely Jacobean floral pattern. On
the coffee table she'd set out little plates, some cookies, a loaf
of homemade rye bread, and a bowl filled to the brim with
butter. We introduced ourselves and shook hands all round.

"Sit down," she said, smiling. "I bring the coffee now."

Tor obligingly sat on the sofa, but I stayed standing for
a moment to look at a little pair of shelves on the wall. They
held china figurines, some from the early 19th century, all of
them antiques of one kind or another. She had good taste.

I sat down next to Tor just as Bryndis returned with a tray laden with cups and a glass carafe of coffee.

For a few minutes we chatted—had we found the house easily, what foggy weather Daly City has—that kind of thing, while we drank the very good coffee. Bryndis cut the loaf of bread, sliced us some, and buttered each slice so thickly that my teeth left marks in the butter when I bit into it.

"This is awfully good," I said. "Thank you so much!"

"Would you like another slice?"

"Yes, please, but could I have less butter?"

"What?" She smiled at me. "You don't like butter?"

I realized that she was teasing, just gently. "I do," I said, "but in moderation."

Bryndis laughed, but she did put less butter on the slice. She sat back in her chair with her coffee mug clasped in her hands and considered the pair of us.

"Well, Torvald," she said. "Your mother has finally told you about Nils."

"Under duress," Tor said. "Liv pried it out of her."

"I don't know why it embarrassed Sirin so much." Bryndis glanced my way. "Have you met her yet, Sirin, that is, Tor's mother?"

"Not yet, no," I said. "She's moved back to Iceland."

"That's a long way, yes. No doubt she'll come for the wedding. But what was I—oh yes. Sirin was very embarrassed, but it wasn't her husband that had the illegitimate son, only her father-in-law, and no one held a high opinion of him as it was."

"That's for sure," Tor muttered.

"Uh, please," I put in. "I'm getting confused. Sirin's father-in-law is your grandfather, Tor?"

"Yeah, my father's father," Tor said. "Halvar Svansson was his full name."

"He was in many ways a hard man," Bryndis went on. "He was Thorlak's father, and also Nils's father. My friend Gerda was Nils's mother, and Sirin is Torvald's mother."

"And my dad was Thorlak," Tor said.

"I've got it now," I said. "Thank you."

Bryndis gave me a quick smile, then continued in a serious tone of voice. "Halvar could be very cruel. He was cruel to Gerda, you see. He slapped her often. Never more than one slap at a time, but still, that is wrong."

I winced and shivered in agreement.

"Finally she left him because of Nils. She didn't wish her son to grow up seeing his father treat his mother so badly. I was afraid that Halvar would try to hurt her, but no, he let her go, the kindest thing perhaps he ever did for her."

"I'm real glad she got away from him," I said.

"Gerda?" Tor put in. "That's not an Icelandic name. It sounds German."

"It is." Bryndis nodded in his direction. "But she was Swedish. Halvar met her in Sweden and brought her home with him. As if he had bought a dog from a shop, the way he treated her! But she stayed because she was glad to be out of Sweden." Bryndis turned toward me. "Do you know the history, the babies that Swedish women had with Nazi officers? The pure Aryan babies, another German lie?"

"I don't, no."

"It was when the Swedes collaborated with the Nazis. The German men in the occupying army wished to get women they considered pure Aryans pregnant, you see, and then raise the children to be the new overlords of Europe. All that nonsense about Aryan blood, and there is no such thing, of course! But some Swedish women were duped and had affairs with these enemies. Gerda's mother was one such. Gerda's father was a German officer. She never knew his last name. He was later sent to Norway. I think her mother told that it was to take charge of a supply train. The Resistance shot and killed him there one winter." She paused to set her empty coffee mug down on the table. "Gerda's mother's name was Rosilde."

I felt Tor turn tense and heard him catch his breath. I would have asked him what was wrong, but Bryndis sat back in her chair with a shake of her head.

"It was very sad for the children," Bryndis continued. "After the war the Swedes turned against these women and put them in prison. They took the children away from their mothers. Gerda was one of them, and she was impounded. The children had nothing to do with their mother's treachery, but they were very badly treated. Many of them killed themselves after they grew up. Gerda did the same when she was sixty. She wrote me just before and said she could not bear to be old, but I think it was the way she was treated, thrown into a stockade like an animal, shunned and mocked and not properly fed after the war. She could never forget."

My eyes filled with tears. I wiped them away with my fingertips. Bryndis handed me a paper napkin and made a clucking sound, sort of like tchah!

"Oh dear, I've upset you!" she said. "But you can see how his mother's—" She hesitated to search for the word. "His mother's melancholy would have infected the boy. And why Gerda never wished to go back to Sweden."

"Oh yes," I said. "I can see it, all right. This is the kind of thing we need to know. Please, don't worry about upsetting me. It's just all so totally sad."

"Yes, very. Torvald mentioned that Nils was still angry about Halvar's will," Bryndis continued. "I doubt if it was the money. He wanted to be included in his brother's family." She nodded at Tor. "His brother, your father, of course, both of them Halvar's sons, but so different in what they had! Being left out of the will must have upset him for that reason, that he still hadn't been allowed into the family. He had money of his own, or so Gerda told me some years ago. He was a stockbroker, yes?"

"An investments manager," Tor said. "On Wall Street. Yeah, he must have done pretty well."

"He was like his father in that, then. Halvar did understand money. But people, no. I remember that when Nils was sixteen, Halvar considered bringing him into the aett." She smiled at me. "That is a very old way of saying, taking someone into your family, to bring them into the aett. But Torvald, your father refused. Nils was older than he was. Your father didn't want an older brother over him. Halvar was a very poor father. Thorlak only received little scraps of love and attention, not enough to share."

"Yes," Tor said. "He told me a lot about that."

I was beginning to seriously dislike Tor's grandfather. Slapping his mistress around, ignoring his sons—what a bastard!

Bryndis talked to us for another hour or so. She had a lot of memories of trying to help Gerda but also of good times they'd shared when both of them had young children. She brought out a photo album and showed us snapshots of her daughter and son along with Nils as a boy. I noticed that in the pictures he always posed a little apart from the other children and rarely smiled. I might have felt sorry for him if I hadn't kept remembering the scene in the art studio, my shredded canvas, and his liquid insult.

By the time we reached the end of the album I realized that Bryndis was growing tired. I prodded Tor, made our apologies, and thanked her profoundly for everything.

"It is nice to see visitors," Bryndis said. "If you do talk to Nils, I would like to see him again too, one day."

"No," Tor said. "You don't want to do that. I'm afraid he's really—" He considered words. "He's not doing real well mentally. I don't think he should ever know that you talked to me about him. I mean it. It could be dangerous."

Bryndis's eyes grew very wide, and she laid a hand on the silver cross pendant at her throat.

"Very well, then," she said. "I'll tell Orvar what you've said, too."

"Please!" I put in. "Maybe he should delete your pictures from his blog. I found you on the Internet. Nils can, too."

Bryndis looked at Tor. "You think Orvar should do this?"

"Yes." Tor's voice was quiet but urgent. "I'd hate to see something bad happen. Just never let Nils know where you are." He paused, then said something in Icelandic.

She nodded and answered in the same. As we all walked to the door, they continued the conversation. I did recognize a few words, like runar and vitki. When Tor and I stepped outside, Bryndis turned to me.

"Well, I'm sorry, we are being rude," she said. "It is a comfort, speaking the old language."

"I can understand that," I said. "I guess I should start learning Icelandic."

"Torvald can teach you." She smiled. "I hope to see you again. At perhaps the wedding."

With that she closed the door and spared me from having to commit to marrying Tor right there and then. I walked a few steps down the concrete path through the lawn, but Tor lingered on the porch. He was studying the plaque above the door, I realized. He raised his right hand, and he was tall enough lay a fingertip on the runes. For the briefest of moments I thought I saw them glow, but that might only have been some trick of the light. Tor nodded in satisfaction and hurried to join me. Together we walked to the car.

"What were you saying?" I asked. "There as we were leaving."

"Oh, I just repeated that I thought Nils was having a breakdown. I wanted her to realize that he could get real nasty. And I asked her if I could charge her runes. She said yes."

"She knows you're a sorcerer?"

"Of course! My grandfather and father were, after all." His tone of voice implied I should have known. "So she figured it's been passed down in the family."

"I thought you said she's a Christian."

"She is. So?"

He sounded so puzzled that it dawned me you could believe in religion and sorcerers, too. Why not? The early Christians sure did.

On the drive home Tor said very little, and I didn't feel much like talking, either. I resented feeling sorry for Nils. I wanted to hate him, just like I'd wanted to hate the people whose élan I stole, but I couldn't. I knew what it was like to live with a parent who suffered from depression, and Gerda must have been seriously depressed. My father fell into depression from time to time—his black dog, he called it, and our entire life revolved around his mood whenever the dog came to stay.

When we reached our building, Tor let me out of the car at the curb and drove Gretel into the garage. I noticed that once he got back outside, he fiddled with his smartphone to shut the garage door.

"Did you put the garage on the security system?" I said.

"Yeah. We've got a car worth stealing now. And on Thursday someone's going to install motion sensors out in back. Among the trees, y'know. If Nils tries lurking up there, there'll be lights, and an alarm going off."

We went upstairs in the house that was slowly turning into a fortress. Tor went into the kitchen and got himself a bottle of dark beer. He didn't bother with a glass.

"What did you think of Bryndis?" he said.

"I liked her. Your grandfather, though! I'm sure glad I never had to meet him."

"You're lucky, yeah." He had a long swallow of beer. "I've got a portrait of him if you want a look at him. He had a bunch of portraits painted. Me and Liv each inherited one when he died. So did my dad, so I've got two of them now." He paused to put his beer down on the counter. "I don't think he ever realized that we didn't like him."

Tor kept the portraits downstairs in one of the long drawers of the built-in storage unit. He brought out a big canvas about three feet by four, unwrapped it from the piece of faded gray corduroy that protected it, and set it up on the lectern under the overhead light. Despite its modern wood frame the portrait was conventional, even old-fashioned, painted in oils and then varnished, a frontal view of a middle-aged man in a red velvet chair against a dark background. Despite his gray hair and eyebrows, he reminded me strikingly of Tor. He had the same strong jaw and brown eyes, the same large hands, which in the portrait gripped the arms of the chair as if he bore the wood a grudge. He looked straight out at the viewer without even a trace of a smile.

"A grim old guy," I said. "The painter, though—whoever

did this was technically really competent. I wonder why they didn't sign it."

"Liv wondered about that, too. Probably Grandfather didn't want anyone else's name on it. That'd be like him."

The more I studied the painting, the more uncomfortable I felt. The eyes of any portrait will follow you if the sitter's looking straight out of the canvas. I knew that. Still I felt that he, or someone, or something, was watching me through this particular pair of painted eyes. I remembered Brittany saying that portraits might have frightened Nils somehow.

"Tor, do you think Nils got one of these, too?"

"Probably. Halvar admitted Nils was his kid, after all. Huh, if all Nils got from the will was a lousy portrait, no wonder he's pissed off." Tor grinned at me. "Like that T-shirt joke."

"That's not funny."

"Why?"

"I don't know, but the portrait creeps me out, and if he's got one, I bet it creeps him out, too." I turned away with a little shudder. "I've seen enough. More than enough."

"Okay. I'll put him back in his coffin." Tor picked up the cloth wrap. "That's how I always think of this drawer."

Watching him wrap the portrait up jogged my memory about another grim family story.

"When we were at Bryndis's, y'know?" I said. "She mentioned the name of Gerda's mother. Rosalie, wasn't it?"

"No." He hesitated. "Rosilde."

"Something's bugging you about that, isn't it?"

He shrugged. He put the painting away and shut the drawer, then turned off the overhead light. I followed him when he left the closet-room and went into the library. He strode over to the window, where he stood looking out with his back to me.

"Tor?" I said. "What's wrong?"

"At first we didn't have a source of supplies in the resistance, only what we could steal." He turned around, and I'd never seen his eyes so bleak, so full of remembered pain. "So we stole it from the Nazis. I've told you about the supply trains. And killing their patrols. When we wiped out a patrol, we'd ski down and strip them of everything we could—ammunition, guns, food, anything they carried that we could use. And one time I was stripping a man I'd shot, but he was still alive. I don't think he realized I was Norwegian. I was wearing a Nazi winter jacket I'd taken from another soldier. He looked at me and said in German, tell Rosilde and our little girl I loved them." Tor shoved his hands into his jeans pockets and tipped his head a little back. "So I said I would, and he died."

"Oh god! You don't think—"

"It's not that common a name, Rosilde. Wyrd, Maya. I knew I felt wyrd all around us."

I wanted to tell him that he couldn't possibly remember, that he had to be wrong. That Nazi officer—he couldn't have been Nils's grandfather. Too much of a coincidence—but if everything I'd read about wyrd was correct, then coincidence had nothing to do with it. Over Tor's shoulder I could see, just outside the window, three women standing in the yard. I stared, took one step toward them, and saw them disappear into shadows. I squelched a scream.

"What is it?" Tor said. "What did you see?"

"The Norns. Just for a second."

He nodded, his mouth set and grim. "Wyrd," he said eventually. "I knew that when I found you again, the threads, the knots—they'd start to unravel."

I could think of nothing to say to that. Tor shrugged, and the mood around us broke.

"Y'know," he said, and his voice stayed perfectly calm, "I think I'll cast the rune staves. I want to make sure that Nils isn't going to give Bryndis any trouble. And I want to email Liv, too, and tell her what Bryndis said."

I went back upstairs. I thought about drawing, but I was afraid of the images that might appear. I avoided looking at the writing desk, too. I did keep thinking about wyrd, and the knots and tangles. I felt convinced without knowing why that a lot of those tangled threads led back to Grandfather

Halvar.

Another remembrance of that sour old man sat on Tor's chest of drawers, a leather case embossed with Halvar's initials, obviously an antique. I'd noticed it before, but I'd never seen Tor open it. That afternoon I released the little gold latch and flipped back the lid. On a lining of blue velvet, crushed down and worn in places, lay a pair of military hair brushes, a straight-edge razor, and other toilet articles. The brushes had tortoise-shell backs, but the razor and the rat-tail comb were steel. They must have been manufactured in the 1930s, I figured from the severe Deco shapes. Worn straps kept the brushes in place, but the comb had come free of its restraint. I picked it up and noticed a couple of tiny splinters of wood lying on the velvet beside the razor.

I took the comb and picked out the splinters, then closed the case. Looking at the skinny fragments of wood lying in the palm of my hand gave me an oddly uneasy feeling. When I examined the gouges on the bedroom door, the splinters matched. I went over to the closet door and knelt down. The rat-tail end of the comb fit into the supposed toothmarks in the wood. I remember the non-existent animal hair on the blankets, too. For a moment I wondered if Tor had been faking the shape-change, but I'd seen the pain in his eyes and heard it in his voice whenever he mentioned the bjarki. I'd lived through the bear-nights and listened to him moan and growl.

Besides, why would anyone fake something like that?

I heard Tor come upstairs. I called out, "I'm in the bedroom." He walked in and waved a piece of paper in my direction. I was still kneeling by the chewed-up door.

"The staves looked pretty positive," Tor said, "but not one hundred per cent positive. I want to get a better fix on Nils. I—what are you doing?"

"Trying to figure something out. Tor, look, these marks on the door. Do you remember chewing on it when you were in bjarki form?"

"Not what you'd call remembering." He thought for a moment. "More like dream images, just bits and pieces. Floating around my mind. When I came back, after the bjarki left me, I mean, I saw the damage and sort of remembered chewing." He thought again. "My jaws hurt."

"But you don't have a real clear memory of opening your bear's mouth and putting it on the door."

"No, I sure don't." He stared at the floor and thought for several minutes. Finally he looked up with a shrug. "That's strange, now that you mention it."

"Come look at this."

Tor folded up the paper and put it into his shirt pocket. When he knelt down beside me, he displayed not one little trace of the anxiety or fear of being caught out in a lie. A person who'd made up an elaborate fiction about themselves would have had some kind of reaction. I handed him the comb. He stared at the sharp end of the handle, then at the door.

"Shit!" he said. "Maya, this is really creepy." He twisted around to look back at the door into the room. "Does this match those marks, too?"

"No, but I found these when I looked in your grandfather's leather case, the one on the dresser. They were lying by the razor."

When he handed me the comb back, I dropped the splinters into his open palm. He studied them for a long moment.

"But I remember clawing at the door," he said eventually. "Not real clearly. Not like remembering playing basketball or something like that, but I remember it." He hesitated and held up his other hand. "I remember seeing the gouges appear in the door. I don't remember seeing a paw."

"You told me once you saw a bear in the mirror when you looked."

"Yeah. Now that I do remember." He stood up and glanced in the direction of the bathroom. "In the mirror over the sink."

"How tall is the bjarki? I mean, like, would his head be high enough to see over the sink if he was on all fours?"

Tor shook his head no. He walked over to the wastebasket, and dropped the splinters into it before he said anything. "I don't remember standing up on hind legs, but bears can, y'know, and they can walk or dance like humans. I remember walking in and seeing a bear in the mirror."

I got to my feet. "When you were bitten," I said, "you had rabies shots, right?"

"Yeah. It's a sequence of shots. First you get immunoglobulin, right near the bite, and that hurts like hell." He rubbed his thigh, remembering. "Then there's a series of vaccines."

"They started the shots right away?"

"Oh yeah. I went straight to the ER, down at Marin General. The bite was still oozing. They figured the dog—we all thought it was a dog—had to be rabid. Why else would it have run right up to me and attacked? A healthy lost dog would have tried to get me to take care of it. Y'know, fawned around my feet. That kind of thing."

"Some people say lycanthropy's a virus, don't they?"

"Yeah. Not that any doctor's ever done any kind of study."

"Of course not, but the shots, they're vaccines against a virus, aren't they? What if lycanthropy's related to rabies? Doesn't rabies give people hallucinations?"

"Do you think I did get rabies?"

"No. I'm wondering if those shots weakened the disease. Like, they couldn't prevent it because it's not exactly the same virus, but maybe you didn't get the full effects. That might explain why you feel like an animal, but you don't turn into an actual bear."

Tor stared at me so long and so silently that I began to wonder if I'd said something really stupid. He caught his breath and nodded.

"I bet you're right." He sounded weary. "Huh, I hired you to see through illusions. You're doing a good job."

I forced out a smile.

"I feel like the bear," Tor continued. "I act like one, but I'm still an ape in here. Grab a tool and bang on the door when I want to get out. Think I'm biting it. The sore jaw—just from grinding my teeth in anger, I bet. Y'know, rage. Frustration."

He turned and strode out of the bedroom. I put the comb back into the leather case, then followed. He sat down on the edge of the couch and leaned forward to stare into the empty fireplace. He let his hands dangle between his knees, a gesture that made them look like paws. I sat down next to him.

"If I really turned into an actual bear," Tor said, "I could rip that door right off its hinges, locks or no locks. They're powerful animals, especially one my height."

"A grizzly?" I said.

"Or an Arctic brown. They're big motherfuckers. Y'know, the old legends are full of bears that act like men. Even bears that get women pregnant. That's where the bjarki, the bear's son, legend comes from. Like Beowulf and Bodvar Bjarki."

"Huh! The girls just made that up when their fathers wanted to know who got them pregnant."

Tor managed to smile at that—a weak, brief smile, but a smile. "What I see in the mirror," he continued, "is what I expect to see. I feel like an animal. I was raised on those old stories. What else would I see but a bear? But the hair on the blankets must be real. No, I could be just projecting that, too. You didn't see it."

"And when we went to look for it, you couldn't see it either."

"That was probably because you'd tipped me off that it might not really be there." He thought for a couple of minutes before he spoke again. "When you study sorcery, you learn to see things outside of you that are really inside of you. Inside your mind, I mean. Unconscious content. Once you learn how to project it out, then sometimes you do it without thinking."

"There are some people," I said, "who can hold an image in their mind and then push it out onto the paper where they can see it just like it was really there. An instructor told my class once that people who can cut elaborate silhouettes can do that."

"That's exactly what I mean, yeah. The bite, the virus, whatever it was," Tor went on, "it set me up to act like a bjarki. And feel like one, too. But I must not transform. Not all the way, anyway. I wish there was some way you could see me and tell me, but it wouldn't be safe. I'm enough animal to maybe harm you. We could cut a hole in the door, or no. Maybe I'd do something creepy through it, stick a claw through, something." He shuddered. "Besides, I still couldn't see myself."

"What about a camcorder? We could set one up in a corner of the bedroom."

"Up high, where the bjarki couldn't reach it, yeah. You could turn it on and then lock me in." He shuddered again, violently this time. "Ugly thought. It's probably kind of disgusting. But I've got to know."

I felt totally creeped out, myself. The man I'd been sleeping with, the man I'd come to love—in the locked room he turned into something, someone, different and dangerous. The possibility of seeing what happened terrified me, but like him, I had to know.

"I guess," I said, "we could just set the thing up and let it run. I don't know anything about those. We never had one when I was a kid. Maybe we could ask your friend Billy."

Tor rolled his eyes. "You know what he'd think, don't you?"

"No. What?"

"That we wanted to record ourselves having sex."

Totally squicky! I squealed, not at the idea of recording us, but at the idea of Billy thinking we were going to and maybe imagining things. "Scratch that idea," I said. "Wait a minute! What about those nanny cams? Y'know, you can set one up in your baby's room to watch while it sleeps."

"There we go! I've heard about those. You can control them from your laptop." Tor smiled at me, a lop-sided twist of his mouth. "Nanny to a bear cub."

"Well, when I took the job I told my friends I was an au pair to a bear."

Tor's smile disappeared. "I'm surprised that you'd want to stay with a freak like me."

"Don't say that! Don't call yourself that!"

"Why not?"

"Because I love you. Besides, I'm a freak too, if you're one."

Tor caught my hand in both of his. "I love you, too," he said. "And I always will."

He raised my hand to his mouth and kissed my fingers,

then let me go.

'Always' is easy to say. Deep in my mind a knot of fear remained, like a thorn that's worked its way into your body through the skin: what if he got tired of me one day and turned me out to die? When I remembered his joke about concubines, the thorn stabbed me near my heart.

That night the thorn worked its way into my dreams and turned them into a nightmare. Once again I stood on a nighttime bridge over dark water, but this time I had no idea where I was. I turned and tried to see lights in the distance. None shone. I looked down and saw in a bubble of bluish light a dead woman floating in the water. At first I thought she was the woman I'd been, Magda, but she had long blond hair that tangled around her neck, as if she'd been hanged in her own hair. Her blue eyes bulged out from the strangling and seemed to stare right at me.

"No!" I said. "No no no!" The last 'no' rose to a wail and woke me.

Tor had turned on the lamp on the end table by our bed. He sat up cross-legged next to me. I lay still and trembled.

"Another nightmare?" he said.

"Yeah. The water again and a woman's corpse."

"You need to start thinking about drawing these dreams. And why you don't want to."

"I just don't." My voice whined like a stubborn child's. I took a deep breath. "They frighten me."

"Well, yeah, that's what nightmares do." He smiled briefly. "Maya, you've got to start looking at this stuff."

"What do you mean, stuff?"

"Whatever the nightmares represent. You won't know until you look at them."

I lifted a hand and watched it shake. He caught it between both of his.

"I bet you know what I'm going to say next," he said.

"Yeah. I've got a talent for sorcery."

He grinned, kissed my fingertips, and laid my hand gently on my midriff.

"Is that the big mysterious meaning?" I continued. "I don't see how these nightmares could be telling me that. They're so horrible."

"I've got no idea what they mean. You're the only one who knows. But that's what being a vitki's all about, knowing the meanings of things. Knowing what comes out of your own mind. Knowing the difference between that and things in the outer world. That's why I want to know what I really look like when the bjarki dominates."

I understood him well enough. I needed to draw the images from my mind in order to see them clearly. I feared them enough to resist doing it, but if he had the guts to let me record him after he transformed, I'd have to summon the courage to draw my dreams. Tor got out of bed, put on his jeans, and walked over to the eastern window. He opened the curtains and let in the pale light of dawn.

"Do you feel the élan?" he said.

"No. I never can unless it's coming from a human body."

He unlatched the window and pushed it open. "How about now?"

The air smelled fresh and pure. I took a deep breath. "It's just air. Nice, though."

For a moment he stood at the open window, then turned and stretched out his arms toward me. The flow of élan swept over me like the perfume of a thousand roses. I fed, drank it in, gasped and fed again until I could feel the energy swirling around me, a tangible stroke along my naked skin. I caught it in my hands, wafted it toward my face, and gulped it down.

"Feel better?" he said.

"Much, yeah. Thanks."

"Huh. It's like my body's the athanor, and it cooks what you need to eat. Interesting."

Tears threatened my eyes. "Tor, if you ever get tired of me, you won't let me die, will you? You won't make me just go back to stealing bits of other people's lives, I mean. It's not enough. I know that now. It's just not enough."

"What?" He gaped at me, then laughed with an uneasy

chuckle. "First, I haven't gotten tired of you in a hundred and sixty years. Second, even if I did go crazy and get tired of you, no, I'd never just let you die. I'll swear it on the runes. Okay?"

"Okay. I just wondered. I—" My voice choked.

He strode over to the bed and sat down on the edge beside me.

"Let me tell you what you mean to me," Tor said. "I'm a lot like my grandfather, y'know. All the energy he put into making money I put into sorcery. I don't want to turn into a cold-hearted bastard like he was. I never loved anything or anyone as much as I love the runes until I found you again. Not even my dad, and I did love him. So whatever heart I've got belongs to you. It's like you're my heart, or at least, you keep it safe for me. You're my life, Maya, in a kind of weird way. My soul, I guess I mean. Without you I wouldn't have one."

I sat up and turned into his embrace. He pulled me close, kissed my forehead, my eyes, my mouth, while his gentle hands stroked my back.

"Why are you trembling?" he said.

"Because I don't know if I can live up to that."

"You can. Don't worry. Just be who you are."

He kissed me open-mouthed and passionately. I relaxed into his love-making, but later I remembered what he'd told me. *Just be who you are.* But who was I? My surrender to loving Tor had changed everything. If I was no longer the vampire, no longer the brave girl-artist fighting poverty and a fatal disease—then I had no idea at all.

CHAPTER 13

I've got two samples of the language now," Tor said. "The runes on the gold ornament and the note from the Rime Jötnar. They're both written with the elder futhark. Which helps."

"It's easier to read than the younger one?"

"It represents more sounds. Less ambiguity."

We were sitting at the breakfast bar after a late lunch. Tor had brought out the rubbings he'd made from the gold ornament he kept in the safe. He laid the note from the Frost Giants next to them so I could compare the two. The style of the carved runes differed from those drawn in ink on the note, thanks to the difference in the tools used to make them, but I could pick out the letters nonetheless. My mind had begun to organize and process the vast body of lore that Tor had given me to study.

"One problem," Tor said, "is that the Jötnar can't spell worth shit. They're not real bright, y'know."

"I gathered that from the legends."

"And the other is that I don't know this language. I can pick out roots. I know Old Norse, and German, too, and a lot about Gothic, not that I'd claim to be able to speak it." He grinned at me. "Tolkien was the last person alive fluent in Gothic. And the first one in about four hundred years."

I had to smile at that. "Why do you know so many languages?" I said.

"My college major was Germanic languages and literature.

That includes Old Norse and the daughter languages. I need them all for the rune work. That's where I met JJ, in one of our basic linguistics courses."

"Makes sense, yeah."

"Do you see these rows of dots?" Tor pointed at the rubbing from the gold ornament's back. "They're set up in pairs, so they could be coded runes. There's a system for that. So you can see that the whole thing's a riddle, or maybe a set of riddles."

The riddles began to obsess him. He took to spending longer and longer hours down in his workshop. At times through the heater vents I could hear him chanting over the rune scripts as if a ritual might help unlock their meaning. While he worked, I passed my time online. I watched back episodes of my favorite TV shows—I streamed them on my laptop and used my earbuds so Tor couldn't hear what I was doing. I also caught up with everyone I knew on Facebook. I did make sure to study the books Tor had given me as well. I found the entire Scandinavian culture fascinating, partly because it was so different from my mother's Southeast Asian heritage and partly, of course, because I'd fallen in love with Tor.

Now and then he gave me 'bulletins from the front,' as he called them.

"I've gotten a few more words here and there, after looking through every damned dictionary I own," he told me at dinner one night. "Thief, wolf, property, and a couple of verbs, I think they're verbs, anyway. This language may be older than proto-Gothic. The only thing I know for sure is that the two languages are the same. The one on the note and the one on the gold ornament, I mean."

"Maybe it's the language the Jötnar speak."

"You're brilliant. That could be it, sure. It probably never dawned on the fuckers that I didn't know how to read their lousy language."

"The kid called you a sorcerer. He probably thinks you know everything."

"Yeah, that's our reputation, all right."

"Although he called Nils the silly sorcerer."

"Occasionally the giants have flashes of intelligence, then." Tor grinned at me. "But what in hell do they want out of me?"

"I dunno. Maybe they need you to cast a spell for them."

"Nah, their women can do that."

"Wait a minute, if the language is the same on that ornament thing, maybe they think it belongs to them. Maybe that's what they want."

Tor stared wide-eyed for a long moment. "Shit," he said. "Yeah, that could be it."

"Then all you have to do is give it back to them."

"Why would I do that? It must be something really valuable. Magically, I mean. If it was just a lump of gold, sure. I'd give it back in a minute, but—"

"Tor! They're dangerous. They're frost giants."

"Yeah. So? I'm not giving that thing away until I know what it means. What do you think I am, a coward?"

"No, but I am."

He laughed in a peal of genuine humor. "It's not you they'd go after," he said. "Don't worry about it."

I argued for at least fifteen minutes, that day, but he never gave in or even really listened. I was learning that 'stubborn' is too weak a word to describe a man like Tor. He'd smelled magic the way a bear smells honey and ignores the swarming bees.

It was a couple of days later that my credit card bills arrived along with the rest of the mail. Tor refused to let me look at them, which told me that yes, I'd been assessed some hefty penalties. Since he kept all his financial papers and records downstairs, he took the bills with him when he went down to his workroom. When he came up for lunch, he told me that he'd paid off the accounts.

"One of the things that came today," he said, "is your new credit card." He handed it me. "It's on my account. Go ahead and get anything you need." He grinned. "Well, maybe not diamond necklaces or things in that price range."

"Huh! I wouldn't know what to do with a diamond necklace."

"Okay, good. Just don't try to use your old cards. I cancelled them."

"You did what?"

"You won't need them anymore. There's a real high limit on the card I just gave you. It should cover whatever you want to spend."

"But hey! I need cards in my own name."

"Why?" Tor appeared to be sincerely puzzled. "Besides, your credit score really sucks."

I winced, because I knew he was right. "But you could have at least asked me before you cancelled them. I mean, how did you cancel them? You don't have my online passwords, do you?"

"No." He gave me a sad smile. "I called them on the phone. The old-fashioned way. I was transferring the payments over at the same time. Of course they did what I wanted."

I set my hands on my hips and glared at him. He heaved a sigh.

"Okay, yeah," he said. "I should have asked you first. Sorry."

He did not sound sincere. I went on glaring at him. "I can't believe," I said, "that they didn't ask you for the answer to the security question."

"They did. What was your mother's first name? Kusuma."

"How did you know that?"

He just smiled. I made a squealing sound of sheer rage that had no effect on him whatsoever. I considered continuing to argue, but I remembered his discussion of what 'husband' meant. Waste of breath, I told myself.

Besides, I knew what to do. I'd wait a couple of weeks until all the credit agencies registered the final payment on the old cards. At that point I could get a charge card from some fancy department store. They hand them out like candy, especially when you have a new address and don't put down your middle initial—that way you might luck out and not show up on the credit check as the deadbeat you were. Buy something small every month for say six months and pay it off every time. Getting a real card again is a snap.

When Tor returned to the library room downstairs, I called Cynthia and asked if she wanted to go shopping with me. I needed new underwear and wanted to hit the mall.

"I'd better not," Cynthia said. "I've got too much stuff to do around here. I'll admit to being glad of the week off so I can catch up. I need to debug our wireless set-up. Jim keeps insisting that the old router's okay, so something else is wrong And I've got to clean out the storage area. It's full of junk."

"That's one thing about always being so broke," I said. "I've never owned enough things to have them be a nuisance."

"Well, if you stay with Tor, that could change."

"Maybe so, yeah. Say, if you're busy during the day, do you guys want to get together for dinner?"

"That's a good idea. What about tomorrow?"

"Sounds good. I'll run it by Tor."

Cynthia and I chatted about restaurants while I went downstairs to interrupt him at his brooding over the runes. When I asked him about going out with my friends, he agreed.

"It'll be good to have something fun to look forward to," he said. "This project's driving me nuts."

As I went back upstairs, Cynthia and I arranged the time and place. After we clicked off, I drove down to the mall. I was going to pick up some of my usual cheap French-cut panties at the low-budget department store, but a fancy lingerie store was having a sale. Even at fifty percent off, their goods still cost more than my usual brand. I debated, but I had the card Tor had just given me. The fabric in the expensive underwear was so smooth, so light and soft. The same soft cloth covered the elastic band so it wouldn't chafe like it did on the cheap ones. I gave in and bought them. I also bought some fancy black lace and satin panties and a bustier, the kind that aren't meant to be worn under your clothes.

As I walked back through the mall to get out to the parking lot, I kept looking around me. What if Nils had come after

me at the mall again? With my bindrune pendant I felt safe
from his prying magical eyes, but what if he'd happened to
be driving around and seen Gretel? She stood out even on
a crowded freeway. Keep your eyes moving, I told myself.
Watch for illusions. All those years of hunting for people
whose élan I could tap stood me in good stead. I had the
habits of a hunter, but they could also keep me from being
prey. As it was, I never saw any trace of Nils nor felt anyone
looking me over.

On the way home I stopped at the post office and put in
an application for a post office box. Once I got my new credit
card, Tor wouldn't have to know about it—or about anything
else I had sent there.

When I returned to the flat, Tor had already come upstairs. He was sitting on the couch looking morose. He had
a book in his lap, an academic looking work with a title in
some Scandinavian language.

"What's wrong?" I said. "The translation?"

"Yeah." He laid the book down on the coffee table. "Come
here and kiss me. I need a hug."

Coming from him that cliché made me laugh. "I can do
better than that," I said. "Wait till you see what I bought."

When I held up the shopping bag, he must have recognized the label, because he grinned. "Gonna model it for
me?" he said.

"You bet. I'll just be in the bedroom changing."

He stayed out of the bedroom until I'd stripped and put
on the black satin panties, the kind you don't have to take
off. When he came in, the look he gave me made me forget
about adding the bustier. He strode over, caught me by the
shoulders and kissed me. All I could think about was getting
into bed. Getting him undressed seemed to take forever. His
lovemaking, as opposed to the magical sex, was sweet and
warm even when he was totally aroused. With my other boy-
friends, I always felt that when we had sex they were taking
something from me that they considered theirs. Tor made
me feel like I was giving him beautiful gifts. He never said

anything as goopy as 'thank you,' but his smile, when we finished, and the way he kissed my face, so gently, the way he stroked my hair, let me know what he felt.

We made love twice that day. When we were done, Tor got up and dressed. He muttered something about going downstairs just as I fell asleep. I woke up about an hour later and took a shower. I brought the panties in with me to rinse them out and hung them over the shower door to dry. Once I'd dressed, I went down to see what he was doing.

I found him sitting at the high wooden table. Big books, some of them leather-bound and smelling like mold, lay open in a messy litter around his spread-out papers. Tor looked up from his work and grinned at me.

"Sex must help me think," he said. "I've unraveled a piece of this."

I came over and perched on the tall stool next to him. He pointed to the rubbing of the back of the gold ornament, where a long row of runes, set off by slightly unsteady lines, formed a sort of belt around its edge. He used his index fingers to isolate a particular set of runes.

"Pain at the full moon." Tor announced.

"That's all it says?"

"No. That's all I understand." His smile disappeared. "Shit, the full moon's on its way, isn't it? Only a few days now, and I'll have to make the damned change."

I laid a comforting hand on his arm.

"It'll be worse, this time," he said, "wondering if you'll just run out on me after you see what I turn into."

"I'm not going to do that."

"You'll be here when I come back?"

"I promise. Are you sorry we're planning on recording it? We could wait another month."

"No. Let's get it over with. I'm more worried because of Nils. When I'm in bjarki form, I won't be able to fend off an attack. Maybe you should just leave the flat. Go stay with your girlfriends where you'll be safe."

"No! I won't leave you. What if he sets the house on fire

or something like that? I'll have to get you out of here."

"There you'll be, out on the street with a dancing bear. Too bad you're not a gypsy in this life. You could get me a red fez and a vest with bells on it."

"And one of those special bicycles."

He grinned, and I laughed, but the worry bit hard underneath the joke.

I left him to his obsession. He returned to the upper flat near dinner time and joined me in the kitchen, where I was pouring myself a glass of cola.

"How's the translating going?" I said.

"Maybe I'm getting somewhere. Maybe not." He snarled like an animal and turned toward the refrigerator. "I'll cook dinner."

At that moment the ravens came, a big flock of them, cawing and flapping as they swirled around the house. I watched them from the kitchen window as they settled in the backyard, some on the lawn, some among the purple leaves of the Japanese maple. The largest raven sat on the stone retaining wall and cocked its head to one side. I felt certain that it was watching me watch it.

"Tor!" I called out. "Come look at this."

He joined me at the window. The ravens in the yard rose up, flapping and shrieking, and flew around the house again in a wide circuit. A few at a time they returned and settled down, most of them on the lawn this time, except for that one large bird, which took up its perch on the stone wall.

"A good omen!" he said.

"Good? Ravens? Don't they eat dead things? I mean, like carrion?"

"Hey, it's a dirty job, but someone's got to do it." He grinned at me. "They're Odin's birds." He paused, thinking. "That leftover roast chicken in the fridge. It's been there too long anyway."

Tor got out the chicken carcass and shredded the remaining flesh into a bowl. When he took the bowl outside, I stayed at the window. As soon as he walked into the back yard, the ravens flew, squawking in excitement. He started scattering the chicken onto the lawn. The birds swooped down and landed into a rough semi-circle at the edge of the yard, waiting. He finished distributing the flesh and left. They hopped forward and began to feed. They squabbled among themselves, cawing, occasionally pecking at each other over a particularly good piece, I supposed, but when the largest raven hopped forward, no one interfered with its choice of morsel.

Tor came back upstairs and stood at the window to watch. "That big one?" he said. "She must be the matriarch. The female ravens are bigger than the males."

I realized that I'd half-expected him to think that the large raven was Odin himself in bird form. Maybe I'd been thinking it.

"I didn't know they travelled in flocks," I said.

"They usually don't. It's got to be an omen."

Once they'd finished feeding, the birds rose and flew off. They headed east and disappeared into the darkening sky.

After dinner Tor went down to the library room to find some dictionaries he needed for his work on the rune riddles. I thought about watching a movie on my laptop, but I would have had to put the charge on Tor's card, where he'd see it and bitch. Instead I decided to do some drawing. I fiddled around with some sketchy bits of landscape, got some unsatisfying scribbles, and remembered the ravens.

I had a clear picture in my mind of the birds sitting in the backyard while the matriarch watched from the stone wall. I got the ravens down on paper, but not the view from the kitchen window. As I drew, the backyard changed. The birds seemed to be sitting on the crest of a hill. Instead of the Japanese maple, a dead, twisted live oak tree stood to one side of the scene. The ravens were watching not Tor with the bowl of food but something hanging on a stick.

Or a thing impaled on a stick. Under my unwilling fingers the image developed beyond my power to control it: a wolf's head impaled on a long pole, stuck in the ground and positioned so that the head seemed to look downhill.

"Yuck!" I said aloud.

I was tempted to tear out the sheet and wad it up. What stopped me was my memory of a passage in one of the old sagas, where Egil the Hunchback killed a mare and stuck her head on a pole in order to drive the king and queen of Sweden out of the country. I carried the sketchbook downstairs to show Tor. I found him sitting on the floor in the library in front of a shelf full of thick leather-bound books.

"Would you look at this?" I said. "Maybe I'm just being silly, but I think it could be important. It just kind of came to me."

He took the sketchbook, stared at the drawing, and swore under his breath.

"The nidhing pole," he said, "but I've never heard about a vitki using a dog or wolf before. That doesn't make it any less ugly. Maybe uglier."

"Uh, is that its name? I remember reading about it."

"Nidh is the Norse word. It means scorn. It's an ancient way of insulting and shaming an enemy, but if you're a nasty son of a bitch like Egil, you can use it as a curse. You cut off a horse's head and jam it onto a high pole so that it looks in your enemy's direction. Then you invoke the goddess Hel to follow the horse's gaze and pour out black evil upon the enemy and his family. It's a real powerful spell, and nothing anyone should mess around with unless they've been seriously wronged. Like, someone murdered a member of your family—that kind of wrong."

"Nils feels wronged over a lot less than that."

"He sure does." Tor handed me back the sketchbook and scrambled up. "And he's the one who turns into a wolf. Huh. I told you those ravens were an omen."

"Do you think Nils is working the curse on you?"

"I don't know yet. I'll have to see if I can figure out where it is. We'll have to go look."

"Oh, squicky!" A second thought made me catch my breath. "And dangerous."

"Maybe. I'll take the guys along, the guys you met. We

have a pact. When I really need them, they come with me to the place where I need them. And I'll do the same for any of them."

"Your warband."

He laughed and nodded. "I guess you could call them that. We look out for each other."

But you lead, I thought to myself. I'm willing to bet on it.

Tor called his guy friends immediately, then spent the rest of the evening casting the rune staves and studying the results. I did more drawings of the same scene from different angles in the hopes of giving us landmarks. Eventually the drawings and the runecasts came together in Tor's mind.

"Up in the Claremont Hills in the nature preserve," he told me. "On the high ridge so the head can look all the way down at us." He smiled with a grim twist to his mouth. "Near Grizzly Peak Boulevard. Appropriate."

Early the next morning Billy and JJ arrived in Billy's white Land Rover. Aaron, JJ told me, had an important development meeting at his job. His 'help person' had already made arrangements to be there with him, which made changing the meeting time impossible.

"He's got Asperger's really bad, then," I said.

"Some people would call him autistic," Billy said. "We don't, us guys, I mean. He just can't deal with people sometimes, like in business meetings."

"Those are hard enough for anyone to deal with," JJ said. "I don't see how anyone stays awake."

"Sheer willpower!" Billy grinned at him. "Well, let's go see what the Evil Uncle's shit on now. Don't you worry, Maya. Tor will clean it up."

It finally dawned on me that when his friends called him the 'wizard,' they weren't just making a joke. They believed in his sorcery. And in mine—Billy studied the drawings I'd made with his eyes narrowed in genuine concentration. Watching his belief made my stomach twist. Tor quirked an eyebrow in my direction. I could practically hear him thinking, *you've got talent for this.*

"I might know where this thing is," Billy said. "I hike up there, and that tree's a pretty spectacular ruin. The oak blight epidemic killed it. What do you bet that's the place?"

"You could fool me." JJ flashed him a grin. "I'm a city boy, myself."

We all piled into the Land Rover, Tor in the front with Billy, JJ and me in back. Tor kept my drawings in his lap, but he stared straight out the windshield the entire time. The set of his shoulders made me think he might be casting some kind of spell, scrying for danger, probably. Billy drove way too fast for my taste. He swore at slow drivers on the freeway, changed lanes, muttered profanities. I tried to ignore the driving. Tor never moved or said a word.

Some miles before we reached the Caldecott Tunnel, Billy turned off the freeway onto a side road. At first it led through a residential area, but the higher we climbed, the sparser the houses became. Once we drove into the preserve itself, the road petered out to a dirt track. The Land Rover bounced and jounced around while JJ swore under his breath and I clutched at the seat and the arm rest on my side. Tor stayed so still and focused that he seemed to be riding on a private cushion of air.

The particular dirt track we were following ended in a grove of live oaks. Billy parked the Land Rover facing downhill. "In case we need to make a fast getaway," he said.

"Probably we won't," Tor said. "I'll try not to start any fires."

None of us laughed. We all got out, and I spent a moment tucking my slim-leg jeans into my hiking boots. Ticks were the big summer hazard up in the dry grass of the hills. Billy and JJ treated their own ankles the same. Tor merely stared uphill as he stood a little apart from us with my drawings rolled in one hand. I remembered the flies at our backyard picnic and figured that the ticks would leave him alone.

It was quiet up in the hills under the midday sun. Now and then I heard a insect buzz, and the long grass, pale gold and dead here at the end of summer, rustled as we tramped through it. The noise of the freeway and the vast urban spread of the Bay Area lay a long way downhill in a sea of silence. We'd only gone about twenty yards up when I began to sweat, the cold clammy sweat of spent élan. I waffled, wondering if I should interrupt Tor's concentration, but he turned around, smiled at me, and sent a wave of élan my way. I pretended to be out of breath so I could gasp as I captured and swallowed it.

"Rest break," Tor said. "Maya's not used to this."

"Neither am I," JJ said with a grin. "Not that I expect any sympathy."

It took me a bare two minutes to absorb all of the élan. I felt it flow through my body in a sweet tide that restored the strength in my legs. As we started trudging up the steep slope ahead, the ravens returned. Cawing to one another, the flock swirled out of the eastern sky and flew around us in a wide circle.

"Whoa!" JJ said to me. "This is like your pictures."

"Yeah," I said. "Sure is."

Tor tipped his head back and cawed in return. Unlike most people's clumsy attempt at bird calls, he sounded like a raven. They understood him and took off, heading southeast, but slowly, flapping around us, settling only to rise up again, until they could be sure Tor followed. The rest of us didn't matter. That was obvious from the way the matriarch looked only at him before she called to the flock. We clambered up through the high grass and outcrops of rock, past a scattering of trees, and finally saw ahead the twisted oak of my drawing. With one last outburst of shriek and caw, the ravens settled on the branches, black and shiny among the rust-colored clusters of dead leaves.

Just on the downhill side of the tree stood the ten-foot high scorning pole, jammed into the ground and topped with the head of a husky or malamute dog. The dog's body, a dark blot on the pale grass, lay nearby.

"Maya, get back!" Tor snapped. "You don't want to look at this."

Too late. I'd already seen that Nils had bound her paws

together with wire, slashed her sides, and rammed something sharp and metal up her female parts. Black blood crusted her fur, which meant she'd been alive for the torment. I nearly vomited, turned my back, and staggered a few steps away. JJ and Billy walked over to join Tor.

"Shit!" Billy said. "He didn't just kill her. The slimy bastard! Jesus!"

"Yeah," Tor said. "Well, she's running free in the other world now." He raised his hands above his head. "May someone call her home!" His voice rang over the silent hillside.

In the profound silence I felt a presence, an answer though not in words. I shuddered. JJ returned to stand beside me. He wiped his sweaty forehead on his sleeve and took a deep breath. "I don't even know what to say," he said. "What kind of twisted nutcase would do that to an animal?"

"A twisted nutcase, yeah. I hope he rots in hell."

From behind us I heard Tor speaking in a language that I didn't recognize—much like Icelandic, but the cadence rolled and dipped in a different way. JJ cocked his head to one side and nodded in recognition. "Old Norse," he murmured. "He uses that to invoke the ancestors."

Tor called out one sharp word. Billy said, "One two three!" I heard them grunt. Curiosity got the better of me, and I glanced over my shoulder just as they pulled the pole free of the earth. Even with two of them holding it, the heavy pole swayed, unbalanced by the dead thing at the tip. Tor muttered something and shook the pole. The head came loose and dropped beside the body with a sickening little thud. I watched the ravens rather than think about the dog's slow death. In the tree branches the shiny black birds shrieked and cawed. Some sprang up and flew, swooping low to return and settle.

"What I don't get is, where are all the flies?" Billy said.

"Nils cast an aversion spell," Tor said. "Huh. That's why the ravens came to fetch me. I'll dispel it, and then they can take what's rightfully theirs."

They laid the pole down in the grass. Tor raised his hands

again and spoke in Icelandic, this time. As we were leaving, I glanced back and saw the ravens settling around the dog's corpse to return her substance to the cycle of life.

On the way home I kept brooding about the poor dog, a female at that. Had Nils meant her horrible death to rebound onto me? Since Tor and I were sharing the back seat, once we got onto the freeway and smoother riding, I asked him.

"What else?" he said. "I dispelled that, too. And deflected the curse back to him." His voice dropped to a growl. "We'll see how he likes that."

When we reached our building, Tor invited Billy and JJ in, but Billy had to get back to work, and JJ needed to return to the graduate library—to allow his thesis to continue driving him insane, was how he put it. I practically ran up the stairs to our flat. I wanted refuge from the cruelty I'd seen. I flopped onto the couch and stared at the beautiful Chinese vases and the masterpiece of a jade mountain. Tor paced back and forth in front of the west window.

"I understand one thing now," Tor said. "Why he didn't use a horse's head. It's too public up there. He killed the dog somewhere else and brought her up with him. He couldn't have gotten a dead horse into his SUV, and killing a live one in the open?" He shrugged. "Someone would have noticed. The park rangers if no one else."

"They would have found the pole eventually, wouldn't they? Despite that spell, I mean."

"Oh yeah. Aversions don't make people blind. But if we'd left it, it could have done a lot of harm. Look. I agreed to stay on defense, right? We both felt sorry for crazy old Nils. No more. He tried to hurt you. I want to send him howling like the coward he is. I want to terrorize him so bad that he'll stay away from us forever. The full moon's nearly here. I'll make my first strike once it's over. Assuming he hasn't made one on me first."

I'd been raised to value compassion as the One Great Thing, the lesson every sentient creature needed to learn from incarnation. But the scene I'd witnessed rose in my memory—the tortured dog on the mountainside—and warned me that Nils had slipped over the edge into dangerous madness.

"Okay," I said. "That's fine with me."

The image of the dead dog on the mountain haunted me. When Tor made lunch, I could barely eat. How could anyone do that to an animal, especially a dog, who would have loved its owner? As my mind kept bringing up the ugly scene, pieces of a different puzzle finally fell into place. Hiking in the Catskills, a rare blood disease, and a werewolf here in California who just happened to run across Tor in the local wilderness?

"What is it?" Tor laid his half-eaten sandwich down on his plate. "You look kind of strange."

"I just realized something. Nils isn't going to attack us at the full moon. He won't be able to."

"What? Why—"

"Because he has to be the lycanthrope that bit you. Anything else would be too much of a raw coincidence. Didn't you tell me that the wolf came right up to you? In daylight? He must have been tracking you."

Tor looked at me for a long moment, then laughed with a sharp bearish chuff. "Of course," he said. "Revenge, and he'd been watching, waiting to see where he could get at me."

"What I wonder is how he knew you'd be on Mount Tam. I mean, he must have gone over there before the full moon. He couldn't drive in wolf form."

"I'd scattered Dad's ashes up there the year before." He shoved his barstool back and got up. "He loved the mountain, and he had a favorite place, a kind of hollow on the mountain side, and in the rainy season there's a stream and a lot of ferns. That's where he wanted to rest."

"Is it near where you got bitten?"

"It *is* where I got bitten. Nils must have been watching, must have known." Tor went very very still. His voice growled when he spoke. "The bastard." He stood with his head thrown a little back, his hands curled into fists, his mouth tight and thin, his eyes narrow with rage, and yet his body stayed quiet, tense but quiet, like a sword blade. "I'm going to get my revenge on this guy. It's not enough to just drive him away. I—" Tor broke off and looked my way. "What's wrong?"

"I'm terrified, that's what!"

"Don't be. He's not going to be able to—"

"Not of him. Of you!" I was shaking, so chilled and sick that I couldn't lie. "I've never seen you—I've never seen anyone look like this, say things like this. Tor, please!"

"I'm sorry." He spoke quietly. "But if I don't make him pay for this, I'm not going to be able to live with myself."

In that moment I understood everything I needed to know about the old sagas.

"Honor," I said. "That's it, isn't it?"

"Damn right! He profaned my father's grave. He's going to pay for that. And for threatening my woman, he'll pay again. And incidentally, for what he did to me, he'll pay a third time. Fucking right he's going to pay in full." He smiled, but there was no warmth in it. "And no, I don't want you to help me. I blew it once, dragging you into this. I'm not going to do it again."

"I want to watch. I want to be there."

"No."

"Tor, I'm afraid of what he might do. I want to see. I might be the one who's got to pick up the pieces afterwards."

He blinked at me.

"Well?" I got up and faced him. "Don't I have to take care of you when you're in bear form? I'll do the same if you're exhausted from whatever it is you're planning. I'll need to know what happened."

He stared at the floor for a long moment. "Okay," he said. "You can come down and watch when the time comes. Once the moon starts to wane."

He turned and strode off downstairs. I heard him slam the door at the bottom. I went into my bedroom and checked the writing desk. The green lion lay on his back, dead in a circle of hovering ravens. Tor stayed downstairs all afternoon, and I was too afraid to go down and ask him what he was doing there.

Yet, when we met Jim and Cynthia for dinner, Tor acted perfectly normally. While we waited for a table at the restaurant, the two guys discussed baseball, whether the A's had a chance to redeem their awful season, if the Giants could stay hot for the rest of theirs. Cynthia had invited Brittany and Roman to join us, but neither of us expected Brit to be on time. Just as we were seated, though, she did call—on my smartphone, not Cynthia's, which was odd since Cyn had made the invitation. I found out why right away.

"Maya," Brittany said, "is Roman with you guys?"

"No. Was he supposed to meet us here?"

"No. I was just hoping that maybe he would." She paused for a long moment. "We might be having our first crisis. The relapse. I mean, they usually do backslide at least once."

"Oh shit!"

"Yeah. Look, tell Cynthia I'm sorry, but I'm going to stay here. He might show up. I'll phone you if he does."

"Please. I don't care how late it is. I'll take the phone to bed with me."

"Okay. Talk to you later."

I clicked off. My hands were shaking so hard that I had trouble getting the phone back into my shoulder bag. My voice shook, too, as I explained the situation to everyone else. Tor turned in his chair to watch me with narrow eyes.

"Oh my god!" Cynthia said. "Maybe we should go into the city and just be there while Brit waits. I hate to think of her being there all alone."

"Can't we eat first?" Jim said. "Brit seems to have one of these crises every goddamn month."

"Aw, honey, that's not fair!" Cynthia turned toward him. "There haven't been that many."

Jim opened his mouth to reply, but Tor got in first.

"You guys stay and eat. Maya and me will drive in. Okay? Our turn." Tor glanced at me. "Why don't you call her and tell her that help's on the way?"

"I'll do that, sure," I said, "and thank you." I gave Cynthia as reassuring a smile as I could manage. "He's my brother. It's my problem."

Jim and Cynthia both relaxed. When the waiter appeared with menus, Tor stood up and greeted him.

"I'm sorry," Tor said. "We have to leave. Medical emergency." He pulled a twenty dollar bill out of the pocket of his slacks and handed it to the startled young waiter. "Here's something for your trouble. Looks like it won't be a party of six after all. Our friends will be staying, though."

The waiter took the money and thanked him. Tor slipped his arm through mine and steered me through the restaurant while I called Brittany. When she heard that we'd be coming over, she nearly cried in relief.

Before we headed for the freeway and San Francisco, Tor drove us home, much to my surprise. He put Gretel into the garage, then backed my old Chevy out while I waited on the sidewalk. He got out and secured the garage with his smartphone.

"I've been thinking," he said. "You should wait here while I go get Roman. Where I'm going, Gretel would be stripped in about ten seconds. No one's going to notice this car. I'm hoping I won't have to get out of it, but you never know."

I gaped at him. "You know where Roman is? How?"

"How do you think I know? Now, you go upstairs and—"

"No! He's my brother, and he'll listen to me better'n he'll listen to you."

Tor thought this over while I fumed.

"Okay," he said. "Get in the car. We're going to grab him before he does something really stupid. He's hanging out in San Francisco. Over in the Crocker-Amazon." He paused and went totally still for a few seconds, then nodded. "Yeah, not far from the Daly City line."

I groaned and got into the car. Don't get me wrong. A lot of decent, hard-working people live in that district, and a lot of students. You can find whole streets of nicely painted houses, but they'll all have grates or bars over their front windows.

Cheap rental buildings and liquor stores, the scruffy bars on Mission Street, the empty lots and the trash blowing around, and the way the cops avoid the area unless they're cracking down on someone—it all combines to attract weak souls and their predators.

By the time we got across the bridge and down to the southeastern edge of San Francisco, the last light of the day was fading. The fog came pouring in, covering the sky a few tendrils at a time, turning the world cold and gray. We left the freeway and eventually found a desolate stretch of Mission Street, fringed with old stucco buildings and the occasional row of cheap little stores. What traffic there was moved fast, especially the big gray and red city buses, as if the drivers were hurrying to get out of the neighborhood. Tor kept in the right lane. We drove north, back toward the city, until we came to a block with a couple of empty lots and a bright pink Mexican restaurant, a stucco cube that could have been imported whole from Tijuana. That's not a compliment.

"I spotted him around here," Tor said. "But if he's going to shoot up, he'll be inside somewhere."

"I don't think he uses needles. I've never seen any tracks."

"That's a good sign, then."

Tor made a U-turn in an empty intersection and headed back south. Near a big, well-lighted gas station I finally spotted Roman. He was leaning against the outside of a bus shelter, his hands shoved in his jacket pockets while he kept watch up a side street as if he were waiting for someone. When Tor pulled up at the curb, I unbuckled my seat belt fast and got out.

"Ro," I said, "what are you doing out here?"

He spun around and stared at me. In the fluorescent light from the gas station, his skin looked gray, and his eyes were dark and huge.

"I could say the same for you," he said. "Shit."

"Get in the car. Brit's worried sick."

"Can't. I'm meeting someone."

"Yeah, I bet. One of your dealers?"

He turned his back on me. Tor got out of the car and strode over to face him. Roman spun around only to see me still there. He turned back, tried to take a step sidewise and rammed into the side of the bus shelter. When he nearly fell, I grabbed his arm by the elbow and steadied him. He reeked of bourbon.

"For chrissakes," Roman said. "So I didn't want to go out to fucking dinner with my little sister's fucking ever so clean and nice fucking friends."

"Yeah, and this is better?" Tor said. "Come on, Cantescu! I know what's going on. You keep seeing re-runs of the action in your head. Someone's face exploding when you—"

"Shut the fuck up!" Roman said.

"Was it a woman, and you thought it was a guy with an IED, but she was carrying a baby?"

Roman swung at him, a hard right straight for his head. Tor stepped to one side as fast and smoothly as a dancer and grabbed Ro's arm in both hands. He twisted and pulled. Roman started swearing in a stream of profanity so foul it was surreal, but Tor kept the pressure on, stepped forward, and forced him to his knees.

"How many, Cantescu?" Tor said. "How many re-runs? You need to blot them out, don't you? Every death. Every scream. Booze won't do it anymore. Especially when you remember your dead buddy."

Roman looked up at him and started to cry. He sobbed, the tears ran, he caught his breath in big gulps and wept the harder. Tor let him go, then bent down and helped him to his feet.

"Come on," Tor said. "Get in the car."

I opened the back door. Roman stopped crying. He got in and slumped down, half-lying, half-sitting across the entire seat. I got in the front seat and turned around to lock the back door. Roman looked up at me, started to speak, then wept again. I just managed to buckle my seat belt before I started weeping with him. I finally got control of myself after Tor had driven us halfway across the city. I opened the glove compartment and took out the box of tissues I'd always kept there. I pulled out a handful and then handed the rest over the back of the seat to my brother.

Brittany lived in San Francisco because she got free rent in return for helping her grandmother, who owned a place out in the Sunset District just off Nineteenth Avenue. Her Grandma Wilson lived in the bottom floor flat while Brittany had the top unit of a building designed to fit in with the Victorian optique—big bay windows, a fancy double-door entrance with stained glass—but in the style of the 1930s. Stucco, gray, drab, in short. Sorcerer's luck gave us a parking place right in front of it.

Tor and I got out, and I opened the back door. Tor reached in and hauled Roman out, helped him stand, brushed some dirt off his sweatshirt. Roman stood still like a little boy and let him.

"Okay," Roman said. "You were in the military. Right?"

"Norwegian army, yeah," Tor said.

"With the Coalition, huh? Iraq or Afghanistan?"

"I don't much like to talk about it."

"I can accept that." Roman took a deep breath. "Thanks."

"You're welcome. Look, you've got to tell Brittany what happened. I don't just mean me and Maya fetching you. I mean what happened. Maybe not all of it. For sure not the details. But you've got to tell her."

Under the olive color of his skin the blood left Roman's face. "You're right," he said. "Shit."

I hurried into the entranceway to ring Brittany's doorbell, but I heard her coming downstairs. She'd been watching out the window, she told me when she opened the door.

"Oh god, thank you, Maya!" she said. "And Tor, thank him, too. Or I mean, do you guys want to come in? I'm all to pieces."

"No, you and Ro need to talk without us there. Brit! You've fallen in love with my rotten brother, haven't you?"

"Yeah." She shrugged and twisted her face into a sour expression. "I am so stupid some times! I always loved the

dogs I rescued, too, but this is different. I don't want to give
Roman away to a good home."

Despite everything we managed to laugh. Roman walked
up to us, looked at the steps by Brittany's feet, and mumbled,
"Sorry." Brittany grabbed him by the arm and guided him
firmly inside. I shut the door behind them and went back to
the car. Tor had already gotten into the driver's seat. I got in
and buckled on my seat belt while he watched me.

"Brittany says thank you," I said.

"She's welcome, yeah." He smiled briefly. "That was close
there, when your brother asked me about the military."

"I was getting ready to jump in and lie for you."

Tor smiled again, then let it fade.

"What I wonder," I said, "is how you knew all that, about
his dead friend, and the woman with the baby. Sorcery?"

"No, I was just guessing. Too many women died in Iraq.
Every soldier loses a friend. Someone lost me. If he's still alive,
he must be ninety by now, but I bet he never forgot the guy
I was back then. You don't."

My eyes filled with tears again. I wiped them off on my
sleeve.

"You know," Tor went on, "it's easier to lay aside what
we suffered in the war than what we did. I don't have to go
through what Roman's going through because I was shot
and killed. That made it even. Paid in full. He got out of
there alive."

Tor's statements were always logical, that is, if you could
believe his premises, like this one: *I died, but I remember it all
anyway.* I could think of nothing to say. He sighed once and
started the car.

CHAPTER 14

Tor drove in his usual fast but careful way out of the city and back to the Bay Bridge. Once we'd crossed, I called Cynthia and told her that we'd found Roman and returned him to Brittany. She thanked me, because she'd been worrying—just as I knew she would.

"Do you think he'll do this again?" Cynthia said.

"I don't know. I hope not. But I think we'd better be ready for it. Brittany warned us it's a long process, pulling someone back."

"So she did. Well, take care. I'd better go. Jim's grumbling."

When Tor and I got home, he turned on both lamps in the living room. The bright colored glow through the Tiffany shades comforted me. I flopped into an armchair and stretched my aching legs out in front of me.

"You need chi," Tor said. "Then I'll fix something for dinner. I'm really hungry."

Tor turned off the air conditioner and opened the east window. The night air, scented with the neighbor's honeysuckle, swept over me. Tor pulled élan from the night air and sent it flowing over me. I opened my mouth and gulped it in, swallowed and savored it, as if I drank down some beautiful liquor. I could see its color in my mind, a deep ruby red, and feel the warmth as it spread through my body.

"I like watching you feed," Tor said. "You look so happy."

"I am happy. You're wonderful."

He grinned and went into the kitchen. I lay back in the chair and looked out the east window. The bloated moon, too close to full, had just risen over the distant hills. Moon in Virgo, I thought. By then the month had changed over to September.

Thanks to his TV phobia, I'd been thinking of Tor as a luddite, but he had no trouble buying and installing the nanny cam. When he figured out how to route it over his wireless connection to his laptop, I realized that he had to be serious about hating television in particular, not technology in general.

"It really scrambles your brain waves," he told me when I asked. "I'm not kidding. It changes the entire pattern of how you think. From what I've read, the digital monitors are better than the CRTs. It's the pattern of lines that carry the signal on a CRT that does the brain wave damage. It's like hypnosis. But the shows aren't any better no matter what you bring them in on."

I stared in complete non-understanding. I had heard something about the changes to brain waves somewhere, I realized, but I'd never thought twice about it.

"Whatever," I said. "I wanted to ask you something. What are we going to do about the élan I need? When the bjarki's dominant, I mean. Last time I ran really low and hurt all over."

"I can feed you right before you lock me in, feed you as much as you can absorb."

"That'll help." I thought back to the other time he'd made the transformation. "I was low to begin with, that first time. Besides, I didn't know what to expect. I still don't, really. I've only been here for one change." I ran the timeline in my mind. "I've only known you for six weeks, haven't I?"

"You've known me a hell of a lot longer than six weeks."

I rolled my eyes. "I mean now. Here. In this life."

"It's all one life. It's just hard to remember the earlier parts. The memories turn into pictures, and then pieces of pictures, and after a while they're gone."

"After a while? After a couple of lives, I suppose you mean."

"Yeah. Talking about this frosts you, doesn't it?"

I shrugged and realized why I felt like sulking. "I'm sorry," I said. "I'm just plain nervous, I guess, about what's going to happen tomorrow."

"You and me both."

"Are you sure you want me to use the nanny cam?"

"Oh yeah. It's always better to know than wonder." He looked at me and smiled in a particularly smug way. "About all kinds of things. Like what's behind those shutters. Remember them?"

I turned and walked off before I said something nasty. He followed me into my bedroom and stopped by the writing desk. I was going to refuse to look at it, but curiosity won. On the lid two figures were fighting with swords, a black man with the sun for his head, and a white woman with the moon for hers. Tiny red lions formed the circle around them, a sign that they were releasing a lot of power.

"What does that mean?" I said.

"They're trying to achieve a balance between them. They're doing it wrong."

"Like we are?" I heard my voice snarl.

"That's not what I meant!" Tor crossed his arms over his chest.

I realized that we stood on the edge of our first fight. Not now, I thought. Totally wrong time!

"I'm sorry," I said. "Look, you need to rest up for tomorrow."

"You're right. I'm sorry, too." He hesitated, then laughed, but the throaty sound merged into a growl. "Ever hear that old expression? Irritable as a bear with a sore paw?"

"Yeah." I managed to smile at him. "I have. Come lie down, and I'll rub your back."

"Thanks. That'll help." He glanced at the bed and winced. "But not in here."

On the carved headboard of the bed, the moon lacked only a sliver before it would turn full.

Somewhere in the night, when we were both asleep, the transformation moved into its first stage. I woke in the gray dawn to find myself about to fall out of bed, because Tor had edged me way over and curled up in the middle of it. He'd curved his back and folded somehow at the waist, drawn up and tucked in his long legs, and bent his head so that his chin nearly touched his knees. I surrendered to the pull of gravity and got out of bed. His eyes opened. He stared unmoving at me as if he'd forgotten who I was, then sat up with a strange sound, not really a growl, more of a snort, but animal all the same. I took a couple of big steps back, but he came to himself and smiled at me. He uncurled, stretched, swore at how stiff he was, and slid over to his side of the bed.

"Might as well get up," he said. "I'm glad I went to the store yesterday."

I dressed, but he put on only a pair of jeans. He padded barefoot into the bathroom, then went to the kitchen. When I followed, I found him rummaging through the refrigerator—him, the man who never ate breakfast. He pulled out a flat package of sausages.

"I guess I should cook these," he said. "Before I eat them, I mean."

"Yes, you should. They're pork."

He got out the frying pan, set it onto the stove, then turned to me.

"I'd better feed you first."

With a toss of his head he indicated we were to go to the living room. In front of the east window, where sunlight fell in a long stripe across the rug, he gathered élan and let it pour over me. I absorbed all I could, swallowed in big gulps while Tor stood with his arms raised and gathered more of what we both wanted so badly. He tipped his head back in order to soak up the élan he needed for himself, but I could see how tightly he'd set his jaw, how his eyes had gone wide with fear. I gulped a last few shreds until I could take not one slurp or smidgen more, and watched him finish feeding.

He lowered his arms and leaned forward from the waist at an odd angle. "Come lock me in." His voice had coarsened, turned low and grating. "Right now."

He bolted for the master suite. It took me a moment to find the keys. By the time I remembered to look on the mantel, where I'd put them the day before, my pulse was pounding in my throat. My hands shook so badly that I had trouble getting the key into the lock. I made myself stop and breathe, just breathe for a long couple of moments. I could hear Tor pacing back and forth inside. Finally I managed the key, shot the deadbolt, and put on the safety chain. On the other side of the door he moaned, a long drawn-out moan that rose to a growl, then fell back into misery.

"Tor!" I called out. "Remember who you are!"

He threw himself against the door and roared, scratched and scrabbled at the wood. *If I turned into an actual bear, I could pull that door right off its hinges.* He'd told me that. I wanted to scream. Instead I made my voice as gentle as I could.

"I love you, Tor. I'll be right here when you come back."

He fell quiet for perhaps a minute and a half. The moaning started again. I walked away.

I put the sausages back into the refrigerator. The thought of eating anything nauseated me, although I knew I'd have to have food eventually. I had to keep my strength up. I—no, we, both of us—had long days and nights ahead of us. I'd grown so used to being fed whenever I wanted that the thought of being on my own panicked me. Panic only drained élan, I reminded myself. *Breathe deeply, imagine flowers, a field of beautiful yellow flowers*—my heart returned at last to its normal rhythm.

I went to the living room, where Tor's laptop sat on the coffee table. He'd plugged it via a transformer into a wall socket so it wouldn't run out of power—even if I did. I giggled at the thought, a sick little stupid sound. I made myself stop. I could hear Tor whining, moaning, at the door just down the hall. Any time, at any moment, I could boot up the laptop, access the cam, and see what was tormenting him, see him in his strangely transformed condition, see at last the creature he became.

It took me three hours to work up the courage.

The entire time, Tor moaned and growled. Occasionally

he scratched on the door.

Finally, close to noon, after I'd made myself eat, I sat down on the couch and faced the laptop. Even then, I had to take a good many deep, soothing breaths before I could boot up. Even after that, it took me a couple of minutes to access the camera images. I hit "record", sat back on the couch, and forced myself to open my eyes and watch.

Tor crouched in the middle of the unmade bed. He'd stripped off the jeans; they lay on the floor nearby. His body was still human, no pelt, no bear's face, no claws, but his posture, the way he hunched over, the way he swung his head from side to side—pure animal. He tipped back his head and roared with a snap of his jaws. Drool spattered and ran. He rolled over to the edge of the bed and jumped down. On hands and knees he crawled over to the bedroom door, then sat back on his haunches. His hands grabbed at the door knob—both of them, fingers held together, as he tried to grasp it between what he must have seen as paws. The door trembled but stayed shut.

He moaned, whined, swung his head back and forth, then clambered to his feet. He rammed a shoulder against the door, fell back, and moaned so piteously at what must have been the pain that my eyes filled with tears. I broke. I leaned forward, stopped the record, closed down the app, turned off the laptop. I'd promised him that I'd record at intervals during the bjarki's domination. I'd done all I could stand of the first session.

I felt like crawling myself, but I walked over to the open window and the patch of sunlight and sat down in it. Maybe some of the élan would filter into my body on its own if I was lucky. The warmth soothed me, no matter what the mysterious life force was doing. I fell asleep right there on the floor. When I woke, the sun had moved on to the other side of the flat. I heard Tor roaring and growling down the hall in the master suite.

I got up and went into my bedroom. On the writing desk a new figure had appeared: a hairy, filthy man naked except for a wrap of rags around his loins. He crouched on a strip of grass and gnawed on a bone. In a circle around him flew tiny vultures. I wanted to throw a towel over the desk so I wouldn't have to see its images, but I was afraid of offending it. At some point I might need its advice.

At twilight, when the silver glow of the rising moon hovered over the eastern hills, I forced myself to boot up the laptop and camera again. We'd set the system up to record to a three gig thumb drive, so computer memory presented no problems. My own memory was a different matter. I knew that no matter what happened, no matter how many times Tor had to suffer the bjarki's domination or how few, I would never be able to forget what I'd seen.

With the moon shining full and strong, he hurt. His pain was obvious even in the images onscreen. He moaned and whimpered as he crawled on all fours, back and forth, shuffling across the bedroom floor. Now and then he stopped and lay down, stretched out, then curled up, over and over, moaning in agony the entire time. I wept. I could not stop myself. He writhed and rolled, got back to hands and knees, began shuffling toward the window, then turned and shuffled back again. He stopped, lay down, and curled into a fetal ball. He began to lick his right arm as if he were trying to soothe the pain.

I moaned with him and turned off the screen and the speakers, but I let the laptop continue to record direct from the camera. This moonrise phase was important, I figured, and he'd want the data when he came back to himself. I could still hear him, of course, through the door. He'd put the bag of earplugs in my bedroom. I was just about to fetch them when Cynthia called me. I took my phone all the way down the hall past my bedroom to make sure she couldn't hear Tor's moans and roars.

"Say," Cynthia said. "Did you guys want to go to a movie tonight? Jim's actually feeling sociable."

"We can't," I said. "Tor's sick."

"God, that's too bad! What's he got?"

I considered lying. I was going to say 'food poisoning.' I

was too aware that this same curse would fall upon us every month, every damned lunar month, thirteen times a year.

"It's the full moon," I said. "He's under the domination of the bear. The bjarki."

Silence, a long dead-air period of silence.

"Maya," Cynthia said eventually. "You sound so tired and shaky that I'm half inclined to believe you."

"It's true. I am not joking. At the full moon he—well, he doesn't actually turn into a bear." I got a sudden insight. "He gets possessed by the spirit of a bear. That's the only way I can describe it. It's like some entity from the spirit world grabs hold of him. He acts like a bear. He's not a bear. But oh god, he's suffering."

"Maya!" Her voice rose in a small shriek.

"I'm not lying." I snuffled back a mouthful of tears. "Look, call Brittany, will you? Tell her what I told you. She'll explain."

Again the silence, trembling with shock. I wondered if I were about to lose one of my closest friends. Cynthia drew in a deep, audible breath.

"Okay," she said. "I will do that. I did talk with her earlier today. I wanted to see how your brother was doing. Better, by the way. But anyway, she went on and on about Tor being some kind of magician. A runemaster, she called him. Are you going to tell me she was right?"

"Yeah. That's exactly what I'm telling you. But it's real dangerous work."

"Guess it must be. Is that what got him this spirit or whatever it is?"

"Pretty much, yeah."

"Okay." She sighed. "Look, I'll let you go. I'll call back after I've talked to Brittany."

While I waited for her return call, I ate something. I don't remember what. When I finished, I turned on all the lamps in the living room, kitchen, my bedroom, and the bathroom across from it. I wanted to fill the flat with light. I gathered my drawing materials and laid them out on the coffee table near the laptop. I'd just sat down on the couch when Cynthia called. Once again, I took the phone down the hall.

"When I told Brit what you told me," Cynthia said, "she said 'I thought so!' She was just surprised he wasn't a werewolf. Or a tiger, she said. I guess those are supposed to be more common than bears."

"In Indonesia they are, tiger spirits, I mean. My mom talked about them sometimes. But Tor's from the Northlands."

"Okay. If any of this makes sense, that makes sense."

"Do you believe us?"

"I believe you because you guys are you and you are my friends. That'll have to do for now."

"It's enough. Thank you." I choked back tears. "I mean that. Thank you."

"So okay, as Brit would say. Is there anything I can do to help? I'll do it."

I considered. I had plenty of ordinary food. Tor was safely locked in. I was willing to bet that Nils presented no threat, either. The one thing I longed for—another source of élan—was the one thing I would never take from my friends.

"I don't think there's anything you can do," I said. "But thank you."

"I'll call now and then. Just to check in. So will Brit." Cynthia hesitated briefly. "Hang in there. I don't know what else to say."

"Just knowing you guys know—god, it really helps."

"Good. I'm going to go online and see what I can find out about these animal spirits. Knowledge is power and all that crap."

I managed to laugh, and we ended the call.

Knowing they knew, knowing they were still my friends—it gave me enough strength to pick up a sketchbook and draw. The earplugs helped, too. Through them I could still hear him when he roared, but they did cut out the painful little whimpers and moans. I knew he hurt. I could do nothing about it because I didn't dare open the locked door.

Still, at times my eyes filled with tears. I let them fall on the first drawing I made. I drew Tor as I knew him, fully human, dressed in jeans and his Raiders T-shirt. I knew his body so well that I got a good likeness just from memory. The tears splashed onto his chest, where I would have wept had I had been able to hold him.

I turned the page and wondered what to draw next. A wolf, maybe, but not real wolves, not the intelligent pack animals who loved their young and lived in a hierarchical society. No, I wanted to draw the mythical kind, the lone wolves. I was thinking of Fenrir and the wolf in *Peter and the Wolf,* dangerous killers, lean, red-eyed, gaunt bodies, fangs.

Nils. I felt him as I drew as tangibly as if he prowled around the living room. Although his mind registered on mine as under the animal's spell, I felt none of the physical pain Tor was feeling. Nils was confused, easily distracted, but he seemed at home in the wolf body, though he paced back and forth, wherever he was, angry, filled with hate. I kept drawing, gestural studies at first, then stronger lines, more fully realized images. Under the hatred I sensed a different emotion, complex, hard to pin down at first. I turned the page and started yet another drawing.

Disgust. Loathing at what he became under the evil stare of the full moon. Self-hatred mingled with the hatred he felt for Tor, who—the wolf lacked words. He could not tell me or himself why he hated Tor. I could find no image for it. In wolf form Nils's mind only knew emotions and concrete images. I picked up his desire to feed on dead things and to kill Tor. He had reasons to hate Tor, but the wolf could only remember being driven from the pack where Tor's father was alpha male.

He couldn't give form to whatever poisoned his soul, but he wanted something. This thing, an object, was prey, it was safety, it was sex—everything in life that the wolf knew as good and desirable. Tor had it. Tor refused to share it. The only possible object was the gold ornament with the runes, the one that Tor kept away from him in the safe downstairs. A lust for gold would have been too abstract for the wolf to understand, too remote from the animal's world. The Fehu rune had pointed to the ornament. I wrote my thoughts on the same page as the drawing, notes for Tor when he came back to me.

I looked away from the page and for the briefest of moments I saw him, the wolf with human blue eyes, staring at me. I screamed. The sight vanished, but the touch of his mind remained.

I could no longer endure contact with Nils. He sickened me. I shut the sketchbook and flopped it down on the coffee table. The slapping sound it made against the wood broke the spell. I got up and went to the west window. By craning my neck and leaning to one side, I saw the full moon at its zenith. Only half of Night One had passed. I walked over to a floor lamp and held my hands under the light. They looked perfectly normal. So far, at least, my body held enough élan.

I decided to stop being a coward. I sat back down and opened the laptop, turned on the monitor, and realized that with the moon so high above the window level, the bedroom had gone dark. The camera showed mostly lumps of darker shadows. I stopped recording and peered at the murky image on the screen. I could just see Tor, curled up by the bathroom door, asleep. "Thank god," I whispered and shut down the system.

As the days and nights of the full moon crawled by, I worked out a routine of sorts around the sessions of recording from the camera in the bedroom. Watching Tor, hearing him growl and moan, hurt like knives to the heart, but I managed to keep on top of the situation. Well, mostly I did. There were times when I broke down to see him in so much pain. But overall, because I knew what was going to happen, I could at least keep the panic element at bay. Tor would come back. He would feed me all the élan he'd stored against the bjarki transformation. I wasn't going to die. I had friends. Either Cynthia or Brittany called every four or five hours. Talking with Brit about my brother made me remember that other people had problems of their own.

In the intervals I drew. I had a lot of sketchpads left from when I'd first taken Tor's job. Before the full moon came, I'd also bought some new oil pastels as well as conté. I tried to draw normal subjects: the view from the windows, the Chinese vases in the living room. At night, though, in the times when the full moon gleamed in the window like the watchfire of an enemy army, the drawings drew themselves—pictures of Tor under the bjarki spell, of the Norse gods, of Nils, and of my father.

I thought of Dad often when my élan began to run dangerously low. On the third morning, my knuckles swelled and turned red. My legs ached, knees first, then as the day ground on, my hips. I sweated, a constant clammy drip. I'd shower, stay comfortable for maybe an hour, and then the sweat would start oozing out of my skin again. I gulped mineral water by the tumblerful. When I thought back, I couldn't remember my father having symptoms like mine. His hurt lay inside him, in his heart and other vital organs.

That day I slept as much as I could, guarding every precious drop of élan. I told Brittany and Cynthia that I'd become too exhausted to talk on the phone, which was true enough. Yet that night, as it always eventually did, the full moon began to wane. I woke up in the morning to the sound of hissing water that meant Tor was taking a shower. I got out of bed, grabbed the keys, and ran naked to the door of our bedroom just as the water pulse stopped. I could hear Tor calling to me in a human voice. I opened the door and saw him grinning at me, fully human again, and as naked I was.

"I bet I know what you want," he said. "Come here and let me feed you."

"And I bet I know what *you* want." I grinned in return. "I can feed while we make love. Well, assuming you're finished with all that élan you stockpiled."

He laughed and enfolded me in his embrace. We fell on the bed together.

We stayed in bed for most of the day. It wasn't only the élan nor just the good sex that kept me there. Lying close to him, hearing his voice, seeing him smile at me, and best of all, knowing he no longer ached in every muscle and sinew—together they added up to a different kind of joy. I ran my hands through his hair, stroked his chest, kissed the bruises on his shoulders that the bjarki's struggles had put there—"to make them better," I said. He laughed and kissed me in turn, told me he loved me over and over.

"I can't believe you're still here," he said. "I was pretty sure you'd cut and run once you saw what happened."

"No. It hurt to watch, but I wasn't revolted or anything. You don't turn into a bear. I don't care what you see in the mirror. You stay a man, but oh my god, Tor! Do you remember the pain?"

"Oh yeah." His voice turned bleak. "It gets pretty bad at first." He lay on his back and frowned at the ceiling. "I wonder if it's because I don't change all the way. My body keeps trying, and shit, it really burns in here."

"It does ease up after a while?"

"By the third day, yeah."

Not fast enough to spare him much. I sat up and thought about Nils, the contact I'd made while drawing the wolf. "I bet that Nils doesn't feel pain once he's in varg form."

Tor's eyes narrowed with questions.

"Let's get up and get dressed," I said. "I want to eat, and you probably do, too. I've got an awful lot to tell you."

I had a lot to show him, as well. After we'd eaten, we sat on the couch together and paged through the drawings I'd made while the bjarki had held him in its claws. The information I'd gleaned about Nils turned Tor grim. He sat rock-still for a long time, staring at the finished drawing, until eventually he read my notes aloud in a voice that ached with fury.

"Any more?" he said. "Pics, I mean."

"Not of the varg. I did do some drawings of my father in another notebook."

He closed the sketchbook he was holding with a snap. "I'd like to see those one day," Tor said. "Not now. I'm in such a shit mood it would spoil the experience." He laid the sketchbook on the coffee table. "I want to see the recordings. Get it all over with. Let me get a beer first. My back still hurts, and that'll help. Do you want something to drink?"

"A little brandy. Please."

Tor fetched himself a bottle of dark beer and a snifter with a moderate amount of brandy for me. Watching the recordings with him safe beside me was an entirely different experience than making them had been. I could lean back and watch him watch instead of agonizing over the video. Now and then he winced at some of the images, but he seemed strangely detached from the footage, even analytical. About halfway through he leaned forward and stopped the playback.

"That's enough for now," he said. "You were right. What I see during the domination is all illusion. When I'm in there, I look at my arms and see legs. I see paws. I look in the mirror and see a bear's face looking back. I'm covered with a pelt."

"None of that shows up here."

"Damn right." He stood up. "I'm going to get another beer. Want more brandy?"

"No, I've had plenty."

Tor frowned at the empty bottle in his hand. "I'll wait, too," he said. "I want to go down and cast the rune staves."

While he did, I took a shower. I really needed one by then. I dried my hair, put on clean clothes, and came back to the living room to find him looking back and forth from the laptop screen to a piece of sketchbook paper. He was writing with one of my felt-tips. A full bottle of beer stood on the table. He laid the pen down and held out the paper.

"Email from my sister," Tor said. "I told her earlier about your theory. Nils being the varg, I mean. I went onto email just now to tell her you were right, but she'd already answered. So I translated it for you."

I took the letter and sat down next to him.

"Something I have been thinking about," Liv wrote. "Do you remember the pattern of our father's illness? After the marrow transplant he seemed much better, but in a few months the disease returned. The doctors were surprised by this. One told me that it should not have happened, or at least, not so fast. And then the pattern started. At the dark of the moon, he would sink and the blood count would be very bad. He would start to improve and the blood count at the full moon would be much much better. I thought then that it was only the influence of the lunar energies. But what if it had something to do with Nils? At the full moon, he would not be able to attack. At the dark he would be at his strongest."

"My god!" I looked up. "If that's true—"

"Then he's a murderer, not just a dangerous asshole." Tor spoke quietly, calmly, but in his voice I heard rage.

"If it's true, it's no wonder he won't talk things out with you."

"Yeah, you bet. There's no way we're going to compromise like good little boys. I wonder if we'll ever know if he killed Dad or not. Not that I need to know." He picked up his beer, drank, set the bottle back down. "To deal with him, I mean."

His smile chilled my blood. I looked down at the rest of the email.

"I have not told Mama all of this," Liv went on to say. "She is upset enough by what she does know. If she writes you, please guard what you say. She has been having her spells again."

"Spells?" I said. "Is your mother ill?"

"That's not the kind of spells Liv means."

"Sorry. What does she do, what kind of magic, I mean?"

Tor hesitated, considered, finally gave one his shrugs. "She sees visions. When she's on a roll, she can summon a few of the creatures out of them. Just the smaller ones, like the nisse. Or foxes. I don't know why, but she has an affinity with foxes."

"Wait a minute! The nisse here—"

"Was her housewarming present to me, yeah. Right before they left for Iceland."

I sighed and gave him back the letter. What do you say to a revelation like that? I could think of nothing. Tor sailed the paper back onto the coffee table and sat back on the couch with his bottle of beer in hand.

"What was the runecast like?" I said.

"Interesting. Your theory about Nils wanting the gold is

dead on. Or not the gold itself, but the artifact."

"You think the writing's some kind of spell, right?"

"Practically every example of the elder runes that survives is a spell. They weren't used like the Latin alphabet, y'know, for everyday things."

"So it's the spell he wants? Not just the gold?"

"That's what I'm thinking, yeah. Too bad the runes aren't an illusion. You could probably read them if they were."

I heard a challenge in his voice. I ignored it.

"I need to call Cynthia and Brittany," I said, "to tell them you're back."

Tor froze with the beer bottle halfway to his mouth. "They know?" he said.

"Yeah, and Brittany even believes it. I bet Cyn doesn't, and I bet she hasn't told Jim."

"I hope not." Tor paused for a long swallow of beer. "And I hope no one's told your brother, either. He's got enough shit to deal with as it is."

That night I dreamed about the shutters again. This time I walked through my parents' apartment, the nice one in San Francisco's Richmond district that we had before they divorced. I went into my bedroom to look outside, but the shutters covered the window. I woke up fast and lay shivering next to Tor while sunlight brightened on the drapes.

I got up and started the coffee in the kitchen. I'd just poured myself a cup when Roman called me. Even though he stumbled politely around, asking me how I was and how Tor was doing, the shake in his voice told me that he was in trouble. I figured he'd relapsed and gotten himself drugged out. The truth was worse.

"It's my old dealer," he told me. "I owe him a lot of money. He's gonna get violent if I don't pay up."

I made a sound halfway between a sigh and a grunt of disgust. "How much do you owe him?"

"Way too much for me to cover. Look, Sis, I'm sorry. I didn't want to hit you up. I know Thorlaksson's got money, but shit, that should be off the table. Begging my sister's boyfriend for money—I mean, sometimes I see just how fucking low I've sunk."

"Yeah? Then maybe the money's worth it. How much, Ro?"

"He's threatened Brit. I told him I'd kill him if he touched her. He just laughed."

My stomach knotted around a lump of ice. "Ro, please, how much do you need?"

A long silence, followed by a little boy's voice, "Three hundred bucks."

"I can cover that. You don't need to ask Tor."

It took me a minute to identify the peculiar sound I heard over the phone. Tears. My brother had started to cry, then choked it back. He sniffled. I waited.

"Thanks." He cleared his throat. "Jesus fucking god, thanks! How soon can you give it to me?"

"Today. But look, I've got to tell Tor if I'm going to meet you in the city. I don't want to go in alone. It's because of his crazy uncle. And I want to meet you while it's still light out. Like, right away."

"Okay, sure. Tell Tor whatever you want. Least I can do is face up to it, huh? The fuck ugly mess I got myself into, I mean." He took a deep rasping breath. "I'll call The Man and tell him I'll have it for him tonight."

"You do that."

It was some while after we clicked off that I realized how much things had changed. Two months previously I never could have scraped together three hundred dollars to give him. Thirty would have been a big stretch. The amount Ro needed would put a huge dent in my checking account, but I could give it to him and still eat.

CHAPTER 15

Since I refused to let Roman know where Tor's expensive antiques lived, having him come to the house was out of the question. I also didn't want him carrying three hundred dollars in cash back to San Francisco on public transportation. So I arranged to meet him at a place we remembered from our childhood, a dim sum place way out on Geary Street, a long drive in from Oakland. I chose this respectable neighborhood because low buildings lined the wide streets. In daylight we could see any threats coming from a decent distance away. What with the Russian Orthodox cathedral nearby, and lots of little shops and delis to attract customers, we'd have plenty of people around us at all times. I figured we'd be safe there from Nils or from anyone who saw me hand Roman a wad of cash. I didn't worry about Roman's dealer. He'd get his money, and that was all his kind ever wanted.

Before we left, though, Tor cast the rune staves. He disliked what he saw.

"We're not staying long," he told me. "Roman damn well better be on time. I want to meet him, give him the money, and get the hell out of there again."

"Okay." I took a deep breath. "You should take a jacket."

"This time of year?"

"It'll be cold out there. The fog."

"I'll put on a flannel shirt."

I drove Gretel in so Tor could 'keep watch' as he called it while we travelled. He sat straight, unmoving, a grim presence

in the passenger seat. I concentrated on driving. Travel moved
fast on the bridge in the middle of the day, but San Francisco
traffic was its usual snarled self. By the time I finally reached
Geary and started driving west on the boulevard, Tor had
relaxed enough to talk to me.

"I'm not seeing Nils anywhere near the place," he said.
"Good. But stay alert, anyway."

I did, for all the good it did us. We drove under a chilly
gray canopy of fog before we reached the meeting place. Despite the slow-moving snarls of traffic on Geary, Tor's parking luck held. We found a spot right around the corner from
the restaurant. We got out, and he put wards on the car before we walked back. As we turned the corner onto Geary, I
saw Roman, standing in front of the restaurant's pink stucco
front. He waved and hurried over to meet us halfway. He and
Tor shook hands.

"I can't thank you enough," he said to me.

"It's okay." I reached into my bra and took out the fold
of hundred-dollar bills. "Just don't get into this mess again,
will you?"

"You bet." Roman took the money and shoved it into his
jeans pocket without looking at it. "I may be stupid as a fucking mule, but I learn eventually. I—"

Tor yelled and spun toward the street. "Down!" He flung
up his hands with a flash of silver light.

Roman grabbed me and followed orders just as I heard
the gunshots. We fell together onto the sidewalk with his body
covering mine. A nearby woman screamed. Men cursed. Roman jerked and twisted, then swore in agony. I heard more
screaming and the sound of shattering glass. Tor knelt down
beside me. I could just see him over Roman's shoulder. I could
not understand why Tor would be pulling off his flannel shirt
and wadding it up. A trickle of blood ran down Roman's arm
and dripped onto mine. I understood.

"Get free, Maya," Tor hissed. "Call 911."

I squirmed out from under my brother's limp body. Tor
was pressing his shirt hard onto the wound on Roman's back

to try to stop the bleeding. Ro had turned a ghastly sort of pale under his olive complexion. He lay so still that I thought him dead. I grabbed my phone from my pocket.

"I've already called." A gray-haired man with tattoos up both arms stepped into my field of vision. "Take off your jacket and put it under his head. He's in shock. Hypothermia's next."

I slipped out of my denim jacket and folded it into a pillow. When I slid it between Roman's head and the concrete, I could see that he while he'd passed out, he was still breathing. I laid my hand on his cheek. His skin felt cold and clammy. I pushed his sweaty hair away from his eyes. When I looked up, the gray-haired man had stepped back into the crowd of onlookers.

"Good," Tor said to me. "Now get out of the way. Here comes help."

I stood up and walked a few steps away from the street. Sirens came screaming toward us from a great distance away, or so it seemed. I heard people talking, but I couldn't understand a word of it, because they were speaking Chinese. Men came running, swearing, calling out words that I did understand, "What happened? That's blood! Is he all right?"

I wanted to scream at them and say, *no, you stupid bastards! He's been shot!* Instead I leaned up against the wall of a shop and trembled. Out on Geary a man in a long black cassock and an odd cubical hat darted through the six lanes of traffic and fetched up near us. I thought I was imagining him or seeing a figure from the spirit world, until he knelt down next to Tor and began praying in Russian. He was a priest from the nearby cathedral.

With a skid of tires and a blast on an air horn a fire truck pulled up out in the street. One of the men in the front seat jumped down and ran over to Tor and Roman. "Good job," he said to Tor, "I'll take over. The ambulance is on its way."

The priest continuing praying. Shivering in his T-shirt, Tor got up and joined me at the shop's wall.

"Okay," he said. "I should have worn a jacket."

I slipped my arm around his waist and leaned against

him. He put his arm around my shoulders and squeezed.

"Are you okay?" I said.

"Oh yeah. I deflected his second shot, the one at me. The fucker!"

I watched the firemen hovering over Roman. One kept up the pressure on the wound. A second man was giving Ro oxygen. *That means he's still alive.* My heart began to ease off its pounding.

Around Tor and me the onlookers were talking in a murmur of quiet outrage. "Couldn't be a drive-by, traffic's too slow, but he had to come from somewhere, I saw something, a guy, an older guy, but it was so fast, where did he go, I didn't see that, jeez we should get inside somewhere, doesn't matter now, here are the cops."

"Nils?" I said to Tor.

"Has to be. I didn't realize he could leap. Y'know, travel like I can. Bam. Gone. The times he attacked us before, he was in a car. That's what I was watching for."

More sirens, more flashing lights and vehicles screeching to a stop—paramedics came rushing over with a stretcher. Tor released me with a gentle pat on the back.

"Go with the ambulance," he said. "I'll stay here and deal with the police."

The paramedics, a tall blond woman and an Asian man, had taken over from the fireman. I knelt down beside them. "I'm his sister," I said.

The woman looked at my face. "You sure are," she said. "We're taking him to the closest ER. We've got to get him there fast. You can ride along."

They got Ro onto the stretcher, face down, and loaded him into the ambulance. The Asian guy hurried around and got into the driver's seat. As I climbed into the back, I looked over to the sidewalk and saw Tor talking with a uniformed police officer. The crowd around them began to break up. The blonde paramedic shut the doors. The siren started up, the ambulance jerked forward, picked up speed, went tearing through the traffic with blasts of the horn.

"He have any allergies?" the blonde said.

"No."

She snapped a paper bracelet around his left wrist, then brought out a cuff and dial and took Roman's blood pressure. I noticed that the blood from his wound had stopped running, though a red stain still spread through the cloth of his heavy khaki shirt. Capillary action, I thought. My mind had become a jumble of disconnected words. I took Ro's right hand in both of mine. His eyelids moved but didn't open.

"Your brother a vet?" the paramedic said.

"Yeah. Marines."

"They're tough. He'll pull through. The guy with you, your boyfriend. Must be another vet."

"Yeah," I said.

"Um." She nodded and kept her eyes on the dial of the blood pressure unit. "Pretty low."

I felt no élan misting from my brother. What little he had left must have pulled back inside him, wrapped around his vital organs in a desperate measure to keep him alive. I could take élan, but I had no idea of how to give it. I could only keep rubbing his hand and silently begging him not to die.

"Here we are," the paramedic said.

The ambulance jerked into a turn and shrieked to a stop. The jumble in my mind grew worse. The blonde flung open the doors and hopped down. We'd stopped under a carport next to a tall gray concrete building. Glass double doors slid open. Two men came running and unloaded Roman on the stretcher. When I clambered down, the blonde followed. She handed me a clipboard and a pen.

"You need to fill this out," she said. "About payment."

I did, as fast as I could. By the time I got into the ER, Roman had disappeared. I saw a warren of hallways, all painted dull yellow, and a sign saying to follow the green line on the floor. I did and reached an open space labeled Admissions. At the front desk a middle-aged white woman with a mouthful of chewing gum looked me over. I realized that dirt smudged my clothes from my fall onto the sidewalk. She moved her gum to the other side of her mouth with her tongue, then handed me another clipboard, festooned with more forms.

"We need payment information," she said and returned to chewing her cud.

I handed over Tor's credit card, which improved her mood. After I signed a final form that promised them I'd pick up the bill, she pointed me in the direction I needed to go. I wandered down a brightly-lit hall, found a pale-haired nurse in green scrubs, and told her that I was the shooting victim's sister.

"He's being prepped for surgery," she said and pointed. "Wait here."

'Here' was a bleak little room with a TV blaring in one corner. On uncomfortable plastic chairs a dark-haired man sat slumped over with his head in his hands. An African-American woman sat a few chairs away and tried to keep a crying toddler quiet. I took a chair and watched the TV because I didn't know what else to do. Later I had no memory of the show at all. The nurse returned with another clipboard. I filled out more forms, and in return she gave me the credit card back.

"The VA will pick up the bill," she told me, "if you're lucky."

She stomped out as if I'd insulted her. The man raised his head.

"She's a bitch," he said. "The others are better."

"Thanks," I said.

He slumped back in his chair and studied the ceiling.

Tor arrived in the doorway to the waiting area about fifteen minutes later. I got up and ran to his open arms. When I told him what had happened so far, his jaw tightened, and his eyes narrowed.

"Come on," he said. "Let's go straighten things out."

Tor raised hell at the admission desk. I don't know what else to call it. He snarled, barked, threatened legal action for the way I'd been treated, and bullied the woman behind the desk until she handed him all the forms I'd signed. He tore those up, tossed them into a nearby trash can, and told her he'd fill out a new set. She handed him a clipboard by shrinking back in her chair and stretching her arm out as far as it would go, as if she were offering meat to a tiger. Tor signed the forms and handed it back.

"Get that nurse out here," he said. "The one with the pale hair."

"I can't do that," she snapped. "She's with a patient."

Their eyes met. She snorted and turned away to her computer terminal. In a few minutes another nurse appeared, a woman of Indian descent, I figured from her reddish-brown skin and straight black hair. She told us immediately that her name was Devi.

"I'm so sorry you had to wait," she said to me. "Caroline worked a double shift today. Stress, you know. She's off duty now."

"Not with a patient?" Tor snapped. "Whatever."

"It's okay," I said. "My brother—"

"In surgery now. They'll retrieve the bullet and assess the damage. Here, come with me, and you can wait near the recovery room."

Tor turned to the admissions clerk, who was cowering behind her computer terminal. "If the police arrive, tell them where I am. My name is Tor Thorlaksson. Can you remember that?"

"Of course I can." She cracked her gum in his direction. "No need to be so nasty!"

"Yeah?" Tor considered her for a long moment. "I'd say there was plenty of need. It's funny how things turned around when a white guy walked in here."

The woman winced and pretended to ignore him. Devi arranged a poker face and beckoned us to follow her. As we did, I realized that I'd never called Brittany. With Tor beside me I could calm down enough to think. We had the next waiting room, a quiet pale green space with comfortable brown padded chairs, to ourselves. A TV murmured in the corner, but Tor was tall enough to reach the thing and shut it off. I took out my phone, which I'd turned off. I turned it back on and tapped Brittany's number on speed dial. When she answered, she sounded frantic.

"Maya, I've been trying to reach you! Is something wrong with Roman?"

"Yeah, he's been shot, he's still alive, and he's in surgery. Are you home? We're not far from you if you are."

"Yeah, I am. Oh god, I knew it was something awful." She took a deep breath. "I know what now. So okay. Give me directions, and I'll be right there."

I told her the name of the hospital and gave her a rough idea of where we were inside it. After I clicked off, I slid over close to Tor. He put his arm around me.

"He'll pull through," Tor said. "It's a deep wound, but it missed the spine."

I felt every muscle in my body ease, because it never occured to me to doubt him.

When Brittany arrived, some fifteen minutes later, Tor spared me the job of telling her what had happened. I huddled against him and listened to the clear, calm way he organized the details. For the first time that day I understood them.

Roman had taken the bullet meant for me. At first I merely accepted the idea. It made sense, explained why I'd ended up lying on the sidewalk. He'd been covering me up, keeping me safe. Sure, okay. A couple of seconds later it hit me. He'd taken the bullet meant for me. He'd known it could happen. He must have known. He'd seen enough combat. He'd seen enough death. I began to tremble. I could not stop, could not control the shaking, my hands, head, my whole body, not even when I realized that Tor and Brittany were staring at me.

"He could have died," I croaked out the words. "Protecting me."

"Yeah," Tor said. "Which is why neither of you have to worry about the bills for this. I'll take care of it. I don't give a shit how much it costs. What the VA won't pick up, I will."

Brittany sobbed—just once—in relief. "Thanks," she whispered.

"Welcome," Tor said. "Now we wait."

And we did, endlessly, it seemed. Brittany and I talked

a little, but words failed me. She brought out her phone and called Cynthia first, then the place that held the group therapy.

Tor eventually went out to find the men's room. He also found a cart selling coffee and brought three cups back with him. I sipped mine slowly to make it last out of the sheer old habit of being poor. I'd just finished it when Devi reappeared.

"He's out of surgery. He did fine. He's in the recovery room, but he's not awake yet. I'll tell you when he is, and one of you can go in then."

"Good," Tor said. "Did they save the bullet for the police?"

"I'll make sure they do." She glanced at Brittany and quirked an eyebrow.

"His girlfriend," Tor said. "The person he'll want to see first."

Devi nodded, smiled, and left again. I heard men's voices out in the hall and went tense, expecting the police. Instead, two men in civilian clothes walked in, a Hispanic guy in jeans and a Forty-Niners jacket, a brown-haired white guy in jeans and a Giants hoodie. The red and orange of those sports team pieces struck me all wrong, weirdly festive to my addled mind.

"Thorlaksson?" the Hispanic guy said.

"Yeah." Tor stood up.

"We're a couple of Cantescu's buddies. From his group. Y'know?"

"Cool." Tor stuck out his hand.

They shook hands all round, and Tor introduced Brittany and me. Valdez and Williams were their names. Williams never spoke nor smiled. Now and then he'd nod or frown at something Valdez said.

"Group leader told us about your call," Valdez said to Brittany, then turned to Tor. "I thought we'd stop by and see if we could figure out who did this."

"Good," Tor said. "Let me tell you what I know."

This time Tor edited his recital of the facts. Although he left out any reference to sorcery, Valdez struck me as the kind of man who might have accepted the fact that Uncle Nils could teleport or leap or whatever you want to call it. His dark eyes had seen plenty of horror, I figured, and plenty of strange things, too, when he mentioned that he and Williams had spent a lot of time in Afghanistan.

"Marines like Roman?" Britanny asked.

"Nah. Army Rangers." Valdez grinned at her. "But for a Marine, Cantescu's a pretty good guy." He glanced my way. "I wouldn't worry about the guy who shot your brother. We'll find him, unless he's lucky and the police get him first."

"Cops just walked down the hall." Tor kept his voice just above a whisper. "Careful."

"Oh good," Valdez said. "I like to know our police force is on the job."

The statement probably didn't fool the two officers who walked in, but they stayed perfectly civil. What they needed to know, they told Tor, was if they had a homicide on their hands.

"No," Tor said. "He's out of surgery. Doing pretty well."

"Good," the cop said. "Glad to hear it."

The two of them looked Valdez and Williams over, then exchanged a glance. They returned to the hallway—to wait for the recovered bullet, I assumed.

"Tell Cantescu we'll be back tonight," Valdez said, "when he can see visitors. If he gives us the money, we'll get it to The Man."

"Thank you," I said, "but I don't know where his clothes are. He put it in his jeans pocket."

"I'll get it from the nurse," Brittany said.

"Okay." Valdez turned her way. "They're going to give him morphine, y'know."

"Yeah," Brittany said. "It's back to Square One, isn't it?"

Williams frowned, and Valdez nodded. "So it goes," he said. "But they have to give him something."

Valdez said good-byes all round, and the two of them left. Tor and I stayed until Devi returned to take Brittany into the recovery room.

"I won't leave him," Brit announced. "I'll stay here all night if I can."

"I can arrange that," Devi said. "If his sister approves?"
I nodded yes.

"Maya, you look exhausted," Brittany said. "That's not good. I'll call you with updates, and if anything changes. Go home and rest."

"She's right," Tor said. "We'll come back tomorrow."

I followed Tor blindly as we walked through the maze of dull yellow corridors that stank of cleaning products. He found the way to a door that led out to the hospital parking lot. Watery streaks of sunlight broke through the fog above.

"Is it safe to drive home?" I said.

"Probably, as long as it's light. And I've got something planned for Uncle Nils. It should keep him busy for a while." He smiled, the cold twitch of his mouth that always frightened me. "Once it's good and dark. As the moon wanes, he'll wane." He glanced at his watch. "Shit, it's three o'clock already. Let's get over the bridge before the traffic peaks."

As soon as we returned home, Tor fed me élan. I flopped onto the couch while he cooked us both dinner. I considered taking a nap, but once we'd eaten, I felt my strength return. Tor insisted that I rest while he cleaned up the kitchen. I sat down in an armchair and let the last of the sunlight pour over me from the west window. When I looked out I could see the fog returning to distant San Francisco. I took out my phone and called Brittany.

"We're in a private room," she told me. "He's sort of awake. They hooked him up to a morphine drip. The nurse told me they'll switch him over to pills in a couple of days. But it looks like he's going to be okay."

Except for his addiction, of course. They'd renewed it for the best of reasons without even knowing what they'd done.

"He can move his legs," Brittany continued. "That's the best news ever."

For a moment I felt sick. My brother could have been paralyzed.

"Have you talked to a doctor yet?" I said.

"No. They want you to be here for that."

"Okay. We'll come over in the morning. Once we're there, you can go home and check on your grandmother."

"Right. I'll need to. I called her, but I'm not sure how much she understood."

We clicked off so she could eat the dinner Devi had ordered for her. Tor started the dishwasher running and joined me in the living room. He stood arrow-straight at the window, his arms crossed over his chest, and watched the sunset fading in the west. The last of the scarlet light made his face glow like fire.

"When are we going to do the ritual?" I said.

"Soon." He turned around to look at me. "Now remember! I don't want you participating."

"Even if you're in danger? Even if you're losing?"

"I'm not going to lose."

"You told me that you and Nils were pretty evenly matched."

"That was before he lost the last couple of rounds. Involving you is too risky."

I wanted to agree, to be all meek and obedient. The thought of taking part in a sexual ritual again terrified me. I knew now that it meant giving up complete control of my self, mind and body both. I'd be nothing but a battery, a source of power to supplement his. I gathered my courage and stood up to join him at the window.

"If you need help, I'll do it," I said. "It's worth the risk to me."

He tilted his head a little to one side and studied my face. "You really mean that," he said.

"Yes, I do. I love you."

"And I love you, which is why I don't want you running any risks."

"I'd be in worse trouble if something happened to you. Nils would come after me for sure, then."

Tor turned half-away, then back again. "You're right," he said. "Shit! I never should have brought you into this. But I did, and I'm stuck with it now. Look, I'll do my best to leave you out. But okay, if I really need another weapon, I'll ask you join me in the center."

"I'll be ready."

"Something I meant to ask you. How did you know what I wanted, that other time? When I asked you to come to me."

The fear took hold of my lungs with icy hands. "I don't know," I stammered. "I really don't. My dad never would have told me about sex magic, and he's the only person I can think of who might have known about it."

"In this life."

The words hung like a challenge between us. I took a step back. He waited, hands on hips, head thrown a little back. I felt as if I were trapped in a staring contest with a tiger. Eventually his mouth twitched in a smile.

"What's behind those shutters you dream about?" Tor said. "One of these days you'll have to open them."

I broke. I took a few steps away and stared out at nothing. Let the tiger pounce and kill me—I refused to see the view that those shutters hid. I heard him move. He put gentle hands on my shoulders and pulled me back to rest against him.

"I'm sorry," Tor said. "I know better. I shouldn't push on you." He kissed the top of my head. "Still love me?"

"Of course." My surprise that he'd ask that question returned my courage to me. "Do you really need me to love you?"

"That's what I tried to tell you. Without you I'd shrivel up inside. You run that risk when you're a sorcerer. You can turn as dry and brittle as dead leaves."

He let me go, and I turned around to find him serious and oddly sad. I saw in his eyes the deep melancholy you sometimes see in a wild animal's eyes, when they come up to the bars of their cage in the zoo. They stare at you as if they were begging you to let them go, but they know you can't open the cage door.

"It's not easy, being who you are," I said.

"No. I can see why you don't want to open those shutters."

Tor turned away and strode out of the room. I followed more slowly. He paused with his hand on the door that led to the stairs down.

"I'm going to get things ready," he said. "It's growing dark."

When the waning moon finally rose, Tor led me downstairs. We changed clothes, as we'd done the first time I'd watched him work. The clothes he put on surprised me, a pair of red sweatpants and an old Cal hooded sweatshirt in dark blue. I knew from my reading that red was the color of sorcerers, but the blue hoodie?

"It substitutes for the sorcerer's cloak," Tor said. "It doesn't matter what you wear, really. It's just a way of setting yourself apart from the mundane world."

He gave me the same white T-shirt to wear for a tunic, but this time he'd drawn big runes in a bindrune pattern all over it. "Yew," Tor told me, "and Elk for protection." The resulting design looked like a bristling hedge or a wrought-iron fence, the kind with spikes. For good measure he drew a Yew rune on my forehead with a piece of chalk.

From one of the drawers he took out a knife with a wooden handle carved with runes, then led the way into the ritual room. It smelled of different herbs, no fruit and flowers this time around, but bitter things, sharp and vinegary. I noticed that he'd used duct tape to cut the circle into eight sections instead of four.

"Sit in the west again," he said.

I sat down cross-legged against the west wall. Tor carried the rune-knife into the center of the circle and faced north. For about two minutes he spoke not in Icelandic but Old Norse, a tribute to the ancestors. In the corners of the room the candle flames jumped and flickered.

Tor stretched out his left arm and with the knife in his right hand slit the skin from just below the elbow to a few inches above his wrist. I clasped a hand over my mouth to keep from whimpering aloud. The blood welled from the shallow cut along the back of his arm. He turned slowly through the circle, scattering the blood onto the floor as he did. He chanted as well, a long string of syllables and vowels—not loudly, but in

the deep vibrated sounds of raw magic. When he returned
to facing north, he rested for a moment. He began to turn
again, and at each place where a line met the circle he called
out the name of a rune.

I saw them. As he brought them forth I could see them
hovering in the air where he'd placed them. The runes glowed
red, a hot flickering red like fire seen through a crack in a
burning building: Ice at the north, then Thorn, Thorn, Torch,
Torch, Hail, Hail, and back to Ice again at the north-west.
He raised his bloody arm above his head and called forth
Tiwaz, Tyr's Mark. All of them hung reversed except for Ice,
a straight line that has no reverse. On his arm the blood had
stopped oozing, but the scarlet line glowed like the runes
and marked his hand between his fingers. When he lowered
his arm, the blood dripped. A shadowy form built up beside
him. A wolf, I thought at first. Tor snapped his blood-soaked
fingers, and the ghostly form sat on command—the malamute
bitch come to assist at the revenge on the man who had killed
her so shamefully.

"Nils!" Tor vibrated the name like a chant. "Come here!
I summon you!"

I heard a scream, a distant throbbing wail. At first I
thought—no, I hoped—I was only hearing a siren from outside,
a fire engine maybe or a police car, but the scream came again
in a mixture of rage and terror, louder this time. Tor called
out words in Norse. The scream echoed through the room.
Between Tor and the Ice rune at the north a mist formed.
I could see a mask-like face and the furious blue eyes that
glared out of it. The dog-ghost got to her feet. I heard, very
faintly, her growl.

Tor raised the blood-smeared knife and continued speaking. The blue eyes looked this way and that in desperate eva-
sion. The mask of bluish mist tried to turn away. Tor spoke
again, and the mask held steady. Slowly Tor raised his left
hand and grasped the spear-point of Tyr's justice that hung
over his head. He clasped the tang as if it were as tangible as
metal and brought it down, pointed it at the mask, and held

it out in front of him. He spoke. I understood not one word, but it sounded like a list of charges or perhaps the tolling of a bell, a death-bell in slow grim strokes.

Through the mask Nils tried to speak. He gibbered, his eyes darted from side to side, he tossed his head. Tor held the glowing point of the spear rune steady and said one last word. The mask began to burn. Nils screamed as the mask disappeared in flames. A shadowy blue image of his naked body stood in its place. With another growl the dog-ghost leapt for its throat. Nils screamed one last time and fell backwards as the pair of them, locked together, disappeared.

Tor stamped three times on the floor, then slowly turned his way around the circle. As he did, the eight runes at the circle points winked out one by one. He held Tyr's Mark above his head, and for the briefest of moments I saw another hand, huge and glowing white, reach down and take the fiery red rune from him.

"Done!" Tor said.

I caught my breath with a sob. I was shaking too hard to stand up. Tor knelt and laid the knife down in the center of the circle. For a long moment he stayed kneeling, head bent, as if in prayer. He got up, walked over to me, caught my hands, and pulled me to my feet. He threw his right arm around my shoulders to support me.

"He'll never be free of the dog until he dies himself," Tor said. "And for all I know, she'll chase him halfway to Hel even then."

"Is he dead?" I said.

"No. But he's about half the sorcerer he used to be. The dog will keep draining his power, harrying him."

"I thought you wanted her to run free. That day on the hillside, you said—"

"She will, once Hel claims him."

I looked up and saw him smiling, not at me, just smiling in satisfaction at a job well done. What have I fallen in love with? That was my first thought. The second was, It doesn't matter. I have.

The smell of his released élan became irresistible. I bent my head and licked blood from the back of his left hand. He smiled and kissed me. The taste of his blood became our bindrune.

CHAPTER 16

By morning the long cut on Tor's arm had scabbed over, although it opened again when he took a shower. Blood oozed. I treated the cut with an antibiotic ointment, laid on thickly. Tor stood yawning while I tended it.

"Does it hurt?" I said.

"A little. Nothing I can't ignore."

To keep the wound clean, I put soft gauze over the ointment layer and taped it down at strategic intervals.

"It should be okay," I said. "But you look exhausted. I could go to the hospital by myself."

"No, I don't want you to go alone. I'll bet Nils is totally wiped out this morning. I'm hoping he'll stay that way for days. He should. But let's not take any chances."

Tor put on a long-sleeved shirt to hide the bandage, and this time he took a jacket. I took my sweater. Roman's blood had stained my denim jacket and Tor's flannel shirt so badly that we left them downstairs in the sink of that flat's kitchen.

We arrived at the hospital just before noon. Brittany gave us a quick rundown of their night—nothing untoward had happened, except she'd barely slept thanks to the noise—then took off to look after her grandmother. In a web of IV tubes and monitor cables, Roman lay on his side in the hospital bed, propped and bolstered with pillows to keep the pressure off his wound. The drugs had left him wide-eyed, a little sweaty, and comfortable enough.

"It still hurts," he told me, "but with this stuff in your

veins, you don't care that it does."

The doctor, a younger man than I was expecting, arrived on his hospital rounds and talked about 'the prognosis,' which was good. He repeated that the bullet had missed the spine and, surprisingly, Roman's vital organs. There was second-ary nerve damage, but that, the doctor felt, would heal with physical therapy. The hospital administration wanted to move Roman as soon as possible into a VA hospital. The problem was the rehab that he'd need after—budget cuts had closed that part of the operation in San Francisco. He'd end up too far away for Brittany to visit easily, especially with our col-lege year so soon to start.

"I've told them," the doctor said, "that they can't move the patient yet. It would be entirely too dangerous. Eventually the committee will take a hand and overrule me, but we've got a while before that happens. I'd like to get him into con-valescent care somewhere near by."

"Let me to talk with them," Tor said.

The doctor grinned. "From what Admissions told me, I was expecting you to wear a horned helmet and carry a sword."

Roman caught my glance and winked. Tor and the doc-tor left together, talking in low voices.

"Quite a guy," Roman said. "Thorlaksson, I mean."

"Yeah. I think he's pretty special."

Roman smiled, a tight little twitch of his mouth. "I'm go-ing to pass out," he said. "Sorry."

"It's okay, but hey, before you do, thank you."

"For what?"

"Covering me like you did. Taking the bullet meant for me."

"You're the only family I've got in the world. Fucking right I did." He sighed, yawned. "We can talk later. But you're wel-come." He closed his eyes, sighed again, and slept.

In clean clothes, her hair freshly washed, Brittany returned before Tor did. Everything was fine at home, she said. She'd brought a tote bag with her, a needlework project to pass the time. Tor came back with the news that the hospital was beginning to see reason about not moving Roman.

"There's a fight ahead of us," he said to Brittany. "We may have to call your congresswoman. But don't worry, we'll win."

For some hours that afternoon I watched Roman sleep and Brittany embroider. Tor slumped down in a chair and drowsed at intervals. I kept looking at his shirt sleeve to check for blood seeping from the cut, but it stayed clean. I should have brought a sketchbook, but in my worry about my brother, it had slipped my mind. Eventually Brit pointed out that there was nothing more that Tor and I could do.

"I'll be here," she said. "Maya, I don't want to see you exhaust yourself. You know how tired you get."

"Yeah," I said. "I do."

"I'd like to get over the bridge before rush hour," Tor said. "If something goes wrong, we can come back."

"Nothing's going to go wrong." Brittany spoke with calm certainty. "I'm here to make sure of that. So okay. Go!"

Before we left, I kissed Roman on his sleeping cheek. Getting out of the stuffy room was a relief. Although I wanted to drive home, Tor insisted that he felt fine.

"I'm wide awake now," he said. "I'll drive."

"How's your arm?"

"It's fine."

"Yeah, sure!"

"The pain is part of the ritual. A vitki's got to learn to shove the pain out of his mind." He grinned at me. "I need to practice."

Once we got into the car, I noticed him wincing whenever he reached for the turn signal or moved the wheel in a way that put pressure on the left arm. I stayed on alert and watched the cars around us. I never saw any sign of Nils. I figured that if Tor, the victor in their odd battle, had drained so much energy, the loser must have been exhausted. I stopped worrying, although I knew that sooner or later, we'd have to confront Nils again.

"Do you want to eat out tonight?" I said. "So you don't have to lift frying pans and stuff?"

"Good idea. I'll have a beer. The cut's starting to ache a little."

A little! I thought. I could see blood on his shirt sleeve, not a solid line, just a fleck here and there, but a bad sign anyway, that it would seep through all that gauze.

We stopped at a Japanese restaurant near home, a tiny place tucked into a strip mall, but nice inside with real wood tables and fabric-covered walls. It also offered a full bar. Once we were seated, Tor had a double shot of scotch with a beer chaser—one whole bottle of dark beer, that is—before the food even reached us. He drank a second beer with his meal, and finally a third "for dessert," he said. Since he hadn't eaten all day, the alcohol hit him hard, as I tried to point out.

"I'm fine," he said. "It's just beer."

"And scotch, then a lot of beer. I'll drive."

"Are you saying I'm too drunk to drive?"

"Yeah, that's exactly what I'm saying. Oh god, it's been a totally awful day, Tor. Let's not get into an accident on top of everything."

"I'm not going to get us into an accident."

I might have made things worse by snapping at him, but luckily the waitress arrived with the bill. Tor had trouble getting his credit card out of his wallet. I clamped my mouth shut and looked away. Finally he got the bill settled and left a tip in cash on the table. When we got up, he walked steadily instead of weaving around, but he was sweating in the hot night, and I could smell the beer oozing out of his skin.

As soon as we stepped outside, the fresh air slapped him in the face. I saw it in the way he took a step back and caught the wall to steady himself.

"Okay," he said. "You can drive."

"Thanks. I really mean it: thanks."

"I should have used the men's room. Let me just go back in."

While he did, I waited outside the restaurant, then decided to walk out to the car. The sun had just reached its setting point, and the sky blazed with golden light. We'd left

Gretel at the far end of the narrow parking lot near a scatter of other cars. I was thinking about Roman, worrying about whether or not he'd make a full recovery, not paying attention to much else. I trusted in the daylight and the presence of other people just some twenty yards away in the restaurant. It seemed perfectly reasonable to go wait for Tor in the car.

Later I realized that I'd been summoned.

As I walked up to Gretel, an arm flung itself around my neck. That's what it felt like, that the arm had suddenly appeared, even though I knew a man had grabbed me from behind.

"Hold still," he hissed. "Or I'll shoot you."

I felt cold metal laid along the left side of my face. He had a gun.

"Nils." I managed to choke out the word.

"Smart girl! You're coming with me. You're just the bargaining chip I need."

Tor! I cried out in my mind. *Help!*

Nils began to drag me backwards. Gun or no gun, I wasn't going to go with him and let him kill me at his leisure. He could travel like Tor did, in big teleported leaps, which meant I had only the briefest moment to get free. I raised a foot and stamped on his instep as hard as I could.

"Hey!" he snarled. "Play nice, and I won't hurt you!"

For an answer I kicked backward and dug the heel of my shoe into his shin. He growled and shook me. I have a weapon, I thought. He can't know, or he never would have grabbed me. I could feel his élan. I began to gather it, pull it from him, drink it in harder and faster than I'd ever done before.

His arm tightened around my neck. With every gulp, with every smidgen I felt slide down my throat, I felt him grow weaker, but not fast enough. I had to distract him, or as a sorcerer he'd sense what I was doing. I let my knees go limp. He staggered, off-balance. I got my feet under me again and kicked backwards, hit his shin and heard him swear.

"Bitch, hold still!"

His arm choked me, disgusted me, his naked arm, hairy,

sweaty in a short sleeve shirt. I twisted, stamped his instep again, and got my head just free enough to bite him. He screamed. I sank my teeth in and locked my jaw tight. The blood spurted. I fed, oh god it felt so splendid to feed myself, to drain red blood, to strip the élan as it flowed from life's pure fountain!

Nils dragged me a few feet backwards, but I kept feeding, draining him. I felt a weak surge of energy as he tried to leap away from the parking lot. Instead he stumbled and nearly fell. Full of his élan, my mouth red with his blood, I had power. I threw my weight backwards. Down we went, him underneath. The gun in his hand flashed toward my face. I twisted and rolled. I dragged him with me and on top of me. I fell onto my back and threw my arms around his waist. He tried to use the gun to club me, but it only hit my upper arm. Although I could have broken away, my terror made me clasp him tight against me.

If I let him go, he'd get up and shoot me. I was certain of that. *Faint, damn you! Go under!* I felt him weakening, heard his heart pounding a broken rhythm. I lay under him like a succubus and went on feeding.

"Let go!" Nils was sobbing. "Stop! I'll let you go! Stop!"

Someone yelled a word I didn't know, a string of them— Icelandic words. Big hands grabbed Nils's wrist and twisted. Nils moaned and shrieked as bone cracked. The gun went flying. A foot flashed into my side vision and kicked Nils hard in the head. The foreign words sounded again. Nils went limp. I unlocked my bite as Tor grabbed me and hauled me to my feet. I leaned against him and trembled but not from fear. I could feel Nils's élan coursing through my blood. The parking lot stretched out huge around me. The sunset light surged like water in big bright waves of flame.

"Hang on!" Tor said.

I threw my good arm around his neck. He hugged me around the waist and leapt.

We stumbled to a stop in front of our house. Tor let me go and took his smartphone out of his jeans pocket. I stood panting on the lawn and felt the world settle around me, a normal sight again, because he'd siphoned my excess élan to make the long leap. He looked perfectly sober, whether from absorbing the élan or producing raw adrenalin, I couldn't know.

"I'll let you in," he said, "and then I'll go back for Gretel. Where's your backpack?"

"I don't know." I could barely speak. "I must have dropped it."

"Shit! Let's hope no one finds it." He tapped in the security codes. "Go upstairs! I'll lock you in. I'll be back as soon as I can."

I followed his orders because I didn't know what else to do. As soon as I got upstairs I ran into the bathroom. I intended to examine my aching arm, but my image in the mirror horrified me so much that I forgot the pain. Blood crusted on my lips and chin. Drops of blood had fallen on my shirt and dried. Nils's blood. I could taste it in my mouth. I turned to the toilet and vomited.

It took me some time to clear my stomach and flush every last bit of the vomit away. I washed my face, then took off the filthy shirt and threw it into the bathtub. I was going to take a shower, but my arm throbbed and burned just above the elbow, where Nils had clubbed me. Since I could raise it despite the pain, I knew it wasn't broken. A meat-red bruise marked the spot. When I looked in the mirror, I saw blood spots on my bra. I took that off and threw it into the tub with the shirt. My stomach had settled just enough to let me keep a couple of pain pills down.

I left the bathroom and went into my room to get a clean shirt. On the writing desk the image had changed to a skeleton holding up a flask of black liquid. I grabbed the shirt and ran down the hall. In the living room I put the shirt on, then flopped down on the couch. I stared at the empty fireplace and tried to forget the taste of blood. My left arm hurt where left-handed Nils had clubbed me, but my right arm and hand were unharmed. On the coffee table lay a sketchpad and my box of conté sticks. I picked them up and began to draw.

When I was a child and my parents were fighting, I drew pictures from fairy stories and folk tales, princes and magicians and monsters and castles, horses who could talk, cats who wore clothes. When I grew older I sometimes drew maps of the magical places where all these beings lived. As a teenager I laid those stories aside, or so I thought, and drew my friends, my family, the buildings where we lived and where I went to school, views of San Francisco, flowers and trees. Those pictures got my teachers' attention, and they earned me my scholarship to a prestigious school I never could have afforded without it.

But always in the back of my mind the old stories lurked, because I belonged to their world of monsters and dark magics. That night, waiting for Tor to come home, I drew the horrors from my dreams, the man formed of green slime, the strangled woman. When I drew the wooden shutters, I saw that they were elaborately carved with runes, so I put those in. I also did a picture of a blond man in a frock coat with a dueling pistol in his hand. I wondered if I was drawing Tor or Björn. Behind the man I drew the shadowy image of a bear standing on its hind legs. The bear seemed to speak and tell me that I was seeing Tor, though he looked different, back then.

His name was Kristjan. I remembered it, finally, that night. He was a lawyer, not a sorcerer in those days. I was going to divorce Björn and marry him so we could go to America and make a fresh start. Instead Björn killed him, and I followed him into death. I could remember how romantic it seemed, stepping off the dock into death—until the water began to smother me and I floundered, terrified, drowning in the icy cold of the North Sea.

Slowly the sky outside darkened until it was too dark to see the paper. I hauled myself off the couch and turned on both floor lamps and the counter light in the kitchen, too, for good measure. Tor drove into the garage just a minute or two after. I stood at the window and looked out at the distant bridge and the city glowing under its corona of fog until he came whistling up the stairs. Whistling. I spun around as he walked in and saw him smiling at me. He held up my backpack so I could see it, then laid it onto the coffee table.

"It was lying where you dropped it," he said. "No one had come near the car or Nils. The stinking bastard cast an aversion spell before he jumped you. The traces were still there. I banished it and left."

"Did you talk to him?"

"What?" Tor cocked his head to one side in puzzlement. "I saw his body, but I can't talk to ghosts. He's dead."

I'd killed someone. Finally I understood what I'd done, broken every promise I'd ever made to decency and God and my father. I'd fed and killed. Yes, he'd assaulted me, but I'd killed him by doing something I swore I'd never do.

"I'm sorry," I gasped out. "I'm so sorry."

"Why?"

"I killed him."

"Not by yourself." Tor sounded perfectly calm. "I hope, anyway, that I finished him off. When I kicked him in the head. Maya, if anyone's guilty of anything, it's me. I drove him to it, didn't I?"

"Did you? I don't understand."

"He had to use violence because he couldn't best me with sorcery. I rubbed his nose in it. And then I let you down. I never should have drunk that much at dinner. I'm sorry. You were right."

"I'm not blaming you for anything. I thought it was safe."

He sighed in honest relief. Very slowly and carefully I walked back to the couch and managed to sit down before I fell. Tor hurried over and sat next to me.

"Let me see your arm," he said. "You're hurt."

When he reached for me, I flinched and slid away from him.

"Maya!"

"Don't you see?" I was shaking by then. "I never meant to kill him. I thought he'd just pass out, and then I could get away."

"Okay, so you didn't know when to stop. Where would you have learned? Why are you blaming yourself like this?"

"Because I've killed someone. And it hurts."

"I don't see why. He attacked you, Maya. Self-defense. Ever heard of it?"

"It's not that simple. I should have realized I was going too far. I should have felt it or something."

"Or something!" Tor shook his head in sheer annoyance. "I mean, shit! Come on! Nils nearly killed your brother. He tried to kidnap you. Think!"

"That's all true. But that still doesn't give me the right to kill him. That's not justice, it's vengeance."

"Yeah. So?" He smiled. He actually smiled. "I warned you that I was a barbarian." At that moment I saw it very clearly, that he belonged to the world of the old sagas. He would have understood the men around him, and they would have understood him, the vitki who could kill like a warrior. More than understood—they would have honored him. But here he was, adrift in the twenty-first century, in some odd way every bit as lost as I was despite his money and his sorcerous power.

"Besides," Tor said, "could we have brought him to justice? Suppose we went to the police about Nils when all the shit started. Would they have believed us?"

"No."

"Okay, then. We had to settle for vengeance. Second-best, sure, but it's what our kind gets."

Our kind. In my mind, I saw the shutters that haunted my dreams. They trembled and threatened to open, just a crack, onto the view I refused to see. I slammed them shut and slumped back into the cushions. I wanted to rest, but instead I saw memory images of the parking lot shimmering and swelling like waves on the ocean. I could taste the memory of Nils's blood in my mouth. I opened my eyes again. Tor slid over next to me.

"Sweetheart, please," he said. "Let me see that arm."

When I raised it, it hurt, but at the same time it felt disconnected from me, as if I held out a stick of firewood.

"That's a hell of a bruise," Tor said. "You should see a doctor."

"No." I cradled my sore arm in my lap. "They'll ask how it happened."

"It's not like they'd believe you even if you told them the truth."

"I don't care. I don't want to go. Not tonight. I want to stay here. Can't you put a rune on it?"

"Yeah, good idea. We'll see how it looks in the morning. I wish we had a TV. For the first time in my life, maybe. For the news."

"I can get it on my laptop, or on yours. Yours would be better."

We ended up waiting for the late local news. I took a shower. Tor put my blood-stained clothes into the washer, tended my arm, and fixed me some oatmeal to replace the food I'd lost. I felt well enough after the bland cereal to drink a little brandy. He sat on the couch and held me in his lap like a child until it was time to set up his laptop. I couldn't tell you what I thought about during those hours. My mind had gone as dark and full of shadows as the view at night.

As we expected, the TV news led off with the corpse found in an Oakland parking lot. The cause of death had not been released. Nils had been carrying his wallet, so the police were able to identify him immediately. The official speculation ran to his having been killed elsewhere and then dumped. No one at the strip mall had noticed any kind of disturbance.

"The aversion spell worked," Tor muttered. "He had power, Nils."

The reporter pointed out that the dead man had been the suspect in an earlier shooting of an unarmed Marine veteran in San Francisco. A police spokeswoman made dark hints about drug dealing and gang warfare. Some of the ex-Marine's friends had become 'persons of interest.' I figured that Valdez and Williams would have great alibis, since they were innocent.

A car commercial appeared on screen. Tor shut down the

laptop. "There," he said. "No one's going to suspect you or me. You can stop worrying."

"It's not that easy. I mean, no, I'm not worried about the police. But—"

"But what?" He sounded annoyed.

"You're the one who's always talking about wyrd."

Tor sighed, one sharp breath. "You've got a point," he said. "Yeah. There's that."

That night I was afraid to fall asleep. Tor left a light on in the corner of the room and turned up the air conditioning to keep us from sweating. When he got into bed, he pulled me into his arms and kissed me until I could at last relax. Clasped against him I slept without nightmares, but I woke early with the memory of Nils's blood on my lips.

I called Brittany and heard that Roman was doing as well as could be expected. When I passed the news along to Tor, he smiled, pleased.

"We can go in to see him later," Tor said. "We don't have to worry about Nils anymore."

"That's true." I felt the guilt as cold and hard, as if every muscle in my body had clenched tight. Along with the guilt, though, I felt relief, sheer selfish relief that I'd never have to worry about him again. He did attack me, I reminded myself. He nearly killed my brother. Self-defense, not vengeance. I clung to that distinction. Tor was watching me with his head tilted a little to one side.

"You feel better," he said. "About the death, I mean."

"Only a little. I don't have your arrogance."

He winced. "I deserve that," he said. "I was so sure that I'd knocked the shit out of him. I never thought he'd have the strength or the guts to fight back like that, not so soon. I'm still learning. I hate to admit it, but I'm only half a sorcerer. So far."

"I'm only half a vampire," I said. "So I guess we match."

He smiled, then let the smile fade. "I keep thinking about it, my arrogance. When I heard you call me, when I was running out to the parking lot, I felt like shit. It was my fault. I was so damn sure I'd gotten the better of him."

"I was sure you had, too. I can't blame you."

"No, go ahead and blame me. I've got to learn from this. There's one last thing I have to tell you. If he had killed you, I would have joined you. Right away. You wouldn't have had to face the death world alone. Not this time."

In the dark and the cold, the water swirling, and my lungs burning in the cold as they screamed for air—would a hand have reached out to me? Would his cold fingers have clutched mine? Would we have sunk down together toward that point of light? I'd never know. I was glad I didn't have to know. This time.

Before we left for the hospital, Tor and I sat on the couch in the living room to drink our morning coffee. I ate a blueberry muffin for breakfast, too, just like a normal person. The sun streamed in the east window and made a golden road across the rug.

"When I was little," I said, "the sun would come into my bedroom window like that. I'd line my dolls up and tell them we were setting off on an adventure."

Tor grinned at me. "Good idea," he said. "Let's go on one. An adventure, I mean."

"Yeah? What do you have in mind?"

"Getting married."

I stared at him.

"You look frightened," he said. "I know it's a big step."

I wanted to say that I hardly knew him. I wanted to point out that we'd been together for only a couple of months. Neither of those things was true, now that I remembered Kristjan.

"Why?" I stammered. "I mean, why get married?"

"Because if something happens to me, you'll inherit what I own that way."

"Something—"

"Wyrd can be harsh," Tor went on. "I should know that if anyone does."

I finally understood. If he were killed by some sorcerous enemy. Or if he died performing some dangerous act of magic.

I now knew enough to think of possibilities.

"I don't care about inheriting your money," I said.

"But I want you to have it. I want to know you'll be provided for if the worst happens. Look, we can have my lawyer write out a marriage contract. If you get sick of me and want to leave, you'll still get half the property as a settlement."

"I'll never get sick of you."

"Well, then, what's wrong?" He frowned in thought. "I could have said that better, I guess. Not real romantic of me." He sighed. "How about this? I love you. Please marry me."

I fumbled for words and found none. He waited, smiling a little, and sipped his coffee.

I tried to argue with myself, but I knew what I wanted. I was stepping off the edge of another dock, letting myself fall into a different sea, but this time I might float to safety instead of sinking into the dark. Might, maybe, could be, that I could have a life that wasn't a constant battle to stay alive. Not a normal life, no—that would lie forever beyond me—but a life where I could survive, paint, grow, and love. Hope—there are times when hope hurts worse than despair, just from the fear that the hope's only another lie. And then there are the times when even if it should prove to be a lie, hope is all we have.

"Yes." I shoved the fear to one side. "I'll marry you."

His smile, so warm, so vibrant, made me feel that I'd made the right decision. He put his coffee down on the table, and I slid over into his arms. I kissed him, and when I slipped my arms around his neck, I felt like a shipwrecked sailor, clinging to a rock in the sea.

Katharine Kerr spent her childhood in a Great Lakes industrial city and her adolescence in Southern California, whence she fled to the San Francisco Bay Area just in time to join a number of the Revolutions then in progress. After fleeing those in turn, she became a professional story-teller and an amateur skeptic, who regards all True Believers with a jaundiced eye, even those who true-believe in Science. An inveterate loafer, baseball addict, and rock and roll fan, she begrudgingly spares time to write novels, including the Deverry series of historical fantasies or fantastical histories, depending on your point of view. She lives near San Francisco with her husband of many years and some cats.

CPSIA information can be obtained at www.ICGtesting.com
Printed in the USA
BVOW02s1016091213

338591BV00001B/61/P